Life, Love, Death

Encounters in a New York diner

Rosemary Hamer

Acknowledgement: Front cover - painting 'Nighthawks' (1942) by Edward Hopper (public domain).

Copyright © 2024
Author Name Rosemary Hamer
All rights reserved.
ISBN: 9798326629807
Imprint: Independently published

Dedication

To all those strangers, acquaintances, and friends who sometimes fleetingly, and sometimes enduringly, criss-cross your path in the world leaving the imprint of their lives on your very soul.

NEW YORK, 1953

WORLD NEWS
June 2 - Elizabeth II crowned Queen in UK
Hillary and Tenzing summit Everest
Korean War

HOME NEWS
Dwight D Eisenhower inaugurated President, January 1953
'Cold War' – Americans fear Communist spies
Traitors Julius and Ethel Rosenberg condemned to death, executed June 19
Senator Joe McCarthy seeks Commies, blacklists Hollywood stars
Mary Terrell wins segregation struggle in Washington restaurants
Women's income in 1951 less than half of men's
'Women's liberation' phrase first used in Simone de Beauvoir book 'The Second Sex'

EVERYDAY NEWS
Polio peaks 1952
Economy booms - 20% of homes have television sets
Fashion: Poodle skirts are a fad
'New Look' by Christian Dior – full skirted silhouette and tight waists
Young men – 'DA' haircuts and Teddy Boy trend
Music: Radio stations, jukeboxes play crooners like Perry Como
Toys: Tonka trucks, Toy guns, Tiny Tears dolls
Films/Books: 'Here to Eternity', 'How to Marry a Millionaire'

CHAPTER 1
New York - early June, 1953

That morning WABC Radio had gleefully announced another hot June day in the city with the prediction of an even hotter summer, all this sandwiched between news of the new Queen of England's coronation and the Rosenberg trial. Joel Petersen didn't care. Adjusting his well-worn leather pork pie hat and scratching his stubble he stomped along the crowded pavement grumbling to himself. The midday heat burnt into his grizzled neck. His sweaty, gnarled arthritic fingers could barely grasp his battered music case. Ageing joints cracked and ground as he forced his way through the oncoming hordes. Why was it when he was going one way everyone else was going the other? There were too many people. Why hadn't those stupid New

Life, Love, Death

Yorkers deserted the city for their usual summer break? What were they doing congregating in groups round shop windows? Whatever was going on? Joel's usual cord jacket felt stifling despite his rolled-up shirt sleeves. He wasn't one to dress down because of the heat, the last seventy years had seen to that. What had good old Mammy always said, 'Now look here Joel, my boy. A man must be rightly dressed at all times in case…' But 'in case' of what he'd never found out.

Recovering his sense of humour, he cheered up. It had been a good gig in the Village last night but a long one. The afterhours drinking had taken its toll. He felt a hundred and ten. A good cup of joe would set him up. The faint sounds of music alerted him. He pricked up his ears. Maybe it wasn't such a bad day after all. The music grew louder. Searching the shops and alleys as he passed, he looked for the musician but sadly it was only the latest vinyl record being played loudly on someone's balcony. Still and all he recognised it. Who could miss Charlie 'Bird' Parker and the magical chord changes of that smooth tenor Sax? No comparison with the real thing, of course. Nothing could beat the sound of a lone Sax played at night in the depths of a smoky filled bar full of sweating patrons drinking whiskey sours and bourbons straight up. Joel gave a sigh. He was getting old with all this reminiscing. He limped on.

Way up 6th and 33rd, he managed to hobble stiffly into Leo's Diner. Plonking himself in his usual seat in a booth out back he looked across at Adelie. As ever, her black currant-like eyes darted here and there. Perspiration beaded her broad forehead and her once blondish plaits stuck to her head. Her formerly immaculate white overall was soaked with sweat and now decorated with brown and yellow stains as she doled out plates piled high with eggs and waffles. Spotting

Life, Love, Death

him, she came over, fighting her way through the lunchtime crowd and collecting a coffee pot on the way. Poor old Joel she thought as she advanced – his usual ebony black skin looked yellowish gray today, but she greeted him cheerily enough, 'Lovely day, Joel, for the time of year. Feels like more heat might be on the way.'

'Dunno 'bout that,' Joel growled.

'I know,' Addy said consolingly, 'it's coffee you need. Maybe we'll get a bit of civility out of you then. Though it looks to me as if coupla glasses of water would do you a power more good.' She laughed out loud as he grimaced.

'Spect so,' Joel said, 'watching the delicious brown nectar streaming into his waiting cup. Almost before she'd finished pouring, he made a grab for the cup and slurped it down.

'You'll burn your mouth,' Addy warned, 'I don't know how you takes it so hot. Now what's it to be – brunch or lunch?'

Joel flicked an arbitrary eye at the clock. It was already half past twelve. 'Lunch I s'pose, Addy,' he grunted. What's good today?'

Addy sighed. Why did he always ask the same old question? Summoning up longsuffering restraint, she answered, 'The usual.'

'Bring me a coupla eggs. Maybe a hash brown or two, a piece of that there bacon, crispy mind, and a fresh roll.'

'Over easy or sunny side up?'

Life, Love, Death

'Over easy, Addy. Sorry you knows I'm a grouch till after my first cup o' joe.'

'I certainly should after all these years, old man, but I forgive you,' she said fondly and bustled off to serve other customers.

Addy's boss frowned and grumbled under his breath when he saw Joel, murmuring to Addy 'Blacks in my diner – what's the world's coming to? I don' wanna be encouraging more of them in here. It puts off my regulars.'

Addy hit him sharply on the shoulder, 'Look Frankie boy, it ain't 'gainst the law whatever you says. Joel's been coming here some ten years since your dear departed pa took over the joint and you were barely a twinkle in your old man's eye. Once upon a time they was in a band together. Joel's harmless – he's a fixture. Your regulars, as you call them, couldn't give a damn.'

Frankie swore a series of oaths and disappeared into the kitchen. It wouldn't do to offend Addy. She was worth her weight in gold despite the pittance he paid her.

Joel, beginning to feel more human, looked round. It was busy for a Tuesday, what was going on? Then he remembered. Wasn't there something about a new Queen in England. That was what those crowds of people he'd passed must have been doing, trying to get a view on them new fangled television sets in shop windows. Best of luck. They'd hardly be able to see a thing on them tiny screens. Some new Queen in another country wouldn't make a dime's worth of difference to him. After all, he grumbled to himself, we've got good ole Ike now for better or worse, though what good

Life, Love, Death

he'll be to the working man? Jus' another jumped up Republican. One of them 'good ole boys. 'Cos he was a sort of Commander during the war he walks straight into the White House.

Interrupting his thoughts, he noticed Addy pushing through the crowd towards his table followed by a smartly dressed matron. What was going on now? Couldn't a poor old man get any peace? Surely Addy wasn't bringing that woman over here? What was up with Addy today? She never showed people to tables. It was usually first come first served, take potluck, end up on a stool at the counter, or in his case, as far out of sight as they could put him. The woman was whispering in Addy's ear and Addy's face cracked into a beaming smile he'd not seen in years. It was as if the sun had come out. Addy's lined face broke into a mess of dimples. 'Now Joel,' Addy said in a wheedling tone. 'This lady needs a seat. She was feeling a mite poorly up there at the counter due to the heat. I thought you might be willing to allow her to share your table.'

Joel scowled and muttered something incomprehensible.

'That's fine then,' Addy said blithely, pretending not to hear. 'Come along, lady. Joel Petersen here is a real gent. He'll make you welcome. I'll bring you over some water.'

Gingerly the woman sat down smoothing her skirt and trying to smile at the old man opposite. She carefully removed her gloves finger by finger and looking up at Addy said, 'Thank you, Adelie. You've been so kind.'

Addy reddened with pleasure and all but curtseyed, 'Wait a tick, I'll be straight back for your order, ma'am.'

Life, Love, Death

Joel sank his face into his food ignoring his table companion. To his dismay, the woman leant across and lay her ungloved hand on his arm saying, 'Mr Petersen, I know this is an imposition, but I thank you sincerely. I was feeling the tiniest bit faint.'

Joel detected a Southern accent. Without thinking he looked up and was immediately awestruck by the woman's startling blue eyes and found himself saying, 'A pleasure, lady. Nuffink at all.'

'Please let me introduce myself,' the lady continued as if Joel hadn't spoken. 'I am Bedelia Gray. So pleased to meet you, Mr Petersen.'

By now Joel's attention had moved back to his hash browns and, making only the faintest response, carried on eating. Mrs Gray however sat back and relaxed as if she had joined a late afternoon tea party, adding, 'I believe the weather is looking to be fine, Mr Petersen, though a little too hot at midday, don't you think?' Joel ground his teeth or what was left of them amongst his yellowing dentures. There was nothing he could abide less than females prattling about the weather. His best tactic was to pay no heed and she might leave him be.

This was not Bedelia's way. Brought up in Kentucky with the perfect manners her Mama had instilled in her, she remarked, 'Maybe a trifle too hot but of course for us Southerners it can never be too hot. A little mint tea would be so refreshing, don't you think?' Joel was lost for words. Was this a bad dream? Had he and this woman been transported to one of them parallel universes his Pappy used to go on about, to sip afternoon tea in one of those plantation

Life, Love, Death

houses down South instead of sitting in a grimy diner off 6th Avenue in New York. Before thinking he had a screw loose, Addy came to the rescue, forcing her way through the crowds bearing a fresh shrimp salad and of all things a real teapot and teacup on a tray. Carefully she laid it down in front of Mrs Gray.

'Lovely Adelie, lovely. Thank you. It's the little touches that make life palatable.' Addy was overcome and, practically bowing, retreated backwards and on to a young man's foot who screeched in pain, 'Jus' look where you're blooming going, Addy. That was my foot, you've crippled me for life.'

'I've done no such thing. You minds your language,' Addy retorted, 'or you'll be getting my boot up your backside.' Joel was shocked. At no time over the years had he seen Addy behave like this. She's gone loco he thought – it must be the heat. This woman is making us both crazy.

'I'm sorry, Mr Petersen, I didn't quite catch that.'

'Nuffink,' Joel growled, realising he must have said something out loud, 'nuffink, Missus.' All he wanted was to escape, but today was one of those days when he craved something sweet, must have been all that hooch he'd drunk last night. He was trapped. An iced donut would do the trick if he could catch Addy's eye.

Mrs Gray sat up ramrod straight. Fastidiously she picked up her napkin and cleaned her knife and fork, 'Not that they're not clean Mr Petersen, I assure you, but one can never be too careful,' and then continued to daintily eat her salad.

Life, Love, Death

Joel thought it was like a rabbit nibbling on lettuce. What an odd woman! He was beginning to relax and return to daydreaming when Addy appeared again. This time she had a gawky girl in tow. Looking directly at Mrs Gray she said, 'Would you mind very much if this young girl joined your table? It's so busy in here today and I don't want her exposed to some of those lewd men at the counter.'

'Of course.' Mrs Gray said. 'Please come and sit next to me. I'm sure Mr Petersen won't object.'

Joel sighed. Not another dem female. Was he to have no peace today? Nobody had asked him if he minded. What had come over the place? Perhaps he'd have to find himself another diner, but how could he when he'd always looked on this place as home This was his Tuesday oasis overflowing with memories of him and Leo growing up as kids in Brooklyn and playing music together.

The awkward girl sat down with alacrity. Energy radiated from her bobbed hair to her pristine court shoes. 'Thank you so much. I'm Bobby Jo Hudson – but please call me Roberta now I'm in New York. Only my parents call me Bobby Jo. I want to sound sophisticated in the city so Roberta it is – but I can't get used to it. It's so formal and grown up.' On and on she babbled.

Joel wished momentarily he were deaf but then of course how would he hear his beloved Sax. A great wave of girlish noise and prattle engulfed him. He wondered if he'd survive. It was too much for an old man. He thought longingly of the solitude of his basement apartment.

Life, Love, Death

There they all sat that Tuesday lunchtime, the old musician, the Southern lady, and the girl of course. Joel comforted himself that it would soon be over. They would never meet again. Life was like that. Passing strangers who stopped for a moment, stepped out of their lives to exchange stories, and moved on without a backward glance. Joel relished the thought.

That Tuesday evening, Mrs Gray sat on the subway on her way home to Queens adjusting her skirt and hat, crossing her ankles neatly over one another and studying her fellow passengers. Her eyes widened and she scowled when she saw the young woman opposite sit with her leg over her knee exposing a good length of thigh and goodness knows what else. Not only that but she was reading 'Lady Chatterley's Lover' in public. Mrs Gray tutted quietly and suddenly thought of the girl at the diner. What was her name now? Bobby something, like those bobby-soxers on the films? Not that Mrs Gray went to the cinema much these days, so many of the films were either violent or full of sex. What about that 'From Here to Eternity'. Fancy a private having an affair with the captain's wife? That was totally unacceptable!

Dragging her mind back to that girl today it was plain to see she'd been brought up with few manners – talking loudly with her mouth full. Next week, Bedelia mused I'll find another diner. The trouble was Leo's was so convenient and so cheap. Tuesday was her half day treat when instead of taking a box lunch to work she allowed herself a meal out and a leisurely stroll to midtown and the Museum of Modern Art. Maybe if she got there early she could avoid that old man and the girl and get a booth to herself. Smiling smugly, she thought 'that's a plan.'

CHAPTER 2

The following week Bedelia Gray found herself back at Leo's, hovering in the doorway. Before she'd made up her mind to go in she saw the girl from last week waving frantically at her from that same booth. Not only was she gesticulating madly but calling out, 'Mrs Gray, Mrs Gray. Over here, over here.'

Reluctant and flushed with embarrassment, Bedelia moved towards her attempting to compose herself. By now thank goodness the girl had sat down and appeared to be excitedly chatting away to someone Bedelia couldn't quite see. No doubt a boyfriend or girlfriend. Well, this time she'd have to put up with the arrangement but next week would be different. It wasn't until the last minute she realised the girl had been talking to the old man from last week. Now what was his name, 'Peter' something. Was she never to escape these two?

Arranging her face in a smile, she greeted them both. 'What a coincidence for us to be all here together again.'

As before, the old man barely acknowledged her but glowered and carried on eating his brunch. The girl, however, moved up the banquette and patting the seat next to her said, 'Please come and sit by me, Mrs Gray. It's so lovely to see you both again. It makes me feel a lot less homesick to think I've made two new friends. New York can be such a lonely place, don't you think?'

Feeling guilty, Bedelia bestowed on her one of her extra special smiles and, finally remembering the old man's name, addressed him, 'Lovely to see you again, Mr Petersen.' There

Life, Love, Death

was only a grunt from the old man, but there was no holding the girl back. She began to recount all her adventures of the previous week as if Mrs Gray and Mr Petersen were family. Interrupting the girl, who was by now in full onslaught, Mrs Gray said, 'I don't know why we must sit in this back booth, Mr Petersen, so close to the kitchen and the rest rooms. It's hardly hygienic and so ridiculously hot.'

Joel stopped eating and, dragging himself away from his food for a moment, looked her straight in the eye, 'You's don' have to sit here, Missus. It's me they's don' want on show. See,' he tapped forcefully and angrily on his black hand. 'Surely you comin' from the South understand that.'

Mrs Gray winced and looked away, 'I'm sorry, Mr Petersen. I was out of order. The trouble is I've lived in the North for most of my adult life and not thought about the South in a long time,' adding nervously. 'I can assure you, Mr Petersen, my dear Papa when he was alive had no truck with slavery. Our dear Mammy who looked after Roger and me was paid a proper wage. I adored her.'

'Spect it weren't a living wage,' the old man snarled under his breath and, ignoring her, chewed fiercely at a shard of crispy bacon.

Bobby Jo, not wanting to be left out and keen to lighten the atmosphere, asked, 'Is that where you come from Mr Petersen, down South?'

'Nope, Brooklyn.'

Mrs Gray keen to avoid more embarrassment waved at Addy with a lace handkerchief, 'Adelie, my dear – do you

Life, Love, Death

think you could summon up a cup of iced mint tea on such a hot day,' continuing to fan herself vigorously with the same handkerchief.

Hurrying over with a beaming smile, Addy said, 'Surely,' only too willing to oblige, 'I's sure there's a leaf or two of mint hiding in that kitchen. Now what else can I get you?'

'A little of your delicious green salad on a cream cheese bagel please. It would be just the thing.'

Joel smirked to himself at the way Addy kowtowed to this so-called lady and couldn't help noticing Addy was wearing a pristine clean overall, yet it was only Tuesday. She only ever wore a clean one on a Monday which by the end of the week was in a sorry condition, and certainly had never bothered to put herself out for him or anyone else over the years. What was there about this Mrs Gray? Wasn't she too posh to sit with the likes of him and this juvenile? There must be more to her. But he was in no mood to find out.

Mrs Gray, determined to make the best of things, said cheerily, 'Now we're here together again, maybe we should say a little about ourselves.'

Joel grunted and swore under his breath, 'Don' see the need, Missus.'

Ignoring the interruption, Mrs Gray continued regardless, 'As you know I'm Bedelia. My Papa chose the name. I never liked it and prefer Delia. I'm a widow this last five years with two grown sons. One a doctor and one a travel writer. Regrettably, I see little of them. They have their own lives to

Life, Love, Death

live…' her voice tapered off. Suddenly she looked fragile and vulnerable.

Rapt with attention, Bobby Jo listened carefully, elbows on the table. After a while she leaned forward and picking up her hot dog, lathered in mustard and relish, with both hands, munched her way through it with a fine set of gleaming molars.

Doing her best not to shudder at the lack of niceties, Mrs Gray continued, 'When my husband died suddenly, so young, things were difficult. Gus was a doctor at a public hospital … not well paid,' her voice quavered. 'Of course, his heart always ruled his head, funny when he was a cardiologist. There was little money, a poor pension. The house had to be sold,' gamely she added, 'but I enjoy my job at Ohrbach's, you know, the Department store. The apartment in Queens is bijou,' and hesitated, 'but convenient.'

There was a long silence when the only sound that could be heard was the repetitive click of Joel's false teeth moving rhythmically up and down whilst he downed his eggs. Bobby Jo moved closer and, abandoning her hotdog, placed two plump soft hands over Mrs Gray's, looking at her compassionately. Mrs Gray sighed and, carefully removing her hands from the girl's, straightened her shoulders and said abruptly, 'Thank you, dear,' as if she'd let herself down.

Joel merely clicked and ground his dentures even more purposefully. Would these women never shut up? But it was not to be. Bobby Jo decided to take a turn.

Life, Love, Death

Finishing her dog and taking a long drink from her shake Bobby Jo began, 'I'm from Little Chute, Wisconsin. No one's ever heard of it. A little bitty town of eleven hundred people. Most of whom have never set foot outside and certainly not been to New York. Me, I want more. I want adventure, so here I am. Pops is a pharmacist, and Mom, well she's only a housewife.' Thinking better of what she'd said she looked apologetically at Mrs Gray, adding 'though of course she does a lot of charity work for our church. They both wanted me to stay home and marry a nice Dutch American boy. We're Dutch Reform you know,' she said proudly, 'our name 'Hudson', like the river, was the name of an English explorer funded by the Dutch. Their first trading post, New Amsterdam, is now New York.' Gabbling on she suddenly came to a full stop as if she'd run out of steam.

Joel let loose a huge sigh. He wished it had been a belch. It might have frightened these women off. But no such luck, they were now looking expectantly towards him, waiting to hear his story. Infuriated he muttered; 'I's dunno what you's want from me. I's ain't nothing much nor done nothing much either.'

'Am sure that's not true, Mr Petersen,' Bobby Jo cajoled.' Am sure you must have had some great experiences in such a long life.' Noticing his battered old case, she asked 'What instrument do you play?'

Joel was tempted to tell her to mind her own business, but he could never be that uncivil about his beloved Sax. Lifting his head and puffing out his chest, he said, 'That there is my Saxophone, Betsy. She's been with me, man and boy. A companion to depend on.'

Life, Love, Death

Bobby Jo's only reaction was, 'Wow! A real musician,' and was immediately overawed.

Seeing her lost for words, Mrs Gray ventured, 'My goodness Mr Petersen, you must have seen and worked with some great musicians in your time.'

Never immune to flattery and always willing to talk about music, Joel relaxed. The lines on his face softened, his arthritic hands unclenched and signs of the handsome young man he once was appeared. 'Well, there were tha' time I's played a gig at the Vanguard in the Village. Thelonious Monk were top of the bill. What a performer. He and Miles Davis was close though peoples says they wasn't.'

Both women looked blank. Bobby Jo's knowledge of music only extended as far as the latest crooner. Not wanting the old man to relapse into his former grumpiness, Mrs Gray persevered although her own interest in music veered more towards Chopin than jazz, 'Were they Sax players too, Mr Petersen?'

'Course not. Ain't you's never heard of them. Thelonious, he were one of the greatest pianist and composers that ever lived, king of bebop, and Miles, no one ever best him on the trumpet.'

Determined to be included and not show her ignorance Bobby Jo interrupted, 'Mr Petersen, do you think we could take a peek at your Saxophone?'

The old man hummed and harred, but they could tell he was pleased. He unclipped the case and brought out a dented but gleaming Saxophone, 'Here's my Betsy. She's a bit the worse

Life, Love, Death

for wear and seen a lot of action, but she's a joy and my darlin,' he murmured as he stroked the keys.

An overexcited Bobby Jo said, 'Do play us something, Mr Petersen, please.'

Joel frowned, 'I's don' know…get thrown out.' But he couldn't resist her imploring face and his own urge to play. Quietly he began to play the first notes of 'Moonlight in Vermont.'

The diner's hullabaloo quietened down. Customers moved out of their booths, gathering round Joel's table. Addy stopped in her tracks, an enthralled expression on her pudgy face. Then out of the blue came a loud shout and Frankie bounded out of the kitchen yelling, 'No more, old man. Stop. You're outta here. I don' have a music license. Get on out.' He quickly bundled Joel, who was hurriedly trying to place Betsy back in her case and the two women towards the door.

The stunned trio ended up standing on the pavement shell shocked. Bobby Jo couldn't stop apologising, 'I'm so sorry Mr Petersen. It's my fault. I'll go back and explain.'

Joel shrugged, 'It won' do no good. He's been trying to get rid of me for a while.'

Mrs Gray laid a comforting hand on his shoulder, 'We loved your playing. I didn't realise the Sax had such a soulful sound.'
Joel brightened up, 'She can produce any sound you like can Betsy. She's real adaptable.' He laughed, 'She's a lady like yourself, Mrs Gray. A lady of shade and mood.'

Life, Love, Death

Addy showed up at the door, 'Now don' you be worrying, you three. That Frankie's bark is worse than his bite. I've sorted him. He's quiet as a lamb now. We'll see you all here next Tuesday. I'll reserve your table as usual.' Without another word she scuttled back inside.

They looked at one another. It seemed they had no choice. Whether they wanted to or not they were booked to have lunch there the following week and together. Nodding a scant farewell to one another, each of them wondered what they had let themselves in for.

CHAPTER 3

Bobby Jo, or Roberta as she now called herself, had stood for hours in front of the mirror in the bathroom at the Barbizon Hotel for Women whilst the rest of the inmates banged on the door. At last, giving up in frustration, they went off to find another bathroom. Bobby Jo wasn't happy with her looks. The day she'd left home she'd thought herself modern and sophisticated compared to her parents. They'd stood, shedding the odd tear, at the train station in Little Chute waving her off as if she were leaving for some dark mysterious continent never to return. Her mother's beige woollen twinset had seen better days and her father's Homberg had started to moult. However, she herself was dressed in her best Peter Pan collar blouse, pleated skirt, frilled bobby socks and new saddle shoes, ready to fit in with the elite, the WASPs of New York.

It was such a relief to leave home and branch out on her own. However, her parents thought otherwise, leaving their 'little Bobby Jo' in the charge of the conductor. How humiliating. After all she was a Rutgers graduate with an arts degree. Perhaps the New York Herald Tribune would finally recognise her maturity and talent. What a piece of luck that a distant cousin of her father's had been able to find her a traineeship at the paper or she would never have escaped Little Chute. This was going to be her chance. She, Bobby Jo, was going to be a famous writer and columnist and hang out with well-known rich people at the Stork Club or the Plaza and mingle with the literati at the Algonquin. There was no going back to Little Chute. It was all about moving forward.

Life, Love, Death

Staring closely at her complexion, she spotted three or four new freckles. Why on earth had she inherited her mother's fair complexion and of all things her red hair – not even a copper version but a good old plain carroty type. At least there was something she could do about that. When she had some money, she would find preparations for those freckles, and get her hair dyed a darker shade of red – one that would make her hazel eyes stand out.

However, since her arrival in in New York she'd seen what the other girls were wearing and realised how young and childish her clothes were. There was nothing for it. Before she started at the paper on Monday she would have to use a portion of her savings to visit the nearest thrift store. A smart skirt suit and high heeled pumps were a necessity for presenting herself at the Tribune offices. Thank goodness she had a week to settle in before reporting for work.

After an exhaustive shopping trip on the Tuesday, Bobby Jo arrived at Leo's wondering if her two companions would be there again. This little diner had been a find. It was close to where she was going to work and so cheap. Hoping the owner was not around, Bobby Jo slunk into the diner trying to look inconspicuous. As ever, Addy was on hand, shouting out, 'Hi, young lady. I've kept your table for you. Go on back. I'll be with you in two ticks.'

A rather uncomfortable Mrs Gray and the old musician were already seated. Mrs Gray seemed relieved to see her, 'Bobby Jo, I'm so pleased you came back and were not put off by last week's debacle. Mr Petersen is here too.' The old man as usual grunted something signifying a greeting.

Life, Love, Death

Haughtily, Bobby Jo said, 'It's Roberta, Mrs Gray. That's what I want to be called in New York.'

Her attempts at assertiveness were completely wasted as Mrs Gray pursued the conversation as if she had never been interrupted, 'My dear Bobby Jo, sit by me. You look hot and bothered. Tell us what you've been doing with yourself and how you like New York.' Joel emitted a whimper. Not all this again. How had he got himself lumbered with this patronising, superior middle-aged woman and this green girl.

Bobby Jo gritted her teeth too in exasperation. Turning to the old musician, she asked, 'No Betsy today. Where is she?'

Feeling more genial now someone had asked after his beloved companion, he said, 'Left her home. Not pushin' my luck.'

'Where do you live, Mr Petersen?'

'The Village. Minetta Street near them clubs.'

Bobby Jo, having no idea what or where the Village was, struggled to keep the conversation going.

'Is that jazz clubs? Is that where you play, Mr Petersen?'

'Not these here days – too old. Jus' a bit o'busking round Times Square.'

'Do you have a family or been married?' Bobby Jo persisted.

Life, Love, Death

'What's it to you? No, I 'ain't bin married or nuffink else. Don' you be asking people 'bout their personal business. You's will come to a sticky end with that nose of yours.'

Bobby Jo sat back and laughed noisily, 'Sorry Mr Petersen. I'm training to be a journalist and like to ask questions.'

'You'll gets yourself into trouble likes them Rosenbergs we keeps hearing about.'

'I hardly think that's the same thing,' Mrs Gray said diplomatically. 'The Rosenbergs are traitors and Communists passing on atomic secrets. They betrayed our country to the Soviet Union.'

Bobby Jo, entirely out of her depth, asked, 'What's wrong with sharing information with the Soviet Union? If both sides had bombs it would cancel out the chance of either of them using them. They would both be afraid of being blown up.'

Mrs Gray laughed and said smugly, 'That's far too simplistic a view, my dear. Someone must take a lead. It's better if our country is in charge. At least we believe in fair play. Now we have a President experienced in war, I would think the last thing he wants is a third World War.'

At this last remark Joel turned up his nose and mumbled, 'I's wouldn't mind seeing them there Upper East Side Whiteys blown up,' adding 'much good this President will do us blacks. He'll keeps his Republican cronies happy, makes sure dem middle-class white folk can buy houses, dang televisions, and refrigerators. People likes me 'as to scratch a

Life, Love, Death

living, worry abouts feeding our families and giving our kids some learnin.'

'But I thought you didn't have any children, Mr Petersen,' Bobby Jo put in innocently.

'That's got nuffink to do with it. It's my people I's talking about. Lot o'good those Republicans are to us.'

Mrs Gray bit her lip. Having been a staunch Republican all her life she found herself at a loss. All her life she had never given her fellow black Americans and their lives a second thought. Even the atomic bomb had never been a subject for discussion when her husband was alive. Tactfully she decided to change the subject. What was it her Papa used to say, 'never discuss a man's politics and religion at dinner'? She supposed that applied to lunch as well. Turning to Bobby Jo, she asked,' When do you start work, my dear?'

'Monday at the Herald Tribune,' Bobby Jo muttered between mouthfuls of hamburger.

'That's exciting,' Mrs Gray extolled. I'm an avid reader of theirs. I'll look for your byline.'

'No chance of that. I'll be a lowly trainee. Don't suppose they'll let me loose on any big stories.'

'Dare say it won't be long before they'll get you nosing up someone's doorstep, and prying into their grief,' Joel said sarcastically. 'You's wait and see.'

The three of them fell silent until Addy came bustling over, 'Now what else can I get you good folks? How about a little

Life, Love, Death

cheesecake or we've key lime pie? Go down well with a little ice cream on such a sweltering day.'

Looking intensely at the menu Bobby Jo declared, 'I'd love a banana split maybe with some chocolate sauce and…maybe some ice cream and…maybe some sprinkles.'

Mrs Gray, Joel and Addy chorused, 'and with a cherry on top.' Suddenly the frosty atmosphere was broken and the three of them began to laugh. A puzzled Bobby Jo sat looking blank, not knowing what was going on,' Why are you all laughing? I can't see anything funny.'

'Never you mind them, honey. They funning you. Take no notice. Be back shortly with your order,' Addy went off smiling to herself. Maybe she'd done some good putting those three together, priding herself she had a sixth sense for lonely people. There was no doubt, as disparate as they were, they had that in common.

Wholly unaware of Addy's motives the three in the booth relaxed, whilst Bobby Jo frantically spooned down her dessert ending up with a chocolate moustache. Mrs Gray tried discreetly to point to the mess but, as Bobby Jo seemed not to comprehend, Joel growled, 'You's got most of that stuff on yours face, young miss. Here, take this,' and handed over a none too clean handkerchief.'

Mrs Gray cringed but Bobby Jo took it nonchalantly enough and cleaned up her mouth, 'Thanks, Mr Petersen.'

'As we seem to be stuck with one another you's might as well call me Joel.'
And that was it, a friendship of sorts had begun.

CHAPTER 4

Standing on the threshold of the Herald Tribune on 41st Street Bobby Jo felt her stomach gurgling, wishing she'd not had that big bowl of fruit loops for breakfast. She was sure the milk had been off. Maybe it tasted different in New York.

A man in a nifty fedora slanted at an angle pushed past her, 'You goin' or comin,' young lady?'

'Coming,' she stammered.

Pushing the heavy door open, the man practically propelled Bobby Jo inside towards a foyer full of chatter. Young women wearing telephone headsets were babbling ten to the dozen to anonymous callers. A bleary-eyed Bobby Jo, feeling slightly queasy, found herself manhandled by the shoulders and prodded towards a blonde Marilyn Monroe lookalike at the nearest desk. 'There you are, lady. Jennifer will sort you out. Can't stop. On a deadline. See you later, alligator.'

Looking down her nose at a blushing Bobby Jo, snooty Jennifer, barely able to make the effort to articulate, asked 'How may I help you?'

A wobbly Bobby Jo managed a shaky reply, 'I'm here to see the editor, Mr Murphy.'

'And do you have an appointment?'

'Well, not exactly,' Bobby Jo stammered. 'I'm Bobby Jo Hudson, I mean Roberta Hudson. My father's cousin spoke to Mrs Reid, the owner, and I was supposed to report here for nine o'clock today.'

Life, Love, Death

Jennifer snorted and tutted, 'I'll ring through to Mr Murphy. He's a busy and important man. You may have to wait.' However, after a brief conversation, Jennifer wrinkled her nose disparagingly, hung up and pointed peremptorily at the elevators, 'Second Floor. Glass office on the mezzanine. Mr Murphy is expecting you.'

More anxious than ever and having no idea what a mezzanine was, Bobby Jo squeezed into the packed elevator. Her legs felt like jelly. Her hands were sweating onto her new red box purse. She wished she hadn't decided to wear this flamboyant chequered red and pink skirt suit and matching pumps. Yesterday she'd felt confident wanting to make a splash on her first day, but at this moment she was having second thoughts perhaps the gray conservative one would have been better. Choosing this outfit had been an act of rebellion against her mother who was always saying redheads should never wear pink or red. Now she had to make the best of it, so with a defiant shrug of her shoulders she stepped out on the second floor.

A wall of noise hit her. In front of her was an enormous room full of desks and people of all shapes and sizes shouting across to one another and speaking quickly down hundreds of telephones. Typewriters were clacking away and telexes spurting out ribbons of tape.

Frozen to the spot Bobby Jo was too intimidated to move. Finally, she spotted the editor's glass office high above the throng. Making her way towards the metal staircase she dodged back and forth between the desks, avoiding the oncoming copy boy pushing a trolley laden with post and newspapers. The staircase was a challenge as she tiptoed up

Life, Love, Death

trying to avoid catching her heels in the metal treads. Gently knocking on the glass door Bobby Jo heard a gruff, 'Come.'

A thickset older man was standing leaning over a desk, striking through print with a blue pencil. Letting her wait he finally looked up and said, 'Well?' as if he'd forgotten she was coming.

An embarrassed Bobby Jo fumbled her way through an explanation. Eventually the older man took pity on her, 'Sit,' he commanded. Studying her he said sardonically, 'You're very young, Miss Bobby Jo or Miss Roberta, or whoever you are. So, you want to be a journalist, do you?' Wishing she could melt into the floor, Bobby Jo nodded. Her courage, if she'd ever had any, had completely deserted her. At that very moment all she wanted was to be back home in Little Chute with her loving parents, married to the boy next door. Sympathising with her predicament, Mr Murphy said, 'As you're a family friend of Mrs Reid I'm obligated to help but you hardly look suitable for the cut and thrust of our profession. It's a hard world out there. You have to be tough to survive it. Anyway, let's see what you're made of.'

Picking up the intercom he said, 'Can Xander Smith report to the editor soonest.'

It only took a few minutes before a lean, hawk-nosed, dark complexioned man threw open the door, 'Got a story for me Sam – 'bout time.'

'Hardly, Smith, after that exposé you did of Joe McCarthy's early life. Nearly ended us in the lawcourts and on Congress's blacklist. We only escaped by the skin of our

Life, Love, Death

teeth and a published apology. You're benched for the time being. I've something safer for you to focus on.'

Showing a set of gleaming white teeth, Xander laughed loudly, 'What else did you expect from me with a name like mine. Remember, Alexander means 'protector of mankind'. So, what else should I do but show up that coward Eisenhower who won't stand up to McCarthy.'

'Thanks for reminding me,' Sam guffawed, 'that name of yours will stand you in good stead at this very moment. I've got this young girl here for you to protect. She's going to be your trainee. You're going to show her the ropes.'

'The hell I am. I'm no wet nurse. What do you take me for?'

'My employee,' Sam said grimly, 'or you'll be out on your ear. This is a protégé of Mrs Reid herself.'

Xander scowled at Bobby Jo, 'So what's your name, fledgling, and why the special treatment?' Looking her up and down, he added, 'Didn't your mother ever tell you a redhead shouldn't wear pink or red?'

Bobby Jo ground her teeth, 'I'm Bobby Jo Hudson but prefer Roberta now I'm in New York.'

'I'll call you Bobby. You need to earn a name like Roberta. It doesn't suit you anyways. You're certainly not New York vintage, more like Bobby Jo from the boonies to me.'

Sam Murphy shook his head and made a swatting gesture, 'Do what you like, the pair of you. Get outta here,' and speaking directly to Xander, 'Smith, make sure everything's

Life, Love, Death

done by the book. Get the kid on payroll and give her something to do.'

'How long for?' Xander persisted.

'As long as I choose, Smith. You're not my favourite person just now. It'll take time to get back in my good books. Go find a 'dog and pony story' that's not controversial. Something to satisfy middle-aged matrons in the 'burbs. Out! And don't slam the door.'

A scowling Xander dragging the reluctant Bobby Jo by the arm, pulled her out of the office, slamming the door so hard the glass shuddered but didn't break. Running down the staircase with Bobby Jo in tow, Xander said, 'Now listen here young Bobby or whatever your name is, I have serious work to do. I don't want you getting in my way. Pushing her towards a couple of desks in the corner he said, 'Sit there. Keep your mouth shut till I tell you otherwise.' Totally ill at ease, Bobby Jo thought this an inauspicious start to her brilliant career as a New York reporter. Would things improve? How was she to cope with this frightening man?

The following day, making her way to Leo's for lunch, Bobby Jo breathed a huge sigh of relief to think that at least she had Delia and Joel. Xander had barely spoken to her all day and when she went home at night the girls at the Barbizon just made fun of her clothes and her accent. Perhaps she'd expected too much thinking it would be straightforward in New York once she had a job and somewhere to live, but the loneliness was unbearable. Most of the time she was terrified and cried into her pillow at night. There were so many people rushing about, yet no one smiled or talked to her. It was as if she was completely

Life, Love, Death

anonymous, adrift in a city of millions. Straightening her shoulders and putting a smile on her face, Bobby Jo entered Leo's, ready to greet the only two people she knew in New York – her friends.

CHAPTER 5

Surprisingly both Bedelia and Joel had arrived early and were making efforts to chat. Bobby Jo heard Joel talking about the Rosenbergs' execution and was taken aback. Joel hardly seemed like a man who followed the news, maybe something in the world of jazz but not anything else.

Delia shuddered, 'What a way to die.'

'I dunno, could be worse ways.'

'Whatever could be worse, Joel?'

'Starvin' to death, beaten to death, lynched.'

Delia's eyes nearly popped out of her head, 'Sounds as if you've first-hand experience.'

'Some,' Joel said sharply, 'and I's tell you's many of them victims would have thought electrocution a kindness.'

Delia, becoming aware of Bobby Jo's presence, said, 'You're quiet today, dear, I didn't hear you join us. Let's change the subject, Joel. It's too fine a day to dwell on unpleasant things.' Turning to Bobby Jo she asked, 'How was your first day at work?'

Shaking her head, Bobby Jo said soulfully, 'Not good. I'm wondering if I belong here or whether I should jump on the next train back to Little Chute.'

Taking on a new belligerent personality, Joel spat out forcefully, 'That's no good, little lady. You's gotta give it a

Life, Love, Death

go. You's will regret it if you's don't. I's know (he tapped his nose meaningfully). I bin there.'

Delia patted Bobby Jo's shoulder, 'I agree with Joel. It's early days. Things will get better.'

A brooding Delia wondered if she was really trying to console herself. Her job in womenswear at Ohrbach's selling discount lines and seconds was not as satisfying as it used to be. The Union Square store was hardly 5th Avenue but what choice did she have after Gus died? Giving up the comfortable house in Hempstead had been a wrench but neither of her boys were interested – one in California and the other travelling the world. At least they telephoned occasionally, and she didn't have to worry about them being drafted to Korea. That was something. The apartment in Queens was adequate for her and Monet, a stray cat she'd adopted, but was this all there was? Thank goodness for Dexedrine. The doctor who'd prescribed it had warned her it could be addictive. But she didn't care, it helped get her through the day.

Just then Addy bustled over, interrupting their thoughts, 'And what'll y'all have today?' Looking directly at Delia, she said, 'We've a nice bit of meatloaf out back, what d'ya think?'

Delia did her best not to make a face, 'So kind, Adelie, but I think I'll stick to my usual egg salad sandwich and maybe some soup if you have it.'

'Only split pea, I'm afraid. Will that do?'

'Perfect.' Delia sat back and relaxed.

Life, Love, Death

'And what about us,' Joel asked angrily. 'I's nothing here. That bitta meatloaf would suit me fine with them there French fries.'

'Hold up Joel, I was getting to you. I took it for granted you wanted your usual.'

'I's can have what I's want,' Joel said angrily, 'I needs a bit of a change is all, and what about her? She look likes she needs summat.'

They all stared at Bobby Jo who, head hanging down, was playing with a napkin. With a face full of anguish she looked up, 'Who, me? I'm not hungry.'

Addy sighed but feeling sorry for the young girl said, 'I know what will do the trick – pancakes with maple syrup. What about that?'

Bobby Jo's face brightened, 'I could manage that…and maybe a vanilla shake.'

Addy nodded, 'Be back in a jiff. Cheer up y'all, it's summertime.'

After the food arrived they concentrated on eating until a revived Bobby Jo said, 'As you're both so much older and wiser than me, can I ask you something?'

Joel sniffed, 'I dunno what you wants from me. I thought all you young 'uns knows best?'

Delia, playing her usual conciliatory role, said, 'I'm not sure being older makes us any wiser but try us.'

Life, Love, Death

'I'm being trained by this older journalist. He's angry about being responsible for me, won't speak or give me work to do. The first day was fine but this morning I sat at my desk doodling. He won't even let me answer the telephone. I feel useless.'

Delia understood only too well. Mr Simmonds, the newly appointed Floor Manager in her department, was proving to be a problem too. Nothing she did was right. Only this morning his majestic three piece suited presence had towered over her. Stroking his pencil moustache he'd said, 'I notice you're not selling many of our Chanel skirt suits, Mrs Gray. I would have thought our clientele would have snapped them up.'

Without thinking, Delia said, 'They're hardly Chanel, Mr Simmonds – only copies. Not good ones at that.'

Raising himself up to his full height, Mr Simmonds practically exploded, 'I'll thank you not to talk to me like that Mrs Gray, or you might find yourself looking for another job at the end of the week. I'm keeping an eye on you.'

As Delia continued comparing her situation with Bobby Jo's, Joel intervened, 'Now you's look here, little lady. You's got to go for it. Read newspapers. Find stories. Come down Minetta Street where I's live. Plenty o' dirt going on there. No good sitting on your ass.'

'Really Joel,' Delia protested, 'you could have put it more politely.'

Life, Love, Death

'I leaves the gentility to you's,' Joel snarled, 'this little gal wants a good dose of common sense or she's never going to get nowhere.'

A confused Bobby Jo wondered if she'd started World War Three but realised Joel was right. What she didn't need was platitudes and sympathy but a kick in the butt. 'Thank you, Joel. I'll do what you say. Perhaps, if you have time I can come to the Village and you could show me around.'

'Maybe,' was the only response she got, as Joel reverted to his former sullen self.

Delia, too concerned with her own predicament, speedily finished her sandwich. Addressing Bobby Jo she added, 'I'm sure things will improve, dear, you'll see. Perhaps Joel has a point. I must go,' and hurried off to her usual visit to the Museum of Modern Art, cheering herself up with the thought of the afternoon ahead.

CHAPTER 6

The following Saturday Bobby Jo was at a loose end. Many of the Barbizon girls had gone away for the summer and those that were left barely gave her a passing glance. Feeling sorry for herself after a trying first week at the Tribune she set out for Times Square. There was always so much life there. Maybe she could find someone to talk to or pick up a free ticket from. Crossing one of the sidewalks she thought she heard music. Was it a Sax? Immediately she thought of Joel, but, no it was another guy busking. One much younger than Joel. Thinking he might know Joel, she hung around until he asked, 'What's up?'

Mentioning Joel's name, the man nodded his head, 'Yep, I know the old dude. Saturdays he's down the Village on the corner of McDougall and Bleecker maybe. Well, certainly somewhere round Washington Square.'

Bobby Jo was excited. She'd heard so much about Greenwich Village, perhaps she should go. Joel hadn't given her an actual invitation but surely he wouldn't mind? Having no idea how to find him she remembered he'd mentioned Minetta Street so she could start there It was a hot day and a long way, but she had nothing else to do and this would be one way of exploring New York.

Stopping for an iced tea and consulting her map, Bobby Jo wandered along admiring the brownstones on the way to Union Square. Ohrbach's store was straight in front of her. Hadn't Delia said she worked there? Should she venture in and look her up? Delia might not be too pleased being a somewhat private person and sometimes rather remote. On the other hand Bobby Jo was tempted. Eventually curiosity

Life, Love, Death

got the better of her. Maybe she could take a sneak look and pretend she was a customer browsing. As it was Saturday afternoon it would be busy. No one would notice her. Not knowing which department Delia worked in, Bobby Jo made her way through the floors, finally catching sight of the Womenswear Department. At once she saw Delia serving a customer and not wanting to be seen hid behind a rack of summer dresses. Delia looked elegant and gracious as she helped a young woman with a new line of frilled blouses.

Everything was going well with the sale when Bobby Jo saw a tall portly figure of a man in a suit with a rapidly receding hairline slide up to Delia, bend down and murmur in her ear. He was obviously the manager. Seeing Delia tighten her lips and narrow her eyes, Bobby Jo gathered this was not a welcome intrusion. After a word or two's exchange the large man stalked off and Delia returned to her customer, attempting to smile. Bobby Jo frowned. This was obviously not an opportune moment to talk to Delia. She didn't want to upset one of her only two friends in New York. Perhaps she'd have better luck with Joel.

As it was lunchtime, Bobby Jo bought a hot dog from a street vendor and spotting the arch of Washington Square moved to sit in the shade. Intrigued by the chess players she stopped to watch them play but was too shy to get close. Her father had taught her to play but neither of them was any good. They usually ended up flinging the chess board over in disgust and laughing uproariously. How she missed him! Little Chute seemed like another world, yet it was only a couple of weeks since she'd left.

With no sign of Joel in sight Bobby Jo continued to the south side of the square, asking for directions from passers-by.

Life, Love, Death

Most people shook their heads and hurried on. The Village seemed to be made up of a series of winding small treelined streets that bore no resemblance to the straight grid-like lines of Manhattan. Becoming tired and dispirited Bobby Jo accosted a tall African wearing a long embroidered robe who shook his head saying, 'Minetta Street - bad place for little gal – much evil – many murders - not safe,' and hurried on.

Never one to be put off by such nonsense, Bobby Jo shrugged and carried on. Turning a corner, she heard the faint strains of music and, making her way towards the sound, sighted Joel with his beloved Betsy. Not thinking and relieved to find someone she knew she rushed up to him, but Joel played on ignoring her. Parking herself right in front of him and determined to be noticed, finally she got a response. Scowling almost menacingly, he growled, 'What d'ya want, little lady? Not your sorta neighbourhood. Get your throat cut if you's not careful.'

'Nothing, nothing, I don't want anything,' Bobby Jo assured him hastily. 'I wanted to see the Village and thought I'd look you up.'

'You's too nosy for my liking. Ain't it bad enough you worm's your way into my Tuesdays, now you's following me home. I's say agin what do you's want?'

'Honestly, nothing,' Bobby Jo flushed up to her roots. 'I'm keen to see everything,' and with a slight sob in her voice she gulped out, 'I'm lonely with no one to talk to. The girls at the Barbizon look on me as a country hick, and that man at the Tribune regards me as a nuisance. I don't know

Life, Love, Death

anyone in New York except you and Delia. I thought you were my friends.'

Joel swallowed uncomfortably, finding it difficult to ignore the note of pleading in her voice. 'Take no notice of me, young 'un. I's a grouchy old man too used to his own company. Stay awhile. I'll play summat for you's. What d'ya wanna hear?'

'Thank you, Joel, oh thank you so much. I'd love to hear you and Betsy play. I don't know much about music. My folks only listened to Mozart and Beethoven. I've only just started listening to the latest music on the hotel's radio.'

Without another word Joel launched into 'These Foolish Things…'and Bobby Jo, recognising it, giggled, 'Is that aimed at me?'

As Joel worked through his usual repertoire, passers-by stopped, admiring his pretty redheaded companion and gave generously. Beaming, Joel said, 'You's might be doing me some good, Missy.'

'I wish I could sing or dance. You could make more money,' bemoaned an enthusiastic Bobby Jo.

'Don' even try,' Joel warned, but at last he was amused and teasing. 'Now I's reckon we's enough for fish supper for us both.'

Bobby Jo was dumbfounded. Was Joel asking her to stay and eat with him? What a surprise! Taking no notice of her reaction, Joel packed up, limping up 6th Avenue to the Waldorf Cafeteria with a bemused Bobby Jo in his wake, and

Life, Love, Death

mumbled, half to himself, 'Cheaper to take out. Have to be my place. 'Spect you'll have a shock. Not what you's used to. No vermin just now though.'

Bobby Jo, not knowing what to expect, waited whilst Joel thrust a pack of fish and chips at her as he picked up Betsy. Following his lead, they made their way back the way they'd come to Minetta Street. Joel slowly eased his way down steep steps to a beaten-up basement door and fumbled for an enormous old-fashioned key. The interior was dark and damp and Bobby Jo did her best not to wrinkle her nose at the smell. In the hallways was a sort of curious sloping hump in the floor. The end of the gloomy hall led into one large room spread across the width of the building. The only furniture was an ancient bed, a table with a wonky leg, two chairs and an old couch with its springs hanging out. A dusty faded curtain hung over an annexe. The only signs that someone lived there was an old wind up gramophone, a stack of records and a wireless. Joel disappeared behind the curtain, reappearing with two plates overflowing with chips and fish. He placed them delicately on the table as if they were eating at a posh restaurant, dusted off a chair with his none too clean handkerchief, and said, 'Best I can do, lady. Here's a fork,' spat on it and cleaned it with the self-same handkerchief. Bobby Jo nearly shuddered but stopped herself in time and reluctantly accepted the utensil. They ate in silence. Joel, unused to company, concentrated on eating his food with his fingers.

Bobby Jo picked at her plate and thought how on earth could anyone live like this? Feeling she should make conversation she asked, 'How long have you lived here, Joel?' nearly making a slip of the tongue and saying instead, 'How long have you lived **like this**?'

Life, Love, Death

'I's dunno. Maybe since I's left Brooklyn. Could be goin' on thirty years. Got a lotta our history here in the Village. After slavery abolished in New York last century, it were home to my people, Africans,' he said with pride. 'I's weren't always here though – first few places in Village weren't good – had to share and was on the road a lot. Slept in vans or backs of cars with other musos or roughed it.' Looking smugly round the room he said, 'This is home, got my music, good ole wireless and my Betsy. That's all I's need.'

Bobby Jo was speechless, beginning to wonder why she felt so sorry for herself when she had a lovely room at the Barbizon, a job and money to buy food with. Taking her silence for encouragement, Joel now he was well fed began to be more expansive, 'Course it ain't all roses living here. 'Bin and still is plenty of murders. The other day a man have his throat and stomach slit on the street – blood and guts everywhere. Probably summat to do with the Crew, you know the Genovese family.' He tapped his nose, 'Mafia. You's need to keep clear of the Triangle Club on Sullivan Street. That's their hangout.'

Hearing all this, Bobby Jo became paler and paler. Just as she was about to faint Joel realised he'd frightened her. Scuttling behind the curtained annexe, he produced a glass of brackish looking water. Bobby Jo, feeling none too fussy, drank it in one gulp. Her colour began to return and feebly she murmured, 'I think I need to go back to the hostel. I'm sorry, Joel. You've been so kind.'

'Don' worry, little miss. I went too far. I's a mate cross the street. He'll run you's back in his van.'

Life, Love, Death

'The mate' and the van turned out to be as old as Joel. After a lot of shuffling about the pair of them cleared a seat for Bobby Jo. After a lot of grinding of gears and sputtering of exhaust, she found herself en route for the Barbizon. Joel stood and waved them off as if he were waving to the Queen of England.

Surprisingly, the antique vehicle made it to East 63rd Street and the Barbizon without being stopped by the police or breaking down. Bobby Jo was so relived to get back; she emptied out her purse, giving the old man tens of dollars to share with Joel. Perhaps the day had been a salutary lesson she decided, seeing how other peoples' lives were so much worse than her own. From now on Bobby Jo resolved, she was going to stop feeling sorry for herself, take a leaf out of Joel's book and be grateful for what she had.

CHAPTER 7

After Bobby Jo's visit to Minetta Street she decided to take Joel's advice about her work and show initiative. On the following Monday morning she reported for duty at the Tribune armed with piles of newspapers, everything from The New York Times to the Daily News and even The Daily Worker. Giving Xander Smith a mere nod, she sat down at her desk carefully perusing the papers one by one, highlighting items, and cutting out stories that interested her. After all, hadn't she obtained a good degree from Rutgers. She was hardly a novice and didn't intend being treated as one.

Looking over at her laden desk Xander smirked knowingly. Perhaps the little girl had guts and backbone after all. Calling the copyboy over, he said under his breath, 'Take that little gal a coffee, d'ya hear. She looks as if she might need one.' As the day wore on, Xander finally approached Bobby Jo who was still thumbing through papers, 'I tell you what, why you don't pick out a news article you find interesting and give me a five hundred word summary by the end of the day.'

A glassy eyed Bobby Jo looked up, rapt with the attention but determined to look nonchalant, and trying to hold back the words that were desperate to spill out of her mouth said coolly, 'Of course Xander, no problem.'

Xander nodded and, going over to a rather battered old typewriter, presented it to her, 'Here, this will do for your first efforts. Let's see what you're made of. I've got to go out for a bit. I'll be back by five, show me your piece then.'

Life, Love, Death

Bobby Jo felt the usual nerves rising in her stomach, but this time accompanied by a feeling of smugness and thrill at the challenge. She would show him.

All afternoon she toiled on a piece about China's attitude to Stalin's death. It was said Mao Tse-Tung wailed when he heard though that seemed unlikely to Bobby Jo with her minimal knowledge of the dictator. Struggling with the words she honed the piece to perfection and typed it out as neatly as she could on the ancient typewriter with its inky ribbon.

Prompt at five, Xander stood in front of her as she typed the last word, peremptorily snatching the sheet from her hand. Sitting down at his desk he took out a red pen, shaking his head as he subbed and crossed out words. Bobby Jo felt like a naughty schoolgirl being taken to task by her teacher. Resentment and fury vied inwardly with exhaustion as she sat waiting. What was he doing to her brilliant prose?

Eventually, Xander looked up, 'Hm – not bad, not bad at all. Too wordy of course. That's to be expected - a novice's error and a bit inflated – but all in all not too bad.' Making the paper into a dart, he threw it back to her. 'Interesting choice of subject. I thought you'd opt for something from Woman's Wear Daily. Didn't think you knew much about world affairs let alone Communist Leaders. A good start, keep it up. I'll want the same tomorrow and the rest of the week. Let the facts speak for themselves – don't embellish – not too many adjectives. Say what you mean and mean what you say.' He got up, threw on his epauletted trench coat looking every inch an East European spy with his swarthy looks and dark hooded eyes, and without a backward glance shouted, 'See you tomorrow, Bobby!'

Life, Love, Death

Goodness, Bobby Jo thought, he knows my name even if he only uses the first part. I suppose that's something. Looking down at the mangled piece of paper which contained her whole day's 'Magnus Opus', she cringed. It was covered in red pen. However, it was a beginning and oddly enough she was less scared of Xander now. Having taken matters into her own hands she realised Joel was right. She had to prove herself worthy of respect.

On the Tuesday, feeling pleased with herself, Bobby Jo arrived at Leo's diner first. Addy greeted her briefly but rushed off to sort out squabbling customers. After a few minutes Joel, looking drawn and weary, arrived with Betsy and sat down heavily in the booth.

'You look tired today, Joel,' Bobby Jo said sympathetically.

'That I's am. Tough times for an old busker. Got moved on three times – slim pickings.'

'Let me buy you lunch, Joel. After all you treated me on Saturday.'

'No, young Missy. I's never takes charity. Pays my own way.' But for once he smiled, and said, 'Thanks.'

They'd already begun their lunch by the time a flustered and upset Delia arrived, complaining, 'It's far too hot for me. There's too many people and no air.'

Bobby Jo, feeling magnanimous to everyone today, said, 'I'll call Addy over. She'll get you an iced tea or maybe some lemonade.'

Life, Love, Death

'Thank you, my dear. I don't feel myself. I've been having problems sleeping in this heat and feel a little nauseous.' For once she was not attired in her usual skirt suit but in a rather fetching short sleeved, full skirted blue dress which matched her eyes.

'What a lovely dress, Delia,' Bobby Jo said admiringly.

Delia smoothed down her skirt and said, 'Yes, it's a new line copied straight from this Spring's Dior collection in Paris. Of course, I get it at a store discount which makes it affordable.' As she talked, she delved into her purse and brought out a bottle of pills. 'I forgot to take these this morning. That's probably what it is.' As soon as the iced tea arrived, she swallowed down a handful of pills.

'Don't abide them there sort of things,' Joel observed. 'A nip of whiskey would do you's better.'

Delia flushed, 'It's since my dear Gus passed. I need something, a little Dexedrine. It's hard to keep going sometimes,' muttering... 'can feel so low and tired.'

Bobby Jo was astounded to hear Delia open up so much. She normally never discussed anything private. She must be feeling ill.

Addy came over asking, 'Anything to eat, Mrs Gray? If you don't mind me saying, you look a trifle peaky. You need a good meal. I've chilli on the stove, not too hot mind, or fresh pancakes with whatever you fancy.'

Delia paled even more, 'No thanks Adelie, just another iced tea and perhaps a little plain toast.'

Life, Love, Death

Addy went away tutting to herself. What had the world come to when folks were eating plain toast.

Delia closed her eyes and sat quietly, whilst Bobby Jo and Joel conversed in hushed tones. Hearing them mention Bobby Jo's visit to the Village on the previous Saturday, Delia's eyes flew open. 'Wasn't it dangerous for you to go all that way on your own, my dear?'

'No, Joel took good care of me.'

Momentarily Delia looked vexed at being excluded but pulling herself together, said frostily, 'I'm sure you had a lovely time together.'

Bobby Jo didn't think it an opportune moment to tell Delia that she'd also called in at Ohrbach's, instead said apologetically, 'It was only chance, Delia, I wanted to see the Village and bumped into Joel,' hoping she hadn't upset Delia. Too exhausted to respond, Delia merely nodded, thinking perhaps she should give the Museum of Modern Art a miss today and go home and rest. A nap might put her in a better frame of mind, 'If you'll both excuse me I think I'll leave you to it and head home.' Not wanting to sound peevish, she added, 'See you next week.'

CHAPTER 8

Later that afternoon, making her way towards the subway after doing some food shopping, Delia found her earlier malaise had lifted. Her mood had changed. The tablets must be doing something she thought and decided to go to the Museum after all. There was a special exhibition of twentieth century sculptures, and the museum was having a late viewing for members.

Visiting the galleries always calmed Delia, particularly after a difficult morning at work. The works of art helped give her a new perspective and remind her that there was a world outside Ohrbach's and people other than Mr Simmonds. That man always gave her a hard time probably because she'd been up for the same promotion. He, being a man, had walked in and been appointed on the spot. It was hardly fair. The only experience he had in retail was door-to-door selling. But as the Personnel Manager explained to her 'We have to give our war veterans priority.' In fact, she'd found out later, Simmonds had only been an assistant quartermaster during the war, sending provisions to NAAFIs, and never leaving American shores. However, here and now in the gallery luxuriating in Matisse, Picasso, and Monet, her senses awash with colours and shapes, all that was best forgotten.

In the sculpture gallery, Delia noticed a man sitting at an easel – an amateur artist no doubt. He had settled in front of a nude bronze where the woman's arm was resting on her knee. Dying to see the man's quick drawing, she edged nearer and nearer, inadvertently dropping her purse on the floor. The man frowned, looking directly at her, 'Can I help you, lady?' he asked in a thick guttural accent.

Life, Love, Death

Delia, disconcerted by such a handsome, darkly tanned, and bearded stranger, could only stammer out, 'I'm sorry. I didn't mean to disturb you. I was curious about your work.'

'That's quite all right, Mevrou. I'm only sketching today. Trying my hand at these exquisite statues. Please to come forward. What is your name?'

'Bedelia Gray…well, Delia.' Delia couldn't help stuttering. Flustered at meeting such a good looking man, she turned away saying, 'I'll go. Sorry to disturb you.'

With a gleam in his eye the man said, 'Being disturbed by a beautiful lady is what I need.' Getting up from his stool he bowed formally, 'I introduce myself too. I am Jan de Vries formerly from South Africa. Pleased to meet with you, Bedelia Gray.'

Delia blushed. Trying to compose herself, she said, 'I've never met anyone from South Africa. How did you come to live in New York?'

'A long story, I'm afraid, in fact a very long story. Please allow me to tell you a little of it over tea in the cafeteria here. I can leave my work for the present.' Not used to meeting or even taking tea with strangers, Delia couldn't find anything to say but agree, 'That would be very pleasant.'

As they sat opposite one another in the busy café, Jan de Vries said, 'If I may say, as an artist, you have the most superb sparkling blue eyes. Has anyone ever told you that?'

Delia was dumbfounded. She couldn't remember Gus, her late husband, ever complimenting her on anything, let alone

Life, Love, Death

her eyes. Most times Gus was so distracted with his work that he barely acknowledged her existence. Even when they first met and were courting, he was always talking about new medical advances, having little time for small talk. During all the years she'd looked after his children, his house, his meals, his clothes, and kept his life running smoothly he'd never even noticed a new dress. Probably she'd been just part of the furniture. It was a shock to realise that, when Gus had been everything to her. Obviously it hadn't been the same for him.

De Vries, sensing Delia's distress, patted her hand, 'Take no notice of me, my dear. Like my fellow countrymen, I can often be too direct. I hope I've not upset you.'

'No, of course not,' Delia murmured. 'I'm just so unused to compliments. At my age few people even look at me, let alone pay me any attention. It's like being invisible.'

'I always look,' De Vries continued. 'Looking and seeing are for me what art is all about. The change of a colour, the nuance of a fold in a dress, the lines of experience on a face, a half-smile, clenched hands.' He reached across and carefully unclenched Delia's fists, which she hadn't realised she'd clamped together while thinking of her life with Gus. 'It's all 'grist to my mill', isn't that what art is about?' he added.

'Are you a professional artist, Mr de Vries?' Delia asked timidly.

'Well, I suppose you could say that. I do exist on the odd commission. But call me Jan – it's the equivalent of your

Life, Love, Death

John, and I shall call you Delia. What a pretty name. It suits you.'

'But isn't it a very precarious way to earn a living?' Delia asked, gaining courage.

'I do have an allowance from some land my father left me in South Africa. Otherwise, it's commissions, and illustrative work for magazines and advertising companies in Madison Avenue and the like. Of course, there is the odd patron or two who like to subsidise my work,' he added with a twinkle in his eye.

'I would love to be able to draw and paint,' Delia said enthusiastically. It's something I envy so much in others.'

'But, my dear Delia, everyone can draw or paint if they wish. Agreed, there are people with natural talent but one can learn if the passion is there. Perhaps one of these days you would do me the honour of visiting my studio on the Upper East Side. I could set you up with paints and show you the basics.'

Delia was elated, not permitting herself to think whether she should accept an invitation from a complete stranger. The Upper East Side at that – he must have money. 'I'd love that,' she blurted out.

'Here's my card,' De Vries said with a flourish. 'Give me a call. I think I get back to work now. It has been a delight meeting you, Delia, and an agreeable interval in a rather tedious day.' He took her hand and bowed over it, taking his leave.

Life, Love, Death

Delia kept on sitting there, smiling smugly. What a man! She even felt beautiful. As she watched him disappear back to the upper gallery, she made up her mind to see him again whatever the consequences. Her sons would never approve, thinking her much too old for romantic liaisons. Nevertheless, Delia felt youthful and gay, practically dancing out of the museum and down the street to the subway. Tossing her pristine lace gloves in the nearest refuse bin, she felt a surge of exhilaration she'd never felt before. She wanted to sing, to dance, to break out. But a little voice in her head wouldn't be silenced, and kept repeating itself, 'What on earth has gotten into you, Delia? Perhaps you should take an extra Dexedrine when you get home.' At this very instant though she was heady with the wine of utter pleasure and determined to make the most of it.

CHAPTER 9

The following Tuesday Delia arrived at the diner bubbling over with good humour. Her two companions looked on in surprise seeing her hatless and without gloves. Her normally tightly coiffured hair was loose and tied back with a fetching bow. A pillar box red purse was a conspicuous mismatch with her stylish green and white striped dress, her black patent leather strappy sandals, and bohemian wicker bag embellished with fruits and flowers. Delia herself was different, gurgling greetings and remarking on Bobby Jo's new blouse and recently dyed copper red bob, 'What a difference, Bobby Jo. You look so grown up and sophisticated. Joel, is that a new shirt, I spy?'

'Naw, it ain't,' Joel spat out. 'Same ole one – just pressed. Nuffink new about me.' But even he could see the fresh glint in Delia's eye. What had happened to the woman since last week? She'd been so morose and down, they'd hardly been able to get a civil word out of her. This transformation summed up his opinion of women. No sooner had a fella got used to them one way than they changed and kept on changing. A fella never knew where he was with them. Thank God he'd never married. It'd been a close call once. He'd had a lucky escape. Suffering badly from too much drink the night before and lack of sleep, he slurped down his coffee in one noisy gulp. 'Dunno what the world's coming to,' he mumbled.

'What do you mean, Joel?' Delia enquired in her absolute best 'tea and sympathy' voice, wanting to spread her feelings of goodwill amongst her companions.

Life, Love, Death

'Bad night last night. Too hot,' Joel groaned, carefully omitting the fact that he'd had too many whiskey sours. 'Was some sort of celebration and dancing in them streets…then them fireworks till all hours.'

'Oh, it must have been the July 4th festivities carrying on after the weekend,' Bobby Jo remarked.

'Ouf, what a fuss! Who the hell cares about American Independence,' Joel snorted, 'nother excuse for people to get drunk and cavort about irritating other people.'

'But it's an important day for us. It's when we gained our independence from England. We must celebrate. Don't you remember it when you were young, Joel, fireworks, hot dogs, barbecues, and fun?'

'Lotta nonsense is all I's can say,' Joel said, determined not to be persuaded out of his bad temper.

Even this exchange couldn't burst Delia's bubble. Swapping pleasantries with Addy, she said, 'Adelie my dear, you look well today. Do you think I could have a turkey club sandwich, fries, and a chocolate shake.' Addy's eyebrows shot up into her blonde plaited hair wondering what had happened to the usually fastidious and particular Mrs Gray. She seemed to have gotten an appetite from somewhere. Making no comment she sped off to the kitchen with her order, leaving Delia looking pleased with herself.

Bobby Jo murmured tactfully, 'Delia, you seem happy today. Have you had good news or perhaps promotion?'

Life, Love, Death

'Hardly,' Delia retorted. 'But I do feel good, much better than I've felt for a long time.'

Bet it's them there danged pills Joel thought to himself. What have we come to when ladies like Delia Gray are popping uppers and downers on a regular basis. He'd seen behaviour like this before but only on tour with musos. One day there was no speaking to them, the next they were slapping him on the back and buying him drinks. Thank the Lord he'd never succumbed. Of course, there'd been the odd bit of weed but those days were gone. It was the grog now that was his downfall.

No sooner was lunch over than Delia shot out of the diner as if it was a matter of life and death. Bobby Jo, dragging her feet, reluctantly made her way back to the Tribune for yet another afternoon of scouring the papers and trying to write something acceptable for Xander. Joel followed, lagging at the back, and pocketing the tips the two women had left. Addy wouldn't begrudge an old man a few cents, after all his need was greater than hers. It was a lovely afternoon but so hot he hadn't the energy to carry on busking. His creaking bones could do with some heat though, perhaps a few hours in Central Park would do him good. It was a hike but he struggled along, taking back streets to avoid the crowds and practically falling onto the first seat at the entrance to the park. Holding tightly on to Betsy he sat back, and his eyelids began to flicker and close. A few minutes' nap was all he needed. Then, with the small amount of dollars he'd earned that day he'd ride the subway home with enough for a bit of bread and cheese and a bottle of Rheingold.

Life, Love, Death

As the warmth seeped into his body, Joel's mind began to wander. What was it that silly Bobby Jo had said that had rankled? Something about 'having fun'. Well, he'd had plenty in his youth. There'd even been one or two women as well. And what about that Delia today? She'd been a surprise. There must be a man involved there somewhere. You never knew with women. He started thinking about women and one woman in particular. It was one of those nights they were playing Smalls Paradise in Harlem during Prohibition. He was doing one of his solos when he spotted her at a nearby table with a thick set white man. She was obviously one of the hostesses. Her beauty took his breath away and made him drop a note or two. Her skin was peachy with hair cascading round her shoulders in long dark curls. But it was the face that was sublime – a cross between the Mona Lisa (though he'd only ever seen pictures of the real thing) and one of his favourite film stars, Louise Brooks, with her sultry looks and glossy red lips.

As soon as the interval came Joel hailed one of the waiters, 'Hey Charlie, do me a favour, get me a bottle of that there bootleg whiskey and whisper in that lady's ear. See if she'll join me for a drink.' Charlie shook his head reproachfully, 'I'll try but it won' do you no good, boss. That there's Dutch Schultz. He's one of our suppliers You'll end up with a pair of concrete boots in the East River.'

Joel pleaded, 'Please try.'

Minutes later Charlie was back, 'You're in luck, boss. Dutch has a bit of business to deal with, or some poor bugger (giving Joel a wink) if you knows what I mean. The little lady will see you later. Meet her in the back dressing room. Don' forget you owe me.'

Life, Love, Death

Joel was beside himself and could barely get through the session. After the band packed up, he made his way down the draughty back corridor. The dressing room was no better than a storeroom with a couple of chairs, a table, a fly blown mirror surrounded by one or two dead bulbs and a tattered wicker screen in the corner. Seeing no sign of the girl, Joel sat down nervously on one of the chairs and uncorked the whiskey. He needed a drink. Before he could get the bottle to his lips a voice called out, 'Who's there?'

'Me,' bleated a sweating Joel.

'And who's 'me'?

'You know, one of the musicians who asked you for a drink? Charlie fixed it.'

'Hold on. I'll be out in a min.'

Joel took a slug of the whiskey to give himself courage. He wished he'd been better prepared and brought glasses but there'd never been many ladies in his life and he was out of practice. He could count on one hand the number of women there'd been, even his mother had abandoned him to his father.

Coming out from behind the screen clad only in a fraying silk robe, Gloria took a good look at Joel. What she saw was a slight, handsome but underfed black guy dressed in an oversized tuxedo and patent leather shoes, clutching a whiskey bottle as if his life depended on it. At his feet was a well-worn music case.

Life, Love, Death

'Hi, I'm Gloria,' she said in an offhand manner. Nodding towards the bottle, added, 'you got any left?'

'Yeah...yeah,' Joel stuttered, hardly able to take his eyes off Gloria's magnificent breasts falling out of her gown. 'Please have a...there's no glasses.'

'The bottle's OK.' Gloria said roughly, 'What can I do you for?' Then sensing his unease, she said, 'Take it easy, kid. I've got all the time in the world, well, until the next poor sap wants to part with his money and have a drink, a dance, or a bit of whatever with me,' giving him a not too subtle leer. Noticing Betsy at his feet she remarked, 'You certainly can play that old thing well. Gets me right down there in my gut,' patting her curvaceous stomach. 'Not bad for a kid.'

'I'm hardly a kid,' Joel protested. 'I's as old as you if not older.'

'OK, kid, just joking. We'll agree to differ. You look so danged young for your age.'

Joel sat up straighter, widened his narrow shoulders, and tried to look more manly. The all-knowing Gloria giggled, 'Oh, that will do it every time.' A deflated Joel sank into the chair, hiding his face in his drink.

'Don' take it to heart, lover boy. You've a sweet face. That's all that matters with the girls.'

'Don' have a girl,' Joel mumbled sheepishly.

Life, Love, Death

'Well, we'll have to do something about that,' and going to the door she flung it open, calling at the top of her voice, 'Desirée, Desirée, come here sugar. Help my friend here out.'

Joel sulked and hung his head. What did this Gloria think she was doing, when it was her he wanted? But a second later he felt a tiny hand creep into his and found himself looking into a pair of luminous green eyes staring up at him from a tiny, exquisite coffee coloured face framed by Afro curls dyed a discreet shade of red. Joel's heart turned over. He'd thought Gloria a beauty but Desirée was something else.

Noticing his confusion, Gloria said, 'Desirée, my sweet, Joel needs a girlfriend. What do you think?'

A tinkling little voice replied, 'Joel, I'm pleased to meet you. I love your playing.' From that moment Joel was gone. Every night after the session he would sit on the stoep with Desirée and tell her the sad story of his life whilst she held his hand looking deep into his eyes, encouraging him to continue.

It was the nights she danced with the customers that he hated. Sitting on the stage he would glower and grind his teeth seeing Desirée in other men's arms, them whispering sweet nothings into her neck. It should be him. She belonged to him. She was his. He'd even started thinking about a future together. Having been on the road so long perhaps it was time to settle down. One night as they gazed at the stars and kissed and canoodled, he said, 'I's want you, Desirée.'

'But Joel, you can have me anytime. I'm yours.'
'No, I's mean I's want to marry you.'

Life, Love, Death

Desirée giggled, 'But you have no money, Joel, and neither do I. How would we live and where could we live with you always on the road?'

'I'll find somewheres.' Joel said fervently. 'We's must be together.'

But the following week the band was off to the Bowery for a gig, then on the road again. Joel tried asking his bandmates for loans but nothing was forthcoming. Money was tight and earnings barely covered lodgings and food. Unhappy about leaving Desirée, Joel begged her to wait for him. Weeks later when he returned to the club there was no sign of Desirée. She'd disappeared. Joel was distraught – not willing to believe she'd deserted him. It was Gloria who had to break the painful news. Desirée had gone off with a guest trumpet player. For the rest of his life Joel would think he'd caught a glimpse of her in the subway or on an elevator or in a crowd. But it was not to be. She'd long gone, his love and devotion with her. No other woman was ever able to compete with her memory.

A football glanced off his shoulder and Joel woke with a start realising he was in the park. A little boy came running up saying, 'Sorry, Mister.' Joel was sorry too. He'd been so sure he and Desirée were soulmates – and were meant to be together - but it had been nothing but a daydream.

Stroking Betsy as he made his way home on the subway, Joel murmured to her, 'At least you's will never leave me, Betsy. You's won't be running off with no trumpet player.'

CHAPTER 10

At the Tribune Bobby Jo was beginning to feel appreciated at last. Xander was not using the red pen so much these days. On the odd occasion he made noises that sounded vaguely like approval even if they were only grunts.

On this particular day he declared, 'You're coming with me today. I've got this blasted story about the heatwave to do when really I should be reporting on the Korean War peace treaty or Che Guevara in Guatemala. I'll be glad when I'm out of Sam's doghouse. Until then you can be my gofer. Grab a pad and pencil. You can write up this insignificant story if I can find one.'

Dragging along a photographer, the three of them made for Lower Manhattan with Xander shouting out instructions to the photographer, 'Harry, take pics of those kids playing in the fire hydrants. Try not to get our cameras wet.' Later they moved on to shots of swimmers in the Hudson, office workers sunning themselves on roofs in their lunch break and kids queuing up at ice cream parlours. 'Call it: 'A Day in the Life – New Yorkers surviving 90 degree heat' or something like that. We'll come back later in the day when it's not so dang hot and get evening shots of people eating out, enjoying a late promenade, and sitting out on fire escapes.'

Turning to Bobby Jo he said, 'Get off to the hospitals. We'll show the other side of the coin – from heaven to hell. See how many people got heatstroke or died. Interview relatives. Take Harry with you. I've a little personal business to see to.'

Life, Love, Death

'Xander, I don't think I'm ready. I've never talked to anyone who's bereaved.'

'Harry will set you right. He's a veteran. Now take off. I'll see you back at the office,' and he raced off at breakneck speed. Bobby Jo wondered where he was going in such a hurry.

Bobby Jo had no idea where to start but Harry, being an old hand, headed them towards Bellevue Public Hospital. 'Look sweetie, see all those poor wretches lining the corridors and hunkering down on the floor in Emergency. Begin there. Talk to one or two poor souls. Your pretty young face will encourage them to open up'.

'But what should I say?'

'Find out how they're coping with the hot weather and why they've come to the Emergency Room. Chat. You'll be surprised how much people want to talk about themselves.' A diffident Bobby Jo approached a rather wan looking young woman leaning against a wall, 'Hi, I'm from the Tribune and wondered if you had time to talk to me?'

'Watcha want? I've been here three hours already and can't find out anything.'

Realising she had found her opening, Bobby Jo said sympathetically, 'Oh that's terrible. What did you want to find out?'

The young woman whose name was Linda, sighed and poured out her story. Despite the terrible heat she and her mom had been out shopping for the family. Without

Life, Love, Death

warning her mother had collapsed in the middle of the road. A kind driver had got out of his car and together they'd carried the poor woman to the sidewalk. As there was no sign of an ambulance Linda tried her best to revive her mother with sips of water and shield her from the fiercest of the sun. One or two passers-by stopped to help until at last a driver offered to take them to the nearest hospital. Once there, the semi-conscious lady had been wheeled away. Linda had been asking and asking where she was but no one would her give her any answers.

Hearing the sad tale, Bobby Jo, her red bob on fire, was fuming and promised to make enquiries on Linda's behalf. After a lot of shouting and using the Tribune's name, she finally got a doctor to tell her that Linda's mother hadn't recovered and had died of a heart attack two hours ago. This was something Bobby Jo had never faced before. Her own grandmother had died with her family around her and it had been expected. Bobby Jo, desperate to know what to do, looked for Harry but he was off taking photographs.

Approaching Linda, Bobby Jo could see the light of expectation and hope in the young woman's eyes. Taking Linda's hand, she said softly, 'I'm sorry Linda, your mother has passed away. Her heart couldn't cope. They should have come and told you.' The young woman almost fell as her legs collapsed under her and Bobby Jo found herself supporting the woman's full weight. Seeing her predicament, a passing nurse said, 'Here, let me take her. It's the shock. It takes people that way. Has she lost someone?' Seeing Bobby Jo nod, she asked, 'Are you a relative?'

'No, I was trying to help her. I'm from the Tribune.'

Life, Love, Death

'Leave her with me. I'll find somewhere for her to lie down. Once she feels better, I'll take her to see…her mother, was it?'

'Thank you, that would be helpful,' Bobby Jo said, feeling as if she was going to collapse herself. Maybe she wasn't cut out to be a tough hard-nosed journalist after all. It was horrible intruding into strangers' lives.

Returning, Harry could see by her face that all was not well. Once he heard her account he said, 'I'm sorry, Bobby Jo, but that's how it goes in this job. It's always hard the first time. At least we've got ourselves a real life story, and I've managed to collect all the relevant facts and stats from the hospital authorities so we can go back to the office.'

Back at the Trib a scowling Sam Murphy was already calling for copy and captions for the photographs, 'Where's Smith now?'

Bobby Jo didn't know what to say. Harry piped up, 'Gone on other business, guv. Don't know where.'

Furiously Sam sifted through the developed photos and throwing a few at Bobby Jo said, 'Right Missy, it's down to you. See what you can do. Captions for these and three hundred words in the next two hours on my desk.'

A fraught and shattered Bobby Jo struggled through copy. Two hours later she stood in front of the editor's desk whilst he scrawled blue lines through much of her prose. 'Not bad, my dear. Not bad for a trainee. Go back, retype it. I want it in my hand in the next fifteen minutes. Use your own byline since that scoundrel Smith has disappeared. Now, what's it to be?'

Life, Love, Death

A stammering Bobby Jo said, 'What do you mean?'

'Your name, your name on the piece.' Sam said testily, 'Come on. I've no time to waste.'

'Roberta Hudson,' Bobby Jo found herself saying.

'That's it then. Be back in fifteen, Hudson. We're ready to go to press.'

It was an hour later when Harry, the photographer, was buying her a much needed drink at the local bar that Bobby Jo suddenly realised she was now a fully-fledged journalist with her own byline.

'What will you have, sweetie? You look all in?'

'I don't know. I don't really drink – only a sherry at Christmas or a watered down Jenever.'

'On this special occasion a brandy for the young lady.' Harry gestured towards the bartender. 'But only the one. Then I think you should go home to bed,' he added in a fatherly way.

'Thanks, Harry. I don't know how I'd have managed without you.'

'My pleasure, young lady.' A gallant Harry bowed and presented her with her drink, 'You never know, I might be helping the next Pulitzer Prize winner. Here's to your future as a journalist, sweetie.'

Life, Love, Death

Reaction set in as soon as Bobby Jo lay on her bed at the Barbizon. Goodness knows what would have happened if she'd not been able to produce the goods. But she had and that was all that mattered. A flush of triumph suffused her whole body. She could hardly wait to see next day's paper and show it to her friends at the diner. Her last thoughts before she fell asleep was how many copies should she buy. Her folks in Little Chute would be proud.

CHAPTER 11

Later that week it was Delia's turn to feel triumphant. A couple of weeks had gone by since she'd visited the Museum of Modern Art but on her return there was no sign of Jan de Vries. She knew she must be brave and ring the number on the card he'd given her. Besieged by doubts and insecurities, she wondered if this was the right thing to do. However, reminding herself of her earlier sense of rebellion and wish for freedom from convention, she made up her mind and rang his studio. A businesslike but brusque voice answered as if the artist was in the middle of painting and didn't want to be disturbed.

'It's Delia,' she breathed into the telephone, 'Delia Gray.'

'Who?'

'We met at the Museum a few weeks ago,' Delia could barely continue, 'you were drawing a sculpture. Remember, we had coffee and you offered to teach me to paint.'

'Of course, of course,' the tone changed dramatically, 'the beautiful lady with blue eyes. Now I recall. Please to forgive a crusty old man whose head is full of his work. When would you like to come?'

'Would Tuesday afternoon next be possible?' Delia asked timidly. 'You see it's my afternoon off,' hesitantly she added, 'there is Sunday of course but that's when I catch up with housework.'

Life, Love, Death

'Tuesday it shall be,' proclaimed the voice. 'Come about three. We shall have tea before we start. Now, do you know how to find me?'

'I'll be fine,' Delia assured him quickly. She was so overwrought with adrenaline and excitement, all she wanted was put down the telephone and hug herself with delight.

'I'll look forward to seeing you, my dear,' Jan said, hanging up.

Delia kept re-running his last words to her as if they were little nuggets of gold. She was finally going to make inroads into her dull, pedestrian little life. What would Tuesday bring? She wished she had someone to confide in. There were her diner companions, of course, but Bobby Jo was much too young to understand and Joel was too old and worn out to care. What did they know about something like this and what it meant to her?

When Tuesday came, she made a huge effort to look youthful and modern. Probably neither her dining companions nor the staff at Ohrbach's would take the least bit of notice. Letting her blonde hair down, she partnered a revealing broderie anglaise blouse with a poppy red full skirt, adding open toed high heeled sandals and a fruit laden straw bag, totally oblivious to the fact that she looked like an Italian peasant who'd wandered in from the vines. Mr Simmonds' eyebrows nearly disappeared into his receding hairline. Coughing he said, 'Mrs (he swallowed, always having difficulty in remembering her name) – uhm – Mrs Gray, I don't think this is an appropriate outfit for the ladieswear department – more suitable for a boating holiday, I would think.'

Life, Love, Death

An insouciant Delia replied cheekily, 'Well, a lot of our ladies like to cruise. I was modelling the latest fashion for them.'

'You're not paid to model, Mrs (uhm) Gray. We have professional ladies for that.'

It was Delia's turn to raise her eyebrows, 'Professional ladies?' she said knowingly.

Mr Simmonds blushed a fiery red and stalked off. If he could only fire that woman. It was only the fact that she brought in most of the revenue for that department that made him think twice.

At the diner Delia's lunching companions also had no compunction about remarking on her attire. 'Wow, Delia,' Bobby Jo said admiringly, 'you look so young and summery. Are you going somewhere special?'

Delia tapped her nose, 'It's for me to know and you to find out,' she said in an unusually playful manner.

Mildly interested, Joel looked up from his hash browns, 'Mighty pretty, Miss Delia. Make men's eyes pop.'

'Certainly hope so,' Delia said smugly, 'maybe only one man's eyes though,' and would say no more.

Bobby Jo and Joel exchanged conspiratorial smiles. Clearly there was a man in Delia's life. Who'd have thought it?

Later that afternoon, Delia slowly wended her way on foot to Jan de Vries' studio. It was too hot and too crowded to

Life, Love, Death

take the bus or the subway. Heads turned as she passed, both men's and women's, and Delia wallowed in the admiration. Never in her life had she turned heads. Of course, at all times she'd looked neat and tidy, and her husband might have mentioned how pristine she dressed. But that meant nothing to her when there was always that other side of her desperate to break out. One that wanted to float about in crazy, brightly coloured clothes that made a statement to the world about her passion and desirability.

Arriving at the artist's brownstone house, Delia climbed the steps and tentatively pressed the bell. There was an enormous clatter inside. The door was flung open and a larger than life Jan de Vries stood there. He was a much bigger man than she remembered and completely filled the doorway. 'Sorry about the mess,' he said. 'That dang cat knocked over my easel when he heard the doorbell. He's got such sensitive hearing. I think he imagines himself a guard dog trying to keep strangers away.'

The front door led into a large extremely untidy living room full of papers and detritus and straight through to a glass ceilinged annexe. A large ginger and white cat was sitting on top of a shelf above the fireplace licking his paint-streaked paws.

'That's Ginger. He's never happy unless he's the centre of attention. A bit like his master I suppose. Come through and let me take your things.' He dropped Delia's bag nonchalantly on the floor as if it was of no account. 'Now let me look at you properly. What a picture. Does my heart good to see such beauty on a hot dusty afternoon. You look so fresh and delectable – positively edible.' He kissed her hand with such relish that Delia flinched, afraid he was

Life, Love, Death

going to actually take a bite out of it and wondering if she had made a terrible mistake.

Aware of her disquiet, de Vries took her by the arm and led her to a seat, 'Tea first I think, or maybe something stronger? Then I'll set you up with paints and drawing materials.'

Delia accepted the tea gratefully, hoping it would calm her nerves, but shook her head at the brandy Jan poured liberally into his own cup. Studying her, he frowned, 'You can't work in that lovely outfit.' For a desperate moment Delia had a horrible thought he was asking her to remove all her clothes. However, he said, 'I've a smock you can borrow. It's a pity you want to learn to paint. I'd much rather have you as a model. Perhaps another day.'

The phrase 'another day' rolled round and round in Delia's brain. It meant he wanted to see her again, but what about her? How did she feel? Feeling too panicky to think clearly, Delia sat quietly, drank more tea and ate a few cookies, which looked like they'd seen better days, struggling to exchange banalities.

Finally, Jan said, 'Ready?' Delia nodded. Delving in the corner of the room, he produced a paint splattered smock and lifted it carefully over her head, 'That should do.'

Throughout the afternoon he demonstrated basic drawing techniques, showing her how to mix colours, and finally allowing her to set off on her own and copy a summer scene he had to hand. Hours went by, Delia had become so involved in her work she hadn't realised it was past seven and said, 'I must go, Jan. It's been a wonderful afternoon.

Life, Love, Death

Have I taken up too much of your time?' Shyly she said, 'Should I be paying you if this is to be a weekly lesson?'

'Of course not, my dear. It's been a pleasure. Perhaps in the future you would agree to model for me. That would be payment enough.'

As they parted, Jan kissed her hand tenderly and going with her into the street hailed a yellow cab, 'Safe home, my dear. I look forward to seeing you next week.'

Delia could hardly breathe on the way home. Her head kept saying, 'What are you doing, Delia? You hardly know this man. What if he wants you to model in the nude? Where is all this going?' But Delia's alter ego didn't care. Feeling as if she was walking about two feet off the ground, Delia floated into her apartment. Picking up Monet she started dancing round and round the room singing until the distressed cat started mewling in fear. 'I'm sorry, Monet, it's such a wonderful life,' and a secret one, one she was going to hold close to her chest well away from prying eyes and certainly well away from Bobby Jo and Joel.

CHAPTER 12

The weeks of July passed rapidly by. Each of the three companions at the diner were preoccupied with their own private lives. It was Bobby Jo who brought up the subject of the Korean War. These days she was taking life earnestly, wanting to sound better informed by wading through the heavier, more serious papers, 'I read that the armistice between North and South Korea was signed yesterday. I never did understand why we were involved.'

Delia chortled in a rather superior way, 'I had no idea, Bobby Jo, you were that interested in world affairs.'

'It's Xander. He says I'm an ignoramus and need to expand my mind if I want to be a top-notch journalist. Which papers do you read, Delia?'

'Well, the Tribune of course mainly the society and fashion columns and perhaps the local news. I'm more of a novel reader really.'

Joel piped up, 'I's don' even take a newspaper, but when it's cold and raining I's goes to the New York Public Library to reads 'the funnies'.

Ignoring Joel's contribution Delia remarked, 'You seem keen to impress this Xander, Bobby Jo. Why him? I'd have thought you'd be more eager to impress your editor. Didn't you say when you wrote that story of yours that Xander had disappeared. It was the editor who let you publish it under your own byline.'

Life, Love, Death

Bobby Jo frowned, 'That's true. But I want to learn all I can. Xander is such an experienced journalist I feel he can teach me so much.'

'Or perhaps,' Delia teased, 'it's because he's young and good looking.'

'I never said that,' Bobby Jo protested as a blush spread up her face clashing with her red hair.'

'You didn't have too, my dear. I'm not too old to be able to work that one out. We've all been young, haven't we Joel, and had crushes.'

Joel growled, 'I's 's'pose so, lady, whatever you say,' and turning to Bobby Jo said, 'Take no notice young 'un. You's can likes who you pleases. That's what it be to be young.'

'Honestly both, I'm not interested in Xander, only what he can teach me. In actual fact he's quite old, in his thirties, so dark skinned with his gleaming white teeth and thick dark hair he looks like a pirate or a spy. Probably more like the latter because of his epauletted raincoats and fedora with the turned down brim. He's always sharp and abrupt with me, making no effort to make me like him.'

Delia laughed merrily, 'For someone you've little interest in, you seem to have noticed a great deal about him. Be on your guard, my dear. That type of man can easily get under your skin.'

'I don't think so,' Bobby Jo said haughtily. 'I may not be from New York but I'm not as innocent as you think. I can

Life, Love, Death

look after myself. He's of as much interest to me as I am to him.'

However, back at the Tribune offices she was very much the subject of discussion. Xander had been called in by Sam Murphy for a stern reprimand, 'I told you, Xander. I wanted no more of your messing about. Where did you vanish to when I told you to get the story about the heatwave. Thank goodness that little girl of yours had the nous to write up a not half bad piece and get herself a byline. Pretty good going for a youngster. I should watch your step. You might find yourself replaced and out of a job. That Roberta definitely has potential.'

For once Xander was nonplussed, 'Sorry, Boss,' he said sheepishly. 'I had to leave the girl,' (and improvising on the spot), added, 'because there was a bit of a family crisis. My mother had fallen and broken her hip. I had to rush her to the hospital.'

Sam Murphy, never a man to be hoodwinked with such a sob story, probed further, 'Now which hospital would that be?' fully aware that Bobby Jo and Harry had been at Bellevue doing their interviews.

There was a minute or two's silence whilst Xander contemplated the situation. Now which hospital would Harry and Bobby Jo have gone to that day? Fairly sure it was Bellevue, he chirped up, 'Presbyterian,' adding nothing more. Never 'over egg the pudding' was the phrase. Keep to the bare minimum when telling a lie.

'And how is your mother now?'

Life, Love, Death

'She's making a good recovery. It'll take time though.'

'And how is she coping? Are you looking after her?'

'No, I live downtown. My cousin's come over to care for her.'

Sam ground his teeth. It was never easy to catch this scoundrel out. The story sounded convincing but then Xander always was. There was something cunning and underhand about him. The trouble was he was a blindingly good journalist with a nose for a story or a scandal. He would have to give him the benefit of the doubt on this occasion. 'Xander, this is your last warning. Don't push me too far or I'll be showing you the door. You need to pay attention to Roberta. Give her the training Mrs Reid and I would expect her to have. Don't abandon her again.'

Xander stood with his head bowed, hiding the smirk that was slowly creeping up his face. He was half listening to Sam, but the other half of his brain was focussed on that girl Bobby with her aspirations to become Roberta, the journalist. He had made a mistake and underestimated her. Perhaps there was more steel in little Bobby than he had first thought. She had certainly fought back since that first day when she was a quivering wreck garbed in that hideous red and pink chequered suit. He felt a burgeoning respect for her, especially getting her own byline on what was essentially his story. She had outflanked him there - probably with Harry's collusion - but, all the same, possibly she was someone he could use and should be cultivated. He would change tack. From now on he would bombard her with his magnetic charm and see what he could make of her.

CHAPTER 13

The August humidity in the city was unbearable. People were leaving in droves heading for the coast, New Jersey, or Long Island. Bobby Jo and Delia arrived at the diner early on their usual Tuesday. It was odd to see no sign of Joel slurping his second cup of joe and chomping away with those clattering teeth of his. Addy rushed over as if it was a matter of life and death, 'Haven't you heard? Haven't you heard? Joel's been arrested.'

Both women were shocked.

Addy said irritably, 'It was bound to happen sooner or later. That old codger would push his luck with the busking particularly when Sergeant Mulroney is on duty. There was a bit of a collision in midtown. One of the drivers said he'd been distracted by Joel and his playing. What a load of …! The driver just wasn't paying attention and crashed into another car, blaming Joel. Anyways, they came for Joel, lights blazing, carting him off in a Black Maria. That Sergeant Mulroney always had it in for Joel. Poor old guy is locked up in Midtown South Precinct. The trouble is I ain't got the time or the money to run over there and bail him out. I'll do a bit of a whip round and see how much we can come up with. Maybe one of you kind ladies would go bail him out. I wouldn't want to see the old chap spend a night in the lock up.'

'Certainly,' Delia said, I'll go. I'm free this afternoon till my art lesson. How much do you think bail will be?'

Addy frowned, 'Not more than a coupla hundred dollars, I hope.' Passing round a hat, she chatted to customers whilst

Life, Love, Death

Frank stood behind the counter scowling. As far as he was concerned, he'd be happy for them to lock Joel up for life and throw away the key. After a lot of counting and double checking of small change, Addy poured the lot into a brown bag and gave it to Delia who hurried off to hail a cab.

'What about your lunch, Mrs Gray?' Addy shouted after her.

'No time for that, thanks Addy. I'll grab a bite later.' The cab sped to West 35th Street and Delia tipped the driver. She was looking particularly charming – in a blue and white checked shirtwaister with matching shoes and bag. Though her look was not quite so flamboyant as the day she'd visited Jan de Vries' studio, she hadn't reverted to her former prim, conservative style. At the precinct an apathetic cop, sweat marks showing through his immaculate uniform shirt, leaned over to ask her what she wanted.

'I've come to collect Mr Joel Petersen, who should not be here,' Delia said assertively. 'I don't know what you're thinking about locking up such an old man.'

After a considerable amount of paperwork and negotiation, the payment of a fine was agreed, and a dishevelled Joel emerged from his incarceration. Rather than be appreciative, he grimaced when he saw Delia, 'Dunno what you's think you's doing here, lady. S'no place for someone like you's.'

Delia ignored his bad humour and taking his arm said softly, 'We had a bit of a whip-round at the diner. I was the one who volunteered to come. Now don't be an old grouch. Let me take you home.'

Life, Love, Death

'I's can find my own way,' Joel protested loudly, but thinking about what Delia had said, murmured, 'everyone put in money for me, did they?' The beginnings of a tear started in his rheumy old eyes and slid down a wrinkled cheek.

Delia squeezed his arm reassuringly, 'They certainly did. Not Frank of course - you know Frank.'

The beginnings of a smile began to wend its way onto Joel's face, 'Mighty grateful. Sorry not myself. They's took my Betsy. I's dunno where she is. I's lost without her.'

'Don't worry Joel. I'll sort it.' Delia marched back to the counter, demanding the Sax. 'I hope you haven't dumped it in lost property, or I'll be very cross indeed,' she said narrowing her eyes and glowering at the young officer.

He cringed and said, 'Wait a moment, Madam. I'll go get the instrument.'

Ten minutes later they were speeding back to Joel's, while he clutched and fondled Betsy, whispering to her reassuringly as if she was a long lost child.

Back at his basement, Delia went out and bought groceries as there was nothing edible in his cupboard. Leaving Joel chomping on bread and cheese and consulting her watch, she realised she was late for her lesson. There was no time to eat so she headed straight for de Vries' studio. When he answered the door she all but fell into his arms, overheated from the rush and faint from lack of food. He took one look at her and picked her up as if she was no more than a feather, carrying her through to the old couch in his studio.

Life, Love, Death

Pouring a little brandy down her throat he said, 'O my goedheid, how did you get in such a state?' He fanned her for a few minutes and disappearing into his makeshift kitchen, returned with coffee and bagels filled with cream cheese.

Whether it was due to the brandy, the heat, or her state of mind, Delia felt strange and distant as if she was another person. There was a languor about the afternoon even when the food had revived her. She started painting as if she was under a spell. Jan kept giving her funny looks as if he too was aware of her preoccupation. All Delia's senses were heightened as if she was waiting for something to happen. Even her finished painting of a vase of flowers had an ethereal look about it.

De Vries studied it in awe, 'Goed, my Delia, what has happened to you? It's as if someone has transformed you!' Without a second thought, he gave her a passionate kiss on the lips. It meant nothing to him - merely a way of expressing his admiration for another artist's work. But to Delia it was a revelation, as if she'd been asleep all her life and suddenly woken up. All her nerve endings were on fire and she felt totally alive. Turning to say goodbye as she left, she was delighted when Jan nonchalantly blew her a kiss, 'See you next week, klein liefling.' What she didn't see was his instant indifference as he returned to his canvas.

On the subway, Delia wondered if it had been a dream, recognising she was behaving like a lovelorn adolescent. Was this what love felt like, this heady feeling of suppressed excitement? Goodness, was she actually in love for the first time in her life? Surely not!

CHAPTER 14

Joel hadn't been the same since the arrest. Even Addy's efforts at trying to tempt him with strudel or donuts didn't work. He'd sunk back into the earlier mood that Delia and Bobby Jo remembered from their first meeting. Each Tuesday, although they still had lunch together, the two women tended to ignore him and sit chatting. They both had other things, in fact men, on their minds but were at this stage loath to confide in one another. Delia wanted to relish this time of being in love, wondering what Jan de Vries would do next, and Bobby Jo was having far too many thoughts and dreams about Xander to make her comfortable around him.

Xander also was having thoughts about Bobby Jo. He'd certainly made a mistake in undervaluing her and probably made yet another mistake in not making use of her from the start. Sam had practically dumped a decoy duck right there in his lap and he'd been too arrogant and self-absorbed to recognise it. From now on Bobby Jo would be his target. There were so many ways she could be useful to him in his other work – as a cover or as a courier - particularly as he was very much aware she had a crush on him. Why not fan the flames? There was no time to waste.

On the Wednesday morning when Bobby Jo entered the press room, she was taken aback to find her old desk in the corner had been moved opposite Xander's. Not able to control her delight, she exclaimed, 'This is a surprise, Xander. I must be doing better.'

'Think nothing of it. Easier to have you on hand where I can keep an eye on you. I've a couple of stories coming up and I

Life, Love, Death

want you to do the background research. Is that alright with you?' But couldn't stop himself adding caustically, 'Do you think you're up to it, Miss Roberta?'

'Absolutely,' Bobby Jo said beaming from ear to ear. 'Ready and willing.'

Despite being prepared to exploit Bobby Jo's usefulness, Xander found it difficult to control his exasperation with such a guileless child - and an enthusiastic one at that. He sighed deeply, 'Don't go getting too eager. Professionalism is the name of the game. Keep some detachment and objectivity or you'll never make a journalist.'

Bobby Jo was instantly deflated. Conscious he'd gone too far, Xander smiled charmingly and said, 'What about lunch then, Miss Roberta? Read the papers in the meantime and we'll discuss the details of new stories over food. I have to pop out to see a contact. I'll be back by one. Will that suit?'

Bobby Jo nodded. It would more than suit her. She was so glad she'd worn her new yellow gingham dress and the red court shoes though the heels were killing her. Hopefully they wouldn't have to walk far for lunch. With her newly bobbed copper hair, she was beginning to feel more like a New Yorker every day.

Xander returned before she had time to catch her breath. Taking her arm, he whisked her off down a series of back streets to a dark, dingy hotel. Standing in reception, all Bobby Jo could think about was her poor feet, probably badly blistered by now. Xander waved to the manager and they were shown though to a back room and one of the more secluded booths. Bobby Jo felt edgy and nervous, wondering

Life, Love, Death

what was going on. After a few minutes, a dark complexioned man joined them. 'This is Stefan,' Xander announced casually, 'He and Edith,' (he gestured to a rather large woman in a tweed jacket and mannish trousers who had just entered the room) write for the Daily Worker and are joining us for a drink.' Bobby Jo was perplexed. How could they talk about Tribune work when there were journalists from another paper present.

Xander, noticing Bobby Jo's bewilderment, said quietly under his breath, 'Don't be alarmed. These are fellow journalists and good friends of mine. I thought it would be good for you to meet a couple of old pros.' Both Stefan and Edith grinned at one another as if there was something they knew that Bobby Jo didn't. Some sort of private joke. Hailing a passing waiter, Xander continued, 'Whiskey sours for you two?' and handing Bobby Jo the menu practically bowed to her, saying reverentially, 'Now Miss Roberta, pick what you fancy. Mind, no lobster and champagne.' The three of them laughed raucously.

Bobby Jo was incensed, realising they were laughing at her though she didn't know why. Trying to control her irritation, she concentrated on the menu. Half listening, she heard them mention something about the Korean War and wanting to prove she wasn't a rookie piped up, 'I thought an armistice had been agreed back in July, though I never did understand why we were involved in a war in Asia?'

Edith, the older woman, laid a hand on her arm and explained in a softer tone as if to make up for their earlier behaviour, 'My dear, you're right. The war's over now. It was Harry Truman's Doctrine that got us into it. An

Life, Love, Death

undertaking to aid democratic countries and to hold back Communism.'

Irritably, Xander said, 'Now don't let's go into all that now, Edith. Let this child have something to eat. I'll explain it all to her later. Now Miss, what will you have?'

Not keen at being called a 'child', particularly in front of these hard bitten, worldly, journos, Bobby Jo said sourly, 'A burger, fries and a Pepsi, thanks.'

Once the two journalists left, Bobby Jo and Xander got on with the business of eating. Xander, with a mouthful of pastrami and pickle sandwich, said, 'There's a couple of stories we must cover this September. I thought you'd like to report on Senator Kennedy's wedding. It'll be a prestigious affair knowing the Kennedys. Harry will show you the ropes and do the photos.'

Wrinkling her nose, Bobby Jo couldn't help showing her disdain. Still smarting from his friends' earlier derision, she gave vent to her frustration, 'Is that all I'm good for to cover some society wedding? Doesn't the Tribune have a fashion columnist? I thought I was going to learn first-hand from you.'

Xander laughed, 'You have to start somewhere, my little chickadee. This is an important political wedding. Who knows, John Kennedy might be President one day – well that's certainly what his father wants. Anyway, I've more important things to get my teeth into now Nikita Khrushchev is going to take over in Russia.'

Life, Love, Death

Trying to sound knowledgeable, a subdued Bobby Jo said sullenly, 'I thought Stalin was in charge.'

Xander raised his eyebrows, 'Not anymore, my dear Miss Roberta. He died back in March. Don't you remember writing that piece for me some weeks ago?' Observing her crestfallen face, and attempting to make amends Xander said teasingly, 'Don't you read them there papers, Miss Roberta, or take in what they say? I see we'll have to seriously tackle your education, don't you think?'

Bobby Jo clenched her teeth but made efforts to smile. As they returned to work, Xander tucked her arm into his and said, 'I think I'm beginning to enjoy working with you, Miss Roberta. We're going to get along just fine.'

Thrown off balance, Bobby Jo didn't know how she felt. At times Xander could be kind yet at others… He was so unpredictable. The problem was she desperately wanted his approval and that meant putting up with whatever he handed out.

CHAPTER 15

The next Tuesday at the diner Bobby Jo arrived in a quiet and pensive mood, unlike her usual exuberant self. Jostling with his troublesome dentures Joel was too busy to notice, extending his machinations to delving round his gaping mouth with none too clean fingers. Trying to avoid looking at him, Delia sighed deeply and turning to Bobby Jo enquired, 'You seem quiet today, Bobby Jo. Is everything alright?' Bobby Jo was loath to say but needed to talk to someone. After a long pause, she began, 'Last Wednesday, Xander took me out to lunch.'

'That was nice of him,' Delia murmured absentmindedly toying with her salad and trying to ignore Joel's continuing unmannerly behaviour as he poked further into the dark chasm of his open mouth. Finally successful, he let rip a great explosion of, 'Goddammit, 'I's got the little blighter at last,' and fished out a long length of charred rind.

Delia shuddered in disgust, 'Honestly Joel, your behaviour hardly measures up to that of a gentleman.'

'Never says I's was no gentleman either. But lady, you's got to get these scraps out or they's irritate all day, and you's wouldn't want that would you's?'

Managing to maintain her composure, Delia returned to Bobby Jo, 'Carry on, my dear, now the floor show's over.'

Bobby Jo continued as if she'd never been interrupted, 'Sure, it was kind of Xander but two other journalists joined us for a drink and they were strange.'

Life, Love, Death

'In what way?'

'The lady was dressed like a man in oversized tweeds and trousers, the other man was foreign and spoke to Xander in a language he seemed to understand. Maybe Russian. I'm not sure. I think Xander mentioned they wrote for the Daily Worker. Also, they kept calling him 'Karl' which I couldn't understand.

Delia shrugged, 'Perhaps it was a sort of joke between them, my dear, a skit on 'Karl Marx' if as you say they were journalists from the 'Daily Worker. 'What did they talk about?'

'The mannish woman, Edith, tried to explain to me about the Korean War. They had a good laugh about what I was going to eat. I had no idea why I was the butt of their jokes. Later Xander corrected me when I said I thought Stalin was still in charge in Russia and hadn't realised he'd died earlier this year. I felt like an idiot, out of my depth. There was a mention of some Doctrine and how our country is trying to drive back Communism and that's why we got involved in in Korea.'

Delia looked apprehensive, 'It's probably newspaper talk, dear. The way journalists discuss politics when they get together. There's no need to worry. You'll get used to that kind of talk. As for the threat of Communism, that's real enough. During the war we were afraid of German spies and Fifth Columnists. It was Fascism then, now it's the Russians and the 'Red Scare.'

'What's that?' a perplexed Bobby Jo asked.

Life, Love, Death

Delia groaned inwardly. What it was to be young and live in your own little bubble. 'Haven't you heard about it? The papers and wireless are full of it these days. It's that Joe McCarthy, the Senator for your state, a right wing Republican. He constantly berates the government about employing Communists and yells about 'Reds under the Bed'. You must have read about him persecuting Hollywood stars. They have to appear in front of Grand Juries if they've ever been members of the Communist Party.'

Embarrassed about her lack of knowledge, Bobby Jo was belligerent, 'I can't see that matters. Don't we live in a free country. People should be allowed to believe and say what they like even if they're Communists.'

An exasperated Delia nearly gave up, but persevered, 'You're right, we do live in a democratic country. The Constitution gives us freedom of speech and we want to keep it that way. That means supporting other countries like South Korea to avoid them being taken over by Communists.'

'But what's wrong with Communism? Isn't it about equality? Everyone owning everything?'

Becoming increasingly irritated, Delia remarked sharply, 'Didn't they teach you any of this in school?'

Mortified, Bobby Jo stuttered with tears in her eyes, 'I'm sorry I'm so stupid but I went to a private girls' finishing school. No one discussed politics there. It was all about becoming a good wife and mother.'

Life, Love, Death

Delia was silent. It was no good haranguing this poor child. Hadn't it been the same for her? That was all she was ever expected to be – a perfect homemaker, wife and mother. Quietly she said, 'In this country we believe in the American Dream, that every person has the freedom to say or do what they like with their lives, become President, make a lot of money or whatever. In Russia, the State owns and controls everything. People are not free to say or do what they like. Don't you see how lucky we are to be Americans!'

Joel, who had been quiet up till now and could see Delia was flagging, decided to throw his hat in the ring. Determined to call a 'spade a spade' he barked, 'Look girlie. Those Commie Russkies is coming here, stealing our atomic secrets, and riling up labor strikes. There's Commie Americans working for Russia right here in Manhattan. Spies is everywhere. Look at them Rosenbergs. You's have to be careful what you's say, even in the Village. Of course, from what I reads in that there library it's said them Communists supports my people but who knows. No one's ever on the side of us blacks.'

Bobby Jo was still frowning, trying to absorb everything they'd said. She wished she'd paid more attention at college, but a liberal arts degree hardly set her up for becoming a hardnosed reporter. She'd only agreed to go to Rutgers to get away from home and because of the college's links with the Dutch Reform Church her parents had been willing. Most of her time there had been spent socialising or writing poetry for a small obscure literary magazine. This had given her a taste for writing and the idea of becoming a journalist or a writer. Politics was completely outside her province. Of course, her parents were staunch Republicans as was the Tribune. Bobby Jo felt embarrassed to think she'd never

Life, Love, Death

voted, gone to rallies or even joined political clubs. Trying to cover her awkwardness, she said, 'I think I must take a leaf out of Joel's book, visit the library and do some studying. At any rate I'm reading the papers now every day.'

Delia, feeling sorry for the embarrassed girl, said, 'Don't take any notice of us. Joel and I have been around a long time. When we were your age, we never paid much attention to world affairs either. You'll soon learn. This Xander sounds as if he's taken you under his wing.'

Bobby Jo reddened, 'He has. I do like him. I hope he likes me too and doesn't only feel sorry for me.'

Delia smiled wryly. How was it she and this young girl were in exactly the same position? The only difference being that Bobby Jo at her age was entitled to have infatuations but not Delia, a middle aged woman. Jan de Vries was always on her mind and she couldn't stop herself hoping this was more than an adolescent crush. Just like Bobby Jo she wanted Jan to like her for herself and not as an object of pity. Thinking of him made her feel warm and shaky inside, longing for next week to come so she could see him again.

CHAPTER 16

Over-anticipation often leads to disappointment and this is exactly what happened to Delia the following Tuesday afternoon. Expecting to find Jan de Vries alone and ready for her painting lesson, Delia had a shock to have the door opened by a frumpily dressed middle aged matron puffing away on a Camel. Her satin cocktail dress barely skimmed her plump figure. Makeup had been lathered on with a trowel over a heavily wrinkled face. Topping it all was a cascade of peroxide curls in the style of Marilyn Monroe. 'Do come in, my dear,' she gasped between puffs. 'You must be Jan's little protégé. He's told me all about you. I was under the impression you were younger. Silly me, probably got the wrong end of the stick.'

Delia was too shocked to respond, and lamely followed the woman through to Jan's studio. Showing herself to be very much at home, the woman threw herself on the couch and knocked back a large glass of gin that had been waiting for her. Jan waved to Delia, 'Goeie middag, Delia. I see you've met Helena. She's going, aren't you, my little chicken,' he said pointedly to the recumbent figure.

'Oh, one more minute, dear Jan. I'll get hiccups if I drink this down any quicker.'

'Being it's your third or fourth,' Jan said dryly, 'I would think you've had enough. Now be off with you and leave me to my pupil.'

Reluctantly, Helena dragged herself up and made for the door. 'You're so cruel, Jan. I don't know why I bother with you. Don't you love me anymore? I've even left you a little

Life, Love, Death

something under the china dog. See, next to that rascal Ginger.' Swaying, she waved her hand in the direction of Jan's big ginger cat who was perched as usual above the fireplace. 'See how good I am to you. You don't deserve me. I'm off. You'll miss me when I'm gone,' and drunkenly weaved her way out of the room. Jan shrugged and turned back to his painting.

Delia heaved a great sigh of relief. What was going on here? Who was that woman and what was she to Jan? Surely, she wasn't paying him, was she, and what for?

After a minute or two, Jan noticed that Delia was still standing in the middle of the room shifting from foot to foot. 'Don't worry about Helena,' he said, 'she's a very old friend, one of many of my so charming American lady friends. She was my landlady when my mother and I first came to New York and often drops in for a drink or three. She's harmless but useful for contacts. I know it's hard to believe but she comes from a renowned New York family, is related to one of the richest people around.' He put his finger to his mouth, 'I couldn't possibly mention their name. She hit the skids some time ago but still receives the monthly check from the family.'

Studying Delia intently, he remarked, 'You look a little tired today, mein klein gerub. Was the store busy or that nasty Mr Simmonds giving you trouble?' This was uttered in such a tender manner that Delia all but swooned, forgetting all about the dreadful Helena and trying to remember when she'd confided in Jan about her manager. Perhaps it was when Joel got arrested. She was in such a state that day. Realising that Jan was waiting for a reply, she said, 'No, the

Life, Love, Death

normal. Of course, being summer there are a lot more visitors and tourists to cope with.'

Making every effort to show an interest in her life, Jan said, 'I hope that business with your musician friend and the police was sorted out satisfactorily.'

'Yes. Joel seems to be getting over it. He's a grouchy old man at the best of times so you never know.'

The afternoon slid by peacefully as Delia wallowed in Jan's presence. However, she couldn't help dwelling on his earlier reference to 'my charming American lady friends'. How many were there? What part did they play in his life and what exactly had Helena left under the china dog? Could it have been money, but what for?

At the end of their session, Jan said casually, 'I wondered if next week instead of painting you might model for me. There's an illustration I have to do for an advert in 'Mademoiselle'. What about that outfit you wore a few weeks ago. It was charming.'

Frowning, Delia protested, 'Surely, I'm much too old for that magazine. Isn't it aimed at younger people – probably college girls?' Inwardly she was pleased and flattered that Jan had remembered what she'd worn. That must mean something.

Jan smiled smugly, 'Well, what if it is? Don't forget it's all down to the artist. I still see you as the young, innocent girl you must have been in your twenties. Have faith in me.'

Life, Love, Death

Delia could feel herself blushing. She felt hot and bothered. What would she be like if he asked her to pose without her clothes? It was beyond thinking.

As she made her way home, overflowing with joy, Delia felt as if she was still that carefree twenty year old. It wasn't until she caught a glimpse of herself in a shop window that reality set in. There she was as clear as day – a tired middle aged woman, shoulders stooped with the fatigue of holding a paintbrush all afternoon. Far from sashaying down the street, she was slowly limping along the sidewalk on painfully aching high heeled feet. Looking like that, how could Jan de Vries ever consider her as his model?

CHAPTER 17

The following week Joel was in a particularly good mood. He was humming to himself as he made for his seat at the diner. He waved to Addy, shouting across, 'How are you Addy, my dear? What a beautiful day.' A shocked Addy nearly poured hot coffee into a customer's lap. What had come over Joel? Perhaps he'd come into money or won a bet. Whatever it was, it was a change and for the better.

Joel felt different. It was all down to Betsy. As ever she was sitting beside him on the subway, when he took her on his lap to let an elderly black man sit down. When the man turned to thank him, they recognised one another immediately. 'It must be twenty years… nearer thirty!' they said in unison.

'Sorry,' Joel said, 'I's know the face but the name's gone. Old age, you know. I's remember we played together at Smalls.'

'It's Benny,' said his companion, 'not the Benny Carter who played with Charlie Johnson's house band, the other one. I was a mere stripling in those days, trying to find my way with my trumpet, though not in Dizzy's league.'

Joel's face lit up. Old memories came flooding back, 'I's was a fill-in player myself with my old Betsy,' He patted her case fondly. She's never abandoned me. Still with me after all these years.'

'We must get together,' Benny said, 'knock out a few chords. There's a whole gang of us oldies who meet at Smalls and jam – a warm up act for the dedicated - an informal gig.

Life, Love, Death

You'd be welcome. There's little money in it, but you might enjoy it.'

Joel looked sheepish; 'I's dunno. My playing is all busking these days. I's ain't up to scratch for you fellas.'

'Don't worry,' Benny assured him, 'we're long past our prime. Some of us are either deaf in one ear or even two, almost blind and invariably playing wrong notes. Try it and see. It's usually Thursday night early in the evening. Bring your wife or friends along to support you.'

Wincing, Joel said, 'I's ain't married and not sure I's knows anyone who's would want to come along.'

'Up to you, buddy. Look here's my stop,' hurrying off, Benny shouted, 'be there 'bout seven. See ya.'

Recollecting his time at Smalls as he sat in the diner, Joel smiled to himself and distractedly slurped back his coffee not realising how hot it was. Choking and coughing he found himself slapped on the back by Delia, followed closely by Bobby Jo.

'There, there, Joel,' Delia said as she placed yet another resounding smack between his bony shoulder blades.

'Nough, lady,' he sputtered. 'What you's trying to do, shove me into an early grave? That woman (he pointed over at Addy) is killing me with her boiling hot drinks. Anyways I's alright now. Caught me unawares is all.'

Addy, seeing Joel's gesture, came bustling over and addressing Delia directly as if Joel wasn't there said, 'Dunno

Life, Love, Death

what's up with that Joel today. First of all, he comes in grinning, next thing he's choking on my good coffee and putting off my other customers.'

'Be orf with you,' Joel said roughly finding his voice at last. 'Nawt wrong with me. It's you's be the problem.'

Addy laughed good-naturedly, 'Now Joel, mind yourself. Behave and let me take these ladies' orders. They look hungry as lions today.'

'And so we are,' Delia and Bobby Jo said in accord.

Once Addy had disappeared, Delia bent towards Joel, 'You alright, Joel?'

'Course I's am. Ain't I's always,' but for some reason he desperately wanted to tell them about Benny and Smalls. What had come over him? He never discussed his business with anyone. But he was fizzing with anticipation and excitement about playing at the club again with his old friends. For once he wanted to tell someone. These days there was little to look forward to except aching bones and an occasional fish supper. But it was hard to break the habits of a lifetime. Hadn't his own dear Mammy always said, 'Tell no one nuffink or they'll use it against you.' But Mammy wasn't here anymore to tell him to wash behind his ears or anything else. He began, 'I's met an old friend today.' He stopped. Delia and Bobby Jo put down their forks and waited. It was so unlike Joel to instigate a conversation or say anything personal about himself, they were mesmerised.

Joel cleared his throat, 'It was Benny used to play at Smalls, you know,' he said addressing Delia.

Life, Love, Death

'I'm afraid I don't, Joel,' Delia said apologetically. 'Is that some sort of jazz club?'

'Only were and still the best night club in Harlem. Smalls Paradise be a legend.'

Bobby Jo's eyes were out on stalks, 'Why?'

'Well, it only play black bands but open to folk of all colors.'

'Like the Cotton Club,' added Delia hastily scrabbling through her limited knowledge of jazz clubs.

'Nope, not like that at all. That there club plays black celebrities but only allows whiteys in.'

'What's so special about Smalls then, Joel?' Bobby Jo asked, her eyes glinting with excitement.

'It bin going since '25. I's remembers them waiters dancing the Charleston and roller skating as they carried orders – breaking into song on occasion. It were summat special – opening till 6 in the morning for the 'breakfast dance'. Everyone you's ever heard of played or sung there – Elmer Snowden, Glenn Miller, Buddy Rich, Fats Waller. Even give a start to Billie Holiday, you's heard of her?' Joel said to Delia. She nodded. Goodness, what had come over Joel? She'd never known him be so expansive other than about his beloved Betsy.

By now Bobby Jo was bobbing up and down with enthusiasm like a small child, 'Can we go, can we go there Joel? It sounds swell. Please let's go,' she continued pleadingly.

Life, Love, Death

Drawing himself up and puffing out his chest, Joel said, 'Benny ask me to join the old 'uns for a bit of impro on Thursday night. I's be honoured if you's ladies accompany me. It'd be a warm-up session you understand, early evening before the main bands.'

Delia was hesitant, 'Not sure, Joel. Harlem you say. Would it be safe for us? Isn't Bobby Jo too young to go to a club?'

An indignant Bobby Jo protested, 'Honestly Delia, I'm twenty three, nearly twenty four and on my way to being a professional journalist. I have to experience life in New York. I don't need to be protected. My parents did enough of that.'

'But they would hardly approve of you going to a nightclub in that area.'

Becoming more and more annoyed, Bobby Jo brushed aside Delia's concerns, 'I don't know what they'd think and don't care. They're not here, I am, and I intend going with Joel with or without you.'

'Calm down,' Delia said, 'of course I'll come too. I've never been to a nightclub in my life either. It'll be something new for me, but I insist on us taking a cab. No subway at that time of night.

It was agreed the three of them would meet at the diner and go from there.

CHAPTER 18

Thursday night came round soon enough. It felt strange to meet up in the early evening. Delia, dressing the part as always, wore a navy and white cocktail dress and coat which she felt was dressy but refined. Bobby Jo, having no idea what to wear, had opted for a red poodle skirt, a white roll top and thrown a yellow sweater over her shoulders. Delia winced, but kept her mouth shut not wanting to spoil the evening. It seemed surprising to Delia that Bobby Jo who was so intent on turning herself into a New Yorker still dressed in such an unsophisticated manner. Perhaps she should take her in hand, however it wasn't really Delia's business and Bobby Jo certainly had a mind of her own.

Surprisingly, though Joel had clung on to wearing his battered old trilby he'd made a huge effort with a clean shirt; shoelace tie and a carefully pressed check jacket, one he'd picked up that morning from the local thrift shop. He was pent up with nerves which began to infect all three of them. However, Delia valiantly took it upon herself to negotiate a reasonable fare with the cab driver and they were soon en route for Smalls. It was a bit of a shock to find the club was in a basement, but Delia resolutely took the lead making her way to the entrance leaving Bobby Jo and Joel in her wake. A big black door announced Smalls and Delia stood back as Joel knocked. It was thrown open by a large black man who smiled as Joel doffed his trilby and explained who they were. Waving them in, he pointed to stairs leading to the basement. Before they knew it Delia and Bobby Jo were wafted over to a table in the dark interior as Joel disappeared. The two of them sat there uncomfortably peering at all the empty tables and feeling out of place.

Life, Love, Death

Bobby Jo whispered, 'I wonder if we should have come.' But no sooner had she said that than people started arriving – people of all shapes, sizes, ages, and colours. They were all laughing, shouting loudly for drinks and soon a roller skating waiter came over, 'What can I get you, ladies?'

Delia rarely drank, but feeling she should let her hair down said, 'I'll have a Manhattan.' It was the only cocktail she'd ever heard of. Maybe this was the time to try it. Bobby Jo said, 'Me too.' The waiter looked questioningly at Delia, who shrugged, 'Sure. She's old enough to drink.'

Bobby Jo scowled after he'd left, 'I don't know why everyone insists on treating me like a child.' Throwing back her red bob and putting on a posh voice, she intoned, 'It's so maddening. I may even start smoking, what do you think Delia? Would a long cigarette holder make me look more soigné?'

Delia laughed, 'I don't think so and it won't do your health any good. My father smoked all his life and it killed him.'

Bobby Jo pricked up her ears, always dying to hear more about Delia's background, but by then the drinks had arrived. Both ladies looked at the fancy long stemmed glasses garnished with a cherry and sighed with pleasure until they took a mouthful. Each of them pulled a face. 'It looks better than it tastes,' Bobby Jo commented. 'It's very strong. I've only ever had wine at home and that was bad enough.'

'Perhaps it gets better as you drink more,' Delia said, gamefully taking a large swallow. A minute or two later she wished she hadn't as her head began to swim. 'I think we

Life, Love, Death

should order food or we'll both be too drunk to see Joel perform.'

It was the strangest menu Delia had ever seen. There was whole lot of Chinese food with odd names such as Chicago Chop Suey and Yat Go Mein Noodles. Even the American menu had its idiosyncrasies with such things as a Golden Buck (Welsh rarebit with an egg) and Fried Chicken Liver, Bacon and Spaghetti together. They decided their safest bet was a Club Sandwich. As they ate, more people arrived and the audience was just as Joel had described, 'The Black and Tans' – a mixture of cultures and colours.

The old men of the impro band began to set up. Joel was smiling from ear to ear as he chatted to Benny and the other men. As soon as they began to play it was as if he was transformed into the young man he used to be. The audience had gone quiet except for feet tapping and people swaying to the rhythms.

Delia found herself hypnotised by the beat, feeling she wanted to get up, dance and let herself go. The music opened up something primitive in her, perhaps her real self. Lately, she had begun to wonder if all those years she had spent with Gus and the boys had been a sham. Had she been play-acting the role of perfect wife and mother? No doubt it was the drink encouraging her to discard her inhibitions and do all this soul searching yet it was as if she was suddenly questioning the person she'd become. She looked across at Bobby Jo who'd also drunk her Manhattan, and was now wolfing down several club sandwiches, tapping her fingers and moving her body to the beat. Relaxed and happy, Bobby Jo was smiling, laughing, and waving to their neighbours on the next table. Of course, Delia thought, this is how she

Life, Love, Death

should have been when she was young rather than the uptight proper Vassar young lady she turned out to be. Was it too late to change? Was she to be dull and middle aged for the rest of her life? Bobby Jo seemed to have cast off the shackles of her Dutch Reform upbringing and her rigid parents in one fell swoop and was open to every new experience. Yet, earlier that evening, Delia had thought that she was the person who could turn Bobby Jo into a more polished and refined New Yorker. Possibly 'refinement' was not all that it was cracked up to be, maybe it was better to be yourself, enjoy life and live in the moment.

Bobby Jo looked across at Delia and grinned, 'This is such a wonderful night for Joel. We'll never hear the end of it. It's amazing to see him so happy and relaxed, isn't it?'

At the break, Joel joined their table and they ordered him a beer. 'Nawt of that fancy stuff you's lot are drinking,' he said, eyeing their glasses with contempt. 'Needs to wet my whistle. Did you's hear Betsy tonight? She were on good form and loved being with the old gang,' talking about her as if she was the performer and not himself. The two women chuckled to see him in such high spirits. Addressing them both, he said, 'The guys asked me to hang out a whiles. Will you's two ladies be right to get home?'

'Of course we shall,' Delia assured him. We'll stay a bit longer and get a cab. I'm sure he'll get us one,' she nodded at the bulky doorman.

'See you's ladies on Tuesday then. Thanks for coming,' Joel shouted as he tore back to the stage.

Life, Love, Death

'Goodness, he looks as if he's about twenty,' Bobby Jo remarked, 'the way he ran up there.'

However later, after their gig when Joel sat down with Benny and the others, he felt his age as bones and joints creaked. It had been a longer session than he was used to. He was not only out of puff but weary. Benny took one look at him and said, 'God Joel, you look done in. I'll give you a lift back to the Village.

On the way, Benny remarked, 'You was ace, man, on old Betsy. The guys loved you. Come back whenever you feels like it. We're always there Thursday, and often short of a Sax. By the way, did you hear from that cutie Desirée you was smitten with? You certainly had it bad at the time. I thought you two might have made a go of it.'

'No such luck,' Joel snapped shortly. 'Didn't you's hear she went off with a trumpet player when I's were on the road?'

Benny scratched his head, 'Did hear something. What brought it to mind was I thought I saw her the other week in the Village.' Glancing across and seeing the expression on Joel's face he thought better of it, adding, 'Maybe I was mistaken. My eyes ain't what they used to be. Forget it, old pal, you're better off without her.'

But Joel couldn't forget it. Suddenly old memories were stirred up. He had this terrible longing to see Desirée again. 'Once before I's die,' he murmured to himself as Benny drove away. 'If she's round here, I'll finds her,' he promised himself.

CHAPTER 19

A different Joel arrived at the diner the following Tuesday. He was spruced up; even his battered leather trilby had been given a polish. When Delia and Bobby Jo turned up, he greeted them like old friends. Delia raised her eyebrows, but Bobby Jo giggled behind her hand saying, 'Joel, you look so smart and were wonderful the other night. Betsy behaved beautifully.'

Joel grinned widely, his false teeth clacking together like tombstones, 'Told you's ladies. Smalls is special. It always gets to you's 'ventually. Knew you's would like it. Hope you got home OK. I does feel a bit bad not going with you's, but it were great to see Benny and the gang again. What a night! Best not do it too much – makes my old bones ache real bad.' He carefully omitted mentioning his talk with Benny about Desirée, yet it was as if a spark had been ignited. He didn't care how old she was, he knew he must see her. The flame in his heart had never gone out.

Addy bustled over, surprised to see three smiling expectant faces, 'Well now, ladies and gent, it appears you are all in a good mood today, enjoying life and one another's company.' Shuffling off once she'd taken their order, she congratulated herself on a job well done. 'Not bad at all, Addy my love. See the way they all get on. Took some doing, but there's three less lonely people in New York now.'

However, one of the trio was not quite so happy. Bobby Jo was still wondering where she stood with Xander. He was being as erratic as ever. He would ignore her and then go out of his way to be extra nice, buying her a 'dog or taking her out for a drink. None of this satisfied her and wasn't

Life, Love, Death

what she wanted. But then perhaps she needed to ask herself, 'What did she really want?'

On the work front she was being allowed to write up inconsequential pieces about local events or other trivia but nothing more than that, certainly nothing controversial. Bobby Jo felt as if she was treading water. Letters from her parents kept arriving but she could barely bring herself to read them let alone reply. Finally, her frantic parents telephoned the Barbizon and she was forced to talk to them and answer their innumerable questions. They were hurt and upset that she had no time for them. Mr Hudson asked, 'Should we come to New York and see you or what about you coming home for a long weekend? You must be due leave.'

It was no use. Bobby Jo kept insisting, 'I'm fine truly but busy. I wouldn't have time to see you even if you came here. Maybe I'll get home for Christmas.'

'But Christmas is months away. What about Thanksgiving?' You can't be that busy, you're only a trainee.'

Bobby Jo was adamant and wouldn't be swayed. She marvelled at her own intransigence. It was as if she'd left Little Chute, her parents and all that went with it behind in another life, and now had no time for anything from the past. Worried to death, her poor parents hung up, questioning each other on what they'd done wrong.

At the beginning of September, Xander sat down opposite and said, 'I've got that story I mentioned last month. The Kennedy wedding. It'll be right up your street. Women love weddings.'

Life, Love, Death

Bobby Jo scowled. What was this about 'women'? She was a journalist not merely a woman or a girl.

Taking no notice of her expression, Xander resumed blithely, 'This isn't any old wedding but a significant one. Senator Kennedy marries Jacqueline Bouvier on September 12th It's not only a society event but a political one. You'll do the social bit. I'll handle the political aspect.'

'What's the big deal about this wedding?'

'The Kennedys are one of the richest families in the country. Joseph Kennedy made his money in business and the movies. There were rumours about bootlegging during Prohibition, but they were only rumours. Despite all that he became American ambassador to England. Unfortunately, during the war he damaged his reputation by favouring appeasement and got recalled. After that he planned for one of his sons to run for the Presidency. Joe Junior, the eldest, was killed in an air crash. So it's down to the next in line, John Fitzgerald Kennedy.'

Bobby Jo turned up her nose, 'Sounds interesting, but s'pose I'm to be the one who finds out about bridesmaids, dresses, flowers, table decorations and all that garbage.'

A grinning Xander said, 'Got it in one, kiddo.'

Despite Bobby Jo's supercilious attitude, she felt her anticipation building. On the day of the wedding her expectations were fulfilled. The stunning bride, attired in a dress of ivory tissue silk with a portrait neckline and brocade embellished skirt arrived, at St Mary's Catholic Church, Newport with fifteen bridesmaids.

Life, Love, Death

Bobby Jo was blown away by the glamour, the eight hundred guests, the clothes, the jewellery, and the orchestra playing under a huge canopy. It was unreal. Later, when the Senator and his bride appeared, Bobby Jo felt as if she was watching a movie, a scene from The Great Gatsby perhaps. The young couple were so attractive and charismatic.

Of course, as usual, Xander was nowhere to be seen as he scurried backwards and forwards interviewing prominent guests. Bobby Jo, left alone with Harry, said in awe, 'Isn't it glorious?'

'Dare say,' Harry replied in his usual gloomy fashion, 'wonder how long it'll last. Makes me think of that legend about Icarus flying too close to the sun and meeting a tragic end.' He patted her on the shoulder in his usual fatherly way, 'Never a good idea, Bobby Jo, to worship at the feet of the god of extravagance and excess.'

Bobby Jo pouted, 'You're an old cynic. Am sure the couple will have a brilliant future. They look so happy and stunning together and so much in love.'

Xander wandered over, 'We can pack up now.' Studying Bobby Jo's glowing face and expression, he remarked acidly, 'Fallen in love, eh kiddo? All a bit too cream puff for me. That amount of lavishness and overindulgence makes me sick to my stomach. Think how many poor out of work people could benefit from all this profligacy. To top it all, these elitist WASPs, even if they are Irish Catholics, didn't want any reference made to the name of Jackie's dress designer because she's black and is as American as you and I, and apple pie if it comes to that. Can you believe it?'

Life, Love, Death

They drove home in silence. After Xander's outburst, Bobby Jo felt awkward, not knowing what to say. Never being sure of herself, she often didn't have a definite opinion. Nevertheless, she consoled herself with the thought it had been the most memorable and romantic day of her life, one she would treasure for the rest of her life. Xander was definitely not going to spoil that.

CHAPTER 20

Bobby Jo couldn't wait for the following Tuesday so she could tell Delia about the wedding. Whilst Joel grumbled and moaned about women's talk, the two women and Addy drooled over the photos that Bobby Jo had surreptitiously stolen from work.

'All this fuss about a dang wedding,' Joel groused. 'Don't know why they's bother. Thems always getting divorced these days.'

'It must have been a wonderful day,' Delia said enviously, 'I would love to have been there.'

'It was, it was,' Bobby Jo said enthusiastically. 'It was perfect, though neither Xander nor Harry seemed to approve. They thought it a terrible waste of money, very self-indulgent, and that it would all end in tears. But I loved it – it was every young girl's dream. Xander thought the money could be better spent on the poor and was particularly upset that the bride's black designer didn't get a mention even though the dress was out of this world.'

At this, Joel sat up and paid attention, 'Typical. Them rich white folk use us as servants or doing jobs for them but we's of no account in the long run.'

Later that afternoon, her head still full of wedding photos, Delia herself felt bridal. On arrival at Jan's studio he suggested a walk in Central Park. 'It's such a warm September day, my liefie, let's make the most of it before Autumn begins.' Fondly he tucked her arm into his, hurrying her along. As they ambled through the park

Life, Love, Death

towards Belvedere Castle and the lake, various attractive ladies greeted Jan warmly and he doffed his Panama hat in response. As they walked on, Delia remarked, 'You seem very popular with the ladies hereabouts.'

Jan laughed, 'It's my foreignness and charisma, I can assure you. I must admit though I have made the acquaintance of many beautiful women since my arrival in New York. It's different with men, you see, my liewe. I would need to belong to the right clubs or meet them through work. As I'm a lone artist that would be impossible.'

Delia was not easily diverted, 'But how do you meet these ladies? Surely that's as difficult?'

Chuckling, and in a teasing tone, Jan squeezed her arm, 'It sounds as if you might be a touch jealous, my liefling. Ladies are far easier to know – didn't you and I meet at the Museum of Modern Art? Women are much more sociable than men, often stopping and watching me paint when I'm out and about. Then it's easy to fall into conversation with them. However, I'm here with you today, loving your company and the heat of the sun. Isn't that enough for you, dear Delia?' Taking a flask from his inside pocket he said, 'What we need now is a little pick-me-up to heighten our spirits.'

'I don't know about that,' Delia said doubtfully, looking disapproving as he poured a little brandy into the top of a flask.

'Why not?' Jan said cheerily. 'Go on – it'll warm you up whilst we take our ease on this bench.'

Life, Love, Death

'I don't really drink,' Delia said. But there was no denying Jan. Carefully she took a delicate sip from the cup. The brandy burnt her throat, making her cough uncontrollably.

Jan was not in the least sympathetic as he banged her on the back, bursting out laughing, 'I see you're not a drinker. The second mouthful is always better. Try again.' A reluctant Delia drank again, swallowing a lot more. This time there was no burning sensation rather a welcome warmth suffused her windpipe and stomach. Suddenly it wasn't so bad.

Studying her face, Jan said, 'See I'm always right about these things. Now let's sit quietly, close our eyes and soak in the sun.'

Feeling soporific by this time, Delia felt herself nodding off, hardly conscious of Jan's hand snaking round her waist. Before she knew what was happening, Jan was caressing and kissing her neck and turning her face to his. This was only Delia's second kiss from Jan, but the first one had been a mere peck in comparison. This time it was as if he was sucking the very soul out of her as she moaned and shivered from pleasure, allowing him to feel her whole body even though people were passing. 'Jan, Jan, everyone is watching us. No, no I can't,' she muttered as she pulled herself free. 'Not here, not in public.' But a part of her wanted him to continue.

Why had she never felt like this with her husband? Gus was always businesslike about sex. It had to be in bed and on a Wednesday night because he had an easier operating schedule the next day. There was extraordinarily little

Life, Love, Death

touching in-between. Gus would certainly have frowned on kissing or even holding hands in public.

Jan shook himself hard like a dog emerging from water, 'Sorry my Delia, you're right. I forgot myself. I couldn't resist you.' Whispering in her ear, he added, 'You always look so perfect and poised with your matching outfits and coiffured hair I want to tear off your clothes and ravish you to find out who you truly are.' Delia's eyes widened, nearly standing out on stalks. No one had ever said anything like that to her before. Pre-Gus there had been one college boyfriend but most of their time had been spent reading poetry together.

'I think we should go back to my place,' Jan announced authoritatively. 'We need wine and food. Then we can spend the rest of the afternoon in bed. Come along, my liefde.' En route he bought bagels, cheese, pâté, and rough red wine, smiling and laughing with the cashier whilst keeping a firm hand round Delia's waist as if she might make a run for it. Delia did feel like running away. What did this gorgeous, handsome, virile man expect from her? She was no Mata Hari. Having second thoughts, Delia tried to pull away and say she must go home, but Jan was determined now his prey was in sight.

Murmuring into her neck and softly biting the lobe of her ear, he hustled her along to his studio saying, 'Don't be frightened, kleinding. I am the most generous and gentle of lovers, but we must eat first.' At the studio, he made Delia comfortable on the couch and said, 'I prepare food and we can talk. You can tell me about your late husband.'
Delia was in a daze, but once Jan brought out the feast and the red wine she relaxed. On the verge of falling asleep she

Life, Love, Death

didn't notice Jan leave the room. Scarcely awake by the time he returned, she didn't even register that he was naked before he picked her up and carried her to his bed. Delia, half delirious with wine and passion, was in no state to protest as he removed her clothes. Ignoring her mewing objections, Jan went ahead and taught her all the things that neither she nor Gus had ever done or even thought about. At times, Delia felt she was standing outside herself looking down on two sweating, writhing bodies full of wanting and desiring. By the time it was dark, she fell into a deep comatose sleep sprawled over Jan.

The next morning on waking, Delia had no idea where she was or what had happened to her. Then it came flooding back. Wrapping the sheet round her, she felt awkward and gauche. There was no sign of Jan, but she could hear him whistling to himself in his makeshift kitchenette. Delia started looking for her clothes which had ended up all over the floor, her brassiere hanging from a lampshade. As she made a move to get out of bed, Jan arrived with a laden breakfast tray and intervened, 'Not so fast, my liefling Delia, you need sustenance after such a night. Goodness, I'm hungry and you must be too.' He yawned widely showing his perfect white teeth.

Delia could feel herself flushing all over her body, but at least this time Jan was wearing a fetching apron over his nakedness. Realising how hungry she was, she turned her attention to the eggs over easy, crispy bacon and toast. Jan said in admiration, 'I like a woman who eats, not those picky, skinny ones who are always dieting. We shall have coffee and take the day off – back in bed?' he queried grinning lasciviously. 'Don't you think?'

Life, Love, Death

Delia shook her head forcefully, 'I can't. I really can't. There's work. Mr Simmonds will be expecting me.'

'But what about your clothes,' Jan smirked, 'they're so wrinkled. You can't be seen in yesterday's clothes.'

'I must go,' Delia said desperately, 'I must go.'

'Well, if you must, you must,' Jan said with a shrug. 'I was looking forward to introducing you to a few new tricks I thought you'd like. Sort out your clothes. I'll ring for a cab.'

Delia gathered up her clothes, practically throwing them on. They were in a terrible state. By the time the cab arrived, she was dressed. Jan kissed her goodbye on the cheek in a perfunctory way, saying saucily, 'See you next week, Delia. Perhaps then you'll model for me with that beautiful body of yours that I've got to know so well.'

Delia couldn't get out of his studio fast enough. She headed for home. Once there rang Ohrbach's telling Mr Simmonds she'd come down with a bad cold and wouldn't be in that day. The next day she was relieved to be going back to work. She wanted to forget all about Jan, but she could barely work as her whole body screamed and craved for him. This was a massive shock. How could someone like her be as susceptible to lust as everybody else, and horror of horrors how was she going to cope with these strange newfound feelings of explosive passion?

CHAPTER 21

Since his gig at Smalls, Joel couldn't get Desirée out of his head. He almost wished Benny hadn't mentioned her. How was he to find her even if she lived in the Village? The obvious place to start was the clubs. The Village Vanguard and the Golden Triangle had been going since the '30s but there was no one there matching Desirée's description. Joel had the same result at the White Horse and the Lion. It seemed futile and he began to wonder if she'd moved away from the Village.

Giving it one last shot he put an advert in The Villager, the local free paper, with a rented box number. All Joel had to go on was Desirée's first name. A week or two went by. When he next went to check his box there was one reply on a scrappy bit of paper saying, 'From Desirée – if you wants me. Find me at,' and there was an address on Bleecker Street. Joel could barely contain himself, then had second thoughts. What if it wasn't his Desirée or, if it was, what would she think of this dilapidated old man turning up out of the blue? He hesitated.

The following Tuesday at the diner, and after a lot of clearing of his throat, he explained his dilemma to Delia and Bobby Jo. Delia was completely out of it these days, wandering into Leo's. her hair down, hatless, a dreamy expression on her face, with mismatched shoes and bag. Studying her closely, Joel was not at all sure she could contribute anything worthwhile.

Once he'd finished talking, Bobby Jo exclaimed loudly, 'Wow, how absolutely smashing. You must meet her, you must. This is so romantic.'

Life, Love, Death

Joel gnashed his teeth, 'Keep it down, young 'un. 'Don want everyone knowin' my business. Anyways am still undecided,' he mumbled.

Bobby Jo tapped Delia on the arm, 'What do you think? It's the most spiffing thing you've ever heard.'

A glassy eyed Delia nodded, recommending caution, 'Be careful, Joel. You might regret seeing her again. After all you have a completely different memory of her from – what about thirty years ago – and she of you. It could be a shock and not a good one.'

'You're right, Missus. That's why I's uncertain. I'll sleep on it.'

The next day Joel, taking his courage in one hand and Betsy in the other, walked down Bleecker Street. It was hard to find the number she'd given him. Finally, he spotted it on the side door to a flat above a shop. Knocking on the door, he half hoped there was no one in but minutes later he heard the clacking of heels on the stairs. The door opened and it was like seeing the ghost of the Desirée he remembered. Her red curls were now snowy white although her tiny, exquisite heart-shaped face looked much the same bar lines and signs of world weariness. But what seized him by the throat was her eyes. Those luminous sparkling green eyes were now dull and dark as if a light had gone out.

'Yer, whatcha want?' Desirée asked in a sullen tone.

'It's me,' Joel said, barely able to speak, 'Joel - remember back in the twenties I was the Sax player.'

Life, Love, Death

'Don remember. You dat person advertising for me? Long time ago – thirty years or more, can't remember.'

Joel cleared his throat, trying to get a grip on his feelings, 'You and I used to sit on the stoop of a night and look at the moon. I asked you to marry me.'

'I dunno 'bout that,' Desirée said with the same morose expression. Then a fleeting memory dawned and her face lit up, 'Now I recalls – a shy skinny guy, not so young but real sweet. You used to hold my hand and whisper sweet nothings in my ear when I was a dance girl.'

'That's me,' Joel said reassured, to at last catch a glimpse of his old lost love.

'You best come in,' Desirée said, slurring her words. 'I got Bourbon somewhere. We can toast old times. You can tell me what's been happening to you, old man.'

Not keen to be reminded of his great age, Joel followed her up the stairs and into her flat. It was a shabby joint, worse than his basement, with walls plastered with yellowing newspaper cuttings and photographs of jazz clubs and musicians. Squinting hard he recognised a picture of himself and Betsy playing with the band at Smalls. 'See, Desirée. Here's me here with my Betsy.'

But Desirée was disinterested, 'Sure, lover, I brings you to mind now. 'Bin such a lot of musos in my life – hard to recall y'all.'

The bourbon was brought out, but Joel could see that his once beloved Desirée was already high. By the time she

Life, Love, Death

came back from finding glasses he could see her pupils were mere pinpoints. She'd probably had a quick fix in the kitchen. It broke Joel's heart to see her like this but he sat and drank with her until she passed out. Taking the glass out of her limp hand he covered her with a raggedy old blanket, sitting for a minute with his head in his hands, wondering if life would have been better for her if they'd married. A musician's life was so erratic. Looking round he noticed the empties and the crack wrappers and knew he must help her. There was little food in the fridge. Using his last few dollars he went out and bought bread, milk and eggs and took them back. After cooking up the eggs, he tried to rouse the sleeping woman and get her to eat. Despite her protests, he managed to get her to eat a little, but all she could say was, 'Watcha want? I got nuffink, old man. Go away. Leave me!' … mumbling, as she began to fall asleep, 'they all leaves me in the end.'

She was almost totally out of it as a hurt Joel responded forcefully, 'But I didn't leave you. I came back for you. You'd gone off with some trumpeter.'

'That's right,' Desirée moaned, 'Stevie summat. He was no good either. Y'all left.'

'I didn't,' Joel said again, raising his voice. But it was no use. She was too far gone to hear.

Wondering what to do next he wrote down his address and said loudly, 'I'll help you's come off this rubbish, Desirée.'

Something must have registered in her drugged up, drunken state as Desirée garbled out incoherently, 'Don want to. Need sleep. Go 'way, old man. Nuffink for you here.'

Life, Love, Death

On his way home Joel made up his mind to do something, but what? Perhaps Delia could help. She was an educated woman with a deal of common sense.

Next day he returned to Bleecker Street to see what state Desirée was in. He knocked on the door, but it opened of its own accord. Stepping inside Joel called, 'It's me, Joel. Desirée, I'm coming up.' There was no reply. When he got to the room there was nothing left. The few sticks of furniture had gone and so had all the newspaper cuttings on the walls. Of Desirée, there was no sign. She'd gone again. Joel put his head against the wall and wept. He'd lost her for the second time. The pain was as overwhelming as the first time.

He collapsed on the floor sobbing, 'I would have looked after you, my own dear love, if only you'd let me.'

CHAPTER 22

It was a wounded and battered Joel who turned up at Leo's for the next Tuesday lunch. Bobby Jo was agog to know how he'd got on with his quest but Delia, taking one look at his face and slumped shoulders, placed a warning arm on Bobby Jo's, 'Not now, dear. I think Joel needs peace and quiet.'

Joel felt as if his heart had been wrenched out of his chest. Over the years there had been a certain exquisite poignancy in looking back at that rose tinted memory of Desirée and what might have been. Now that was smashed to pieces. Perhaps he should have listened to Delia and her advice about caution. Would he ever feel content again? Playing at Smalls had given him a new lease of life, and his search for Desirée a purpose and a vigour he hadn't felt in years. But what next? He was aware his two companions were watching him closely with sympathy in their eyes, but he didn't want pity.

When Addy came bustling over, he said quietly, 'Usual, thank you Addy.'

Addy raised her eyebrows but saying nothing laid a comforting arm on his shoulder, 'Right away, Joel. What about you, ladies. Ready to try something more adventurous?'

'Oh definitely,' Bobby Jo grinned, 'and am sure Delia wants something other than her usual rabbit food.'

Life, Love, Death

'Don't be cheeky,' Delia reproved, but ended up laughing, 'Very well, Adelie. Surprise us.' Looking over at Joel she added, 'We need cheering up today.'

'Not me,' Joel said miserably, head down, hunching into his shoulders and bending forward to stroke Betsy. 'I's wants my usual.'

'Okey dokey,' Addy quipped making faces at the girls over Joel's head.

Bobby Jo was flying high. She felt sorry for Joel but she was far too excited about her own life to allow anything to cast a shadow over it. Since the Kennedy wedding, Xander had put himself out to be particularly kind. He would critique her work but often utter an occasional word of praise. At times she would catch him staring at her from under his dark hooded eyes as if he was appraising her but, if caught out, would exude a boyishly charming smile, saying, 'You look so lovely and fresh today, Miss Roberta. I can't take my eyes off you.'

Bobby Jo wished she knew where she was with him. Also, she was not at all sure she wished to be constantly addressed as 'Miss Roberta' with that underlying touch of irony, although 'kiddo' was much worse.

'Now, Miss Roberta,' Xander said thoughtfully, 'I have a job for you. It's a personal errand rather than anything for the paper. You can say 'no' if you wish but it would mean a lot to me if you were willing to do it.'

Bobby Jo, eager to please, shot out a quick, 'Yes, of course I'll do whatever you need.'

Life, Love, Death

'There's a package I want delivered to a building on 7th Avenue. It's to do with a story I'm writing. It's very hush hush. Here, I'll write down the address. It's a red door between a sewing and a typewriter shop. Make sure you're not seen. First of all, you visit the typewriter shop. Say you're interested in their latest model. Whilst the assistant shows you the machine, look through the window. Check you haven't been followed and there's no one watching in the street. Leave the shop, double back and enter the red door. You'll find a letter and parcel rack there. Leave the package in the one marked 'J' and slip out carefully. Take the subway back. Get off a stop before Herald Square and walk the rest of the way.'

Bobby Jo was intrigued, dying to know why all this 'cloak and dagger' stuff but, recognising the expression on Xander's face, she controlled herself. 'Be watchful and vigilant' were his last words to her as she pranced out of the building, thrilled to be doing something for him. At last, Xander was showing he trusted her. She took a peek at the parcel in the briefcase he'd given her. It looked fairly innocuous. It was bulky, well wrapped and sealed with tape. A note on the front said, 'To J from K.M.' and in tiny script, *'Need meeting urgently.'*

Casually, Bobby Jo thought, 'Hope it's not a bomb,' and giggled at being at being silly. Honestly, she was losing it. What about the 'K.M.' – was Xander being 'Karl Marx' again, just like the joke Delia had made a few weeks ago? It was all too much, just like a spy story. But Xander was no spy, what a ridiculous thought! She must pull herself together and follow Xander's instructions. Unluckily, she came unstuck at the typewriter shop. It had a big notice on the door 'Closed for funeral. Reopening tomorrow'. Using

Life, Love, Death

her initiative, Bobby Jo made for the sewing shop but once she got nearer could see there was no clear view of the street from their window. 'Oh dammit,' she said loudly to herself, so doubled back and checking the street made for the red door. Thank goodness. All was as Xander had said and she was relieved to dump the package in the rack. On her way back to the Trib she totally ignored Xander's instructions, taking the subway to Herald Square and stopping off at a drug store for a Plantation Peach before returning to the office. Xander would be none the wiser and if he did happen to find out, would think she was taking extra precautions. As Bobby Jo licked her way through her ice cream, she wondered why there was so much secrecy about an article for the Trib. Thinking back on what Xander had said, she realised Xander had told her two different reasons for the errand. Firstly, he'd said it was something 'personal' and nothing to do with the paper, then he'd said it was 'something to do with story he was writing'. Odd! There was nothing Bobby Jo loved more than a mystery. It made Xander that bit more alluring.

By the time Bobby Jo got back to the Trib people were packing up and going home. There was no sign of Xander. Harry called over to her, 'Xander said to get off home, kiddo. He's with Sam and they may have to pull an all-nighter on a piece of news that's come in.'

Bobby Jo chewed it over as she made her way back to the Barbizon. What was Xander up to? Perhaps he had a second job. Anyway, she was going to make it her business to find out. If she was in the know they might become closer. He was definitely the man she wanted making all those raw young men she'd left behind in Little Chute look like mere boys.

CHAPTER 23

Since her traumatic experience with Jan the previous week Delia was having the jitters. She was all fingers and thumbs at work and was reprimanded by Mr Simmonds for wrongly pricing new inventory. At home she could barely eat and even Monet's affectionate presence on her lap gave her no reprieve from her tortured mind. What was she to do? Rationally she told herself Jan knew so many women he wouldn't miss her and probably wouldn't care if she didn't turn up next week. But it was she who cared, she was the one who couldn't do without him. Even one afternoon in his bed had been like a drug. She was addicted now and had to go back for more. But what about her self-esteem? Having always been self-contained and inhibited it was terrible to be so vulnerable and needy. How she wished she had someone worldly wise to advise her, but neither Bobby Jo nor Joel would be of any use in that way.

However, proving her wrong, - Joel - despite his own misery or because of it picked up on Delia's state of mind. On their usual Tuesday before Bobby Jo arrived, he glanced across at Delia and said quietly, 'You's looks frazzled, Missus. Can I's help?'

Delia nearly broke down, but pulling herself together said, 'Good of you, Joel. But I must sort this out for myself. You understand?'

He nodded, 'Same here, Missus. I thinks we's on our own with our woes. A hard thing, life. It 'don get easier.'

A lively Bobby Jo arrived with a flourish, sweeping away all talk of anguish. Always transparent in her moods, it was

Life, Love, Death

hard not to be caught up in her exuberance. She was full of what she was doing at work and how her relationship with Xander was progressing. There was talk of him giving her a surprise the following week and Bobby Jo could hardly contain herself. It reminded Delia how marvellous it was to be young and not have to concern yourself with consequences or the future beyond next week. Deciding she should adopt some of that same attitude Delia determined to face her situation, go to Jan's, and see what would happen.

When Delia arrived at the studio with all her nerve endings jangling, to her amazement Jan merely gave her a hasty peck on the cheek. Looking her up and down, he said, 'I'd completely forgotten that illustration I was going to do for 'Mademoiselle'. Now they're chasing me for it,' adding accusingly, 'You've got the wrong clothes on,' making it sound as if it was Delia's fault. Delia was too disconcerted to say anything. Talk about Bobby Jo's changes of mood, Jan's were even worse. Why had she got so wound up about seeing him?

Intent on his work, Jan said, 'Never mind, liefling. Go behind that screen. Take everything off. I'll paint in your outfit from memory.'

Delia was rushed behind the screen with a mere pat on the backside from Jan. Before she knew it, she was modelling nude, a swathe of red material round her waist and a flower basket in one hand. Totally exposed, she didn't know where to look but had no chance to complain as Jan manhandled her into the pose he wanted. It was difficult for her to recognise the man she'd been so intimate with the week previous as he either stared at her dispassionately, worked feverishly at his canvas, or mixed paints.

Life, Love, Death

The afternoon grew on. Delia's body began to ache. She yawned, trying to move into a more comfortable position but all she got was growls from the other side of the canvas, 'Mien Gott, Keep still. Not much longer.'

Finally, when Delia could barely stand, Jan threw aside his brush and fell down limply on the couch, 'Come here, mein liefling and take a rest with me.' Delia couldn't help but comply. No sooner had she lay beside him than she realised he'd gone to sleep. Gently removing his arm from around her, she got up and dressed.

Itching to see what Jan had painted, she removed the old cloth he'd shrouded the painting in and was stunned. It was as if he'd painted a youthful version of the young girl she'd never managed to be. There was a lightness of touch combined with the realism of a confident, self-assured girl who knew she looked attractive and was sure the world could see that too.

Jan's memory was extraordinary, as he'd painted on the body the exact outfit Delia had worn at their second meeting. Despite being impressed and wishing she'd been that girl when she was young, Delia felt an underlying sadness and regret that she'd never be even a shadow of that girl. They always said beauty was wasted on the young – how true that was. Now she was middle aged and tired and all she could think about was getting home.

By now Jan was snoring loudly, so Delia tiptoed out of the studio wondering why she'd been so nervous about seeing him. It was all a lot of nothing. Even taking her clothes off hadn't phased her. She hardly recognised the person she was becoming. Of course, there were still elements of her

Life, Love, Death

former straitlaced personality to overcome, but overall she was ready to embrace the idea of becoming a modern Fifties woman. One who could take control of their life and this love affair, if that's what it was, and not allow a lover like Jan to dominate her as Gus and her father had done.

CHAPTER 24

Bobby Jo was so caught up in her feelings for Xander, and trying to figure out what he was up to, she was barely aware of what was happening in the outside world. Russia had built their version of the hydrogen bomb earlier that year, and a concerned Eisenhower had reacted by approving the expansion of America's nuclear arsenal. Consequently, the Cold War continued. On television, the Edward Murrow show was planning to expose McCarthy's anti-communist campaign targeting military and government employees. But life for Bobby Jo went on as usual.

Bobby Jo's interests revolved round: what to wear to work the next day, how to impress Xander with her intelligence, and vain attempts to cultivate friendships with the Barbizon girls. The latter was proving fruitless. The snooty girls would scoff at her efforts and turn away and converse with their friends or bury their heads in the cult book of the year, Fahrenheit 451. Bobby Jo tried to read it but was unconvinced by its improbable view of the future. At the diner she struggled to explain the theme of the book to Delia and Joel.

Joel grunted in his usual fashion and taking no notice of her explanation, said, 'Sounds load o'nonsense. Wha' you's want to know about the future when the present is so bad, some days even worse,' he remarked gloomily. Since the Desirée debacle he'd sunk lower and lower into himself as if there was nothing left to live for.

Delia looked over at him with a pitying glance. If only there was something they could do to rouse his spirits. Trying to respond to Bobby Jo, she said, 'I'm with Joel on this. I think

Life, Love, Death

we should live in the present.' Biting her lip, she added, 'I myself have been at fault living too much in the past. Both my father and my husband led me to believe that all a woman wants is security, a home, and a family. Now I'm not so sure. I feel I've missed out and hardly know myself. Yet I've already lived over half my life. There's so much to see and experience in the world and I've hardly begun. I really need to live life to the fullest and find out who I am before it's too late.'

Bobby Jo's jaw practically fell open. She'd never heard Delia talk like this. Whatever had happened to her? 'Wow, Delia that sounds real cool. How will you start?'

'I don't know yet,' Delia said smugly, 'but I intend to find out and I'll let you know. Now tell us, how are you getting along with Xander? Are you making any progress?'

Joel growled and rolled his eyes. Oh God, these women. Always trying to entrap a poor, clueless man or talk about their innermost feelings. Heartily sick of hearing what antics they might get up to, he hauled himself up from his seat, 'I's off now, ladies – you's can gossip all you's like. I's have to get back to work,' and cradling Betsy he stomped out, throwing coins on the table.

'The poor man,' Delia said softly. 'He's never been the same …I don't know…I wish we could help him somehow.'

Sensing Bobby Jo was about to explode with exasperation, she said, 'Well, tell me everything, dear. I know you're dying to.'

Life, Love, Death

'I don't know where to begin…I can't wait…it's all happening Friday night.'

'What is?' an irritated Delia asked. Why were the young always so pent-up with excitement, when anyone her age was never supposed to show any emotion.

'It's Xander. He said he's taking me to a posh nightclub.'

'Why?' Delia asked bluntly. 'Sounds unusual. He's not shown that much interest in you lately, has he?'

'I know,' Bobby Jo said defensively. 'He's busy with the Vice President's visit to Hanoi later this month.' Miserably she acknowledged, 'You're right. He does blow hot and cold.'

Delia immediately felt ashamed. How could she quash all this young girl's anticipation like that, just because she herself was going through a tricky time. Changing tack, she asked, 'And what will you wear. Do you have an evening or cocktail dress?'

This didn't help bolster Bobby Jo's failing spirits, 'No, I only have juvenile dresses I brought from home.' Her shoulders drooped.

'Perhaps I can do something,' Delia offered. 'I may have a dress you can wear,' then grimaced, 'but my clothes would be much too old fashioned for you. On second thoughts, you can come by Ohrbach's. I'll find something for you there and use my staff discount. How would that suit?'

Bobby Jo brightened up, 'That's swell, Delia. Thank you.'

Life, Love, Death

'I don't know,' Delia tutted, 'where you get all this language from, 'cool', 'swell' makes you sound like one of those Village beatniks. I suppose it must be the cinema,' but she smiled indulgently at Bobby Jo, thinking she could be her daughter.

As it turned out, Bobby Jo had no need of Delia's help. On her return to the Barbizon there was a delivery for her. An enormous package labelled Saks Fifth Avenue was sitting on Reception. All the girls were hovering round it, clacking like hens. They pounced on her as soon as she entered, demanding to know if she had a wealthy lover. At long last, Bobby Jo was able to take her revenge. Picking up the parcel without a word, she made a hasty exit to her room. The crowd of girls was left standing speechless, in awe of this country bumpkin from nowhere receiving a dress from Saks of all places. Perhaps they murmured between themselves they had underrated little Miss Nobody. Maybe she was worth knowing after all.

Bobby Jo was beside herself, anxious to tear off the packaging wondering who it was from. It could be from her mother, though highly unlikely as her mother would never have heard of the store. There was Delia, but she would never be able to afford or even go to Saks. Why would she when she worked at Ohrbach's? By this time Bobby Jo had worked her way through mounds of tissue, she was finally rewarded with the sight of the most glamorous deep emerald taffeta beaded evening dress she'd ever seen. Reverently removing it from its box, an enthralled Bobby Jo held it in front of her. It was her exact size and with it, further down in the box, were long black evening gloves, a green and black beaded bag, and the highest pair of black pumps Bobby Jo had ever seen. Searching through the

Life, Love, Death

wrapping Bobby Jo looked for a sender's card. Right at the very bottom was a gold embossed card with the words, 'Enjoy, X'. It was a shock to think Xander had gone to all this trouble and expense. She remembered what Delia had said about wondering what Xander wanted. But even her suspicions could not dampen her delight. She couldn't wait to try the dress on.

The whole ensemble was so perfect that Bobby Jo twirled and twirled in front of the mirror – blowing pretend kisses to make-believe waiters, running through imaginary scenarios with Xander as he spun her round the floor or topped up her glass with champagne. The high heeled pumps took some getting use to, but she had time to practise before Friday. It was hard to take the dress off, but she hung it on the outside of the wardrobe and sat relishing it. Later that night as she lay in bed, she could see the outline of the dress shimmering in the darkness. It was like a mirage or a dream that she might never wake up from, although she still had nagging doubts about Xander. How could she ever thank him? What was he up to? What did he want from her? Anyway, that was for the morning. All she could do now was sleep and luxuriate in the thought of her new outfit and the coming Friday.

CHAPTER 25

Friday came too slowly for Bobby Jo. As that day dragged on, Xander gave her not the least flicker of attention. Bobby Jo began to feel panicky. Was Xander playing with her? Perhaps the dress was a practical joke. Was he really intending to take her out? It wasn't until towards the end of the day that Xander looked across at Bobby and said, '7.30, okay? I'll pick you at the Barbizon. You better wait for me in the entrance. I don't want those prudish old spinsters knowing my business.' That was it. All he had to say before turning back to his work. Not a mention of the dress. A minute or two later, he cast a beady eye at the time and said, 'You better get going. I know how long you gals take to dress and fuss with yourselves. See you later.' Not allowing Bobby Jo to utter a word, he packed up his papers and disappeared up to Sam Murphy's office.

Bobby Jo did as she was told but didn't like being lumped in with 'you gals' especially as she never took long to get ready. Back at the Barbizon all was peaceful. Most of the girls usually went out for drinks after work on a Friday night. Bobby Jo was so tense, she could barely pin up her copper bob in the French twist Delia had shown her. It took a lot of hairspray but finally she was able to start on her face. Her hand wobbled with the eyeliner and mascara brush. Lastly, she applied the bright red lipstick. Standing back clad only in her fluffy lace petticoat, her new brassiere, girdle, and stockings, Bobby Jo thought she looked far more grown-up than usual. Hopefully that beautiful dress would add the finishing touch. The dress was stunning. Bobby Jo carefully adjusted the neckline to show a little more cleavage. The shoes were another thing. Although she'd practised with them, they seemed higher than ever. Trying to walk across

Life, Love, Death

the room with a type of Marilyn sway, she almost tripped and fell. Steadying herself and studying her reflection in the long mirror, Bobby Jo barely recognised that tousle headed redhead dressed in a Peter Pan collared blouse and pleated skirt who'd left Little Chute in June. The final addition was a tiny, beaded cocktail hat she'd managed to buy in her lunch hour. She'd come a long way. She was a woman now.

Despite looking the part Bobby Jo was jittery, as she made her way to the lobby, hoping not to bump into any of the snooty girls. She was really not as confident as her outfit made her out to be. Perhaps if she pretended she was someone else, maybe one of those Hollywood movie stars from 'Photoplay', she would feel more self-assured.

Xander's cab arrived on the dot of 7.30. He got out to open the door for her and didn't seem in a particularly good mood. As the evening was cool, Bobby Jo had thrown a coat over the green dress. She waited for Xander to make a comment about how she looked but he merely sighed, concentrating on giving the driver directions. After a while, he turned and stared at her with his piecing, dark set eyes and frowned, 'Too much lipstick. You don't need to look like a floozie. Take some of it off,' and handed her his handkerchief. Bobby Jo reddened, feeling humiliated. This wasn't a good start to the evening. She felt like a child rather than the sophisticate she'd imagined herself to be. What was wrong with Xander? He was so hard to fathom. His demeanour didn't bode well for the evening ahead. Bobby Jo sat there, palms sweating, wondering what was going to happen next, whilst Xander remained silent and brooding by her side.

Life, Love, Death

Bobby Jo, having no idea where they were headed and by now loath to ask, was amazed when the cab drew up before a wrought iron gate in Midtown. On its frontage was a lineup of ornamental model jockeys in coloured silks. Bobby Jo could hardly believe it. Was this the '21' Club? All the famous people she'd ever heard of had dined here. Full of expectancy, she looked at Xander questioningly. He nodded, seeming at last to enter into her delight and enjoyment, drawling in a Rhett Butler take-off from 'Gone with the Wind', 'Now Miss Roberta, you are one of the elite and illustrious of New York. May I escort you in?' Taking her arm he helped her out of the cab. Bobby Jo felt as if she was floating. Gone was the earlier unpleasant atmosphere. The doorman doffed his top hat to Xander as if he knew him, saying, 'Have a good evening, sir, madam,' and they were in.

Bobby Jo couldn't breathe. In the Bar Room every inch of the ceiling was hung with sporting goods, memorabilia, and toys. Bemused by it all, she turned to Xander who explained, 'Regulars leave souvenirs. See, there's one of the first ones: a replica of Howard Hughes' TWA plane and Senator John Kennedy's torpedo boat from the war.' The tables were decked out in the same red and white chequered tablecloths they'd had during Prohibition. It was like stepping back in time.

A waiter showed them to a table upstairs and Xander announced, 'I think a drink is called for – some sort of aperitif. Can you recommend one?' he asked the hovering waiter.

'What about a Manhattan, sir?'

Life, Love, Death

Bobby Jo pulled a face. Xander grinned, 'Didn't know you were so up on cocktails, mon petit chou. How is that?'

'Delia and I went to Smalls one night to hear Joel play. I had one there, but it was bitter like cough mixture.'

'Well perhaps we'd better stick to something you might like. What about a Daiquiri for the young lady and a Negroni for me.'

'Excellent choice,' the waiter bowed and moved away.

Bobby Jo was too self-conscious to ask what a Daiquiri was and even more overwhelmed when she was presented with her menu, a great deal of which was in French.

Xander noticing her bewilderment, said, 'Would you like me to order for us both? I'm sure I've some idea what you might like. Let's see – what about starting off with pâté de foie gras, a favourite of mine, followed by a Special Hamburger '21' that should suit you, and then for both of us Profiteroles au Chocolate washed down with champagne.'

The meal was delicious especially as Xander omitted to mention what pâté de foie gras really was. After dinner, Xander regaled Bobby Jo with stories about how '21' had coped during Prohibition. He talked about the camouflaged doors, the invisible chutes, the quick release bar shelving and the club's pride and joy, the wine cellar with its secret two and a half ton concrete door opened with a meat skewer.

Conversation for once was easy. Bobby Jo was in a soporific state, allowing herself to gaze adoringly at Xander. Being as

Life, Love, Death

he couldn't fail to notice, he decided to make full use of the moment. Taking her hand, he declared, 'You know I'm growing increasingly fond of you, Miss Roberta. Now if I wasn't your mentor and your senior, I would be taking full advantage of the situation.' Detecting disappointment in her eyes he added, 'Of course in time to come things may change. We shall have to see how it goes. Now Miss Cinderella, I think it's the witching hour. I must get you back to that den of spinsters before they call out the law.' Paying the mammoth bill without flinching, he bundled himself and Bobby Jo into a hailed cab. In the back of the cab, he pulled her close proceeding to kiss her passionately until her head swam. After kissing her senseless, he whispered in her ear, 'I've a few jobs for you, Miss Roberta. That's just between you and me. Can you keep secrets?'

A stupefied Bobby Jo nodded.

'Excellent. I'll explain when we lunch next week. Later in the week I'm off to Indochina on Nixon's trip. The Trib hasn't got a foreign correspondent at the moment so Sam's asked me to fill in. I must be in his good books again or he's desperate,' he laughed mockingly.

Arriving at the Barbizon and telling the driver to wait, Xander, his arm held tightly round Bobby Jo, walked her to the door, 'Straight to bed with you after all that alcohol. No sitting up chatting. You need your rest.' He kissed her swiftly and returned to the cab without a backward glance.

Bobby Jo was euphoric. How she longed to tell a good friend about the evening, but there was only Delia. She was probably far too old to remember how an evening like this felt.

Life, Love, Death

On her way upstairs, Bobby Jo found a pile of notes in her pigeonhole – all messages from her parents, pleading with her to come home for Thanksgiving. Not bothering to read them, she tore them up and tossed them in the nearest garbage can. Little Chute was a long way away. She wanted nothing to remind her of its existence. Now she was a real New Yorker, and Xander was beginning to show his feelings for her in actions if not in words. He obviously trusted her with his secrets. She would never betray him.

CHAPTER 26

Joel was becoming irritated and bored with his Tuesday lunch companions. It was a terrible thing to say when he had no other friends. He hadn't the heart to play at Smalls with the gang and his old friend Benny Carter anymore. It was as if life had no meaning since the episode with Desirée. He still had his routines and his regular busking spots but even those were becoming problematic. Sergeant Mulroney was always around waiting to pounce. This was a disaster as the lead-up to Christmas was one of his lucrative times. People were queuing for theatres, shows, late night shopping, or gathering at restaurants for after work parties, and music was always popular. There was no doubt he and Betsy could draw a crowd. Grimly, he made his way to the diner after spending all morning playing hide and seek with Mulroney and his fellow cops.

Not acknowledging Addy, he sat down in the usual booth hoping his two companions would have gone elsewhere. But no such luck. Bobby Jo came in first, bubbling over with energy, followed by Delia who was also in good spirits and more assertive than usual. They greeted Joel, but he ignored them. Bobby Jo made rude finger gestures over his head at Delia, who shook her head discouragingly. They ordered, then sat in silence. Delia, feeling great compassion for the dispirited Joel, placed her hand on his and said sympathetically, 'Is there any way we can help?', including Bobby Jo in the 'we', though what good that scatty young girl could be was anybody's business.

Joel, never keen to talk about himself or his problems, suddenly let go and blurted out, 'Betsy and I has to leave New York,' mumbling, 'No good with that Mulroney and

Life, Love, Death

his mates. Can't earn a living heres about. They's constantly on my back. I's dunno what to do.'

Bobby Jo looked blank. However, Delia said, 'Let me think. What about a change of area, Joel, then Mulroney will forget all about you?'

'But I's needs crowds – them queuing up – is generous when entertained.'

'What about changing your time of day and keeping away from Midtown, move to areas where there are off Broadway shows?'

'You may have summat there, Missus.'

'I have another idea too, Joel,' Delia's face lit up. 'What about coming and playing at my store's Christmas party? Am sure I could get you a fee. I know it's a way off yet, but it could help.' Turning to Bobby Jo, she said, 'What about the Trib Don't they have a Christmas party? Could you ask the editor if they want live music. Then perhaps the Smalls' gang could come along with Joel.'

Joel brightened up, actually smiling. 'Thanks, Missus. You's all there, for sure.'

Not knowing whether to be flattered or insulted, Delia smiled. Since taking herself in hand, she'd begun to feel more self-possessed and confident, positive she could solve her own problems and those of the world.

For Joel, it was as if destiny was determined to give him a helping hand too. A few days after the conversation at the

Life, Love, Death

diner, he bumped into Benny Carter again. 'Where've you been, Joel? We're missing you at Smalls. Why aren't you coming on Thursdays? The gang wondered if they'd upset you or something.'

Joel was dumbfounded. Perhaps he had friends after all. Feeling he owed Benny an explanation, he launched into the whole saga of Desirée and stood, head bowed, feeling foolish. Benny took his arm, 'Look, old friend. We all lose our heads over women. It's nothing to be embarrassed about. At least you tried to help her. She was probably too ashamed to let you do anything. Easier to run away again. Look, it's coming up to that season again. Our gang is doing more paid sessions at Smalls. They'd love to have you back. What about it? Better than freezing on the streets. Come Thursday. We'll sort out dates.'

Joel couldn't believe it. Perhaps his fortunes were changing. Maybe Delia had sparked off a run of luck for him. In future he wouldn't turn his nose up at his Tuesday diner friends. To be fair, hadn't they always been there for him? Bobby Jo making efforts to visit him and Delia getting him out of jail. He decided to appreciate them more.

Going back to Smalls on the Thursday was like coming home. Everyone greeted him with affection and enthusiasm. Taking his place with Betsy on the rostrum it was like he'd never left. They soon fell in with the gang's impro and their welcome from the audience warmed his heart once more. Maybe he wasn't finished yet and still had a way to go.

The biggest surprise of all was that the band had a new singer, a beautiful black lady called Blanche. She wasn't the typical sexy, sinuous creature they usually employed but a

Life, Love, Death

sensual, voluptuous, mature woman with graying braids whose mellifluous voice sent shivers down Joel's spine.

During the break, as they had a drink, she smiled at him with her wide coral painted lips, patting a seat beside her. Spellbound, a bemused Joel sat down. His head was spinning. Blanche, noting his confusion, said, 'Glad to meet you, Mr Petersen. Benny's told me a lot about you and Betsy.'

Normally Joel would have growled and been riled to be the subject of gossip, but the mention and inclusion of Betsy appeased him. 'You's a lovely voice, Missus. It got me in me guts. I's could listen all night.'

'Thank you, Joel. I appreciate the compliment coming from a musician like yourself. I'm Blanche DuBois, not the one from the Tennessee Williams play,' she chortled.

Joel looked vacant, 'Sorry Missus, never been to that there theatre or the like.'

Blanche smiled, 'Not a lot of musicians in our business could afford it. Blanche DuBois was a character in 'A Streetcar Called Desire.' My mother was a slave down South but could read and write a bit. She saw the name on a playbill. We never had no surname except the master's so once she and my father moved up North, they gave me that name.'

Joel was impressed. Not many of his people were willing to be so open about their backgrounds, himself included, especially not to strangers. Making a big effort, he held out a hand, 'I's pleased to meet you, Blanche Dubois, I'm Joel Petersen, after my father's master 'Peter'.'

Life, Love, Death

'D'ya know Joel,' Blanche said amiably, taking his hand, 'I think we're going to get along just fine. Don't you?'

'I's hope so, Blanche.' For once, Joel allowed himself some vulnerability, 'I's in desperate need of friends.'

Clinking glasses, they sealed their friendship. Joel began to feel more optimistic as if this was the beginning of a new future, something to look forward to, not the miserable end he'd predicted for himself.

CHAPTER 27

Delia couldn't believe how much her life had changed since meeting Jan de Vries. She was more outgoing at work, and growing so assertive with the dreaded Mr Simmonds that these days he was too intimidated to criticise her. She was not so sure about Jan though. When it came to him she had no control over her emotions, and inwardly knew she didn't trust him.

One Tuesday afternoon when Delia arrived at the studio, Jan said, 'I'm sorry, Delia. I have to go out for a short time to deliver a painting. Make yourself at home. I've set up an easel for you if you feel in the mood for painting, otherwise take a rest till I get back. Then we can rest together,' he added salaciously, punctuating it with a soft pinch of her bottom. This time Delia was not in the mood to be so easily seduced, totally ignoring Jan's innuendo.

Deciding she wanted to know more about her lover, Delia took a look round his studio and apartment, curious as to how he made his money. Since that early visit Delia had not bumped into the dreadful Helena or any other woman for that matter. Probably Jan kept his women separate. Her eye fell on a pile of letters that had been opened but flung carelessly on the bedroom floor. None of the envelopes were sealed. Money spilled out of the top of some of them. Cautiously, Delia bent and picked up a few. Each envelope had Jan's name scrawled in a different hand. There were sheaves of dollar bills and many scribbled notes saying, *'Darling Jan, What a night! Love D'*, or *'Can't believe how you made me feel. See you soon, very soon,'* (underlined in red) *Love R.'* There were so many 'billets doux' Delia was shocked. It was just as she thought, Jan was a paid gigolo. What did he

Life, Love, Death

want with her then? She wasn't wealthy, in fact, she existed from month to month on her salary. After paying bills her budget barely stretched to cover the cost of clothes and food for her and Monet. There was a sudden bang on the outer door. Delia hurriedly stuffed everything back in the envelopes, hoping she'd got them in the right order.

Jan came bounding into the room saying, 'My little cherub, I find I've a lot to do this afternoon. No time for painting with you or doing anything else,' arching his eyebrows coyly. 'I'm sorry, ma petite, to have wasted your time. Shall we meet again next week or perhaps you'd rather one evening during the week?'

'No, no,' Delia said in a rush, 'next week will be fine. I've a lot of shopping to do today anyway. I'll be off.'

'Not without this, mein liefling,' Jan pulled her to him and kissed her passionately, but Delia was barely responsive.

Holding her face between his two large hands, Jan said, 'Are you alright, my darling? You seem rather distrait. Have I done something wrong. Maybe you're cross with me for keeping you hanging round here?'

'Not at all,' Delia was quick to reassure him. 'I'm a little tired you know, with work.'

'Oh bah, that terrible store and the so pompous Mr – what is his name?'

'Simmonds,' Delia answered mechanically.

Life, Love, Death

'Oh, my poor liefling, you need a holiday and so do I. I must see if I can borrow my old friend Helena's summer place on Long Island. No one much uses it in the winter. We can huddle there together in front of log fires, take walks on the beach and watch the wild ocean. Doesn't it sound romantic? What do you think?'

Thrown off balance, Delia demurred, 'I can't get away at this time of year. We're at our busiest with the run up to Christmas.' The last thing she wanted to do was go away with Jan. She needed to get out of here, go home and think.

Jan, never one to be put off, said, 'Let's talk about it next week. I can see you're in a hurry to leave.' He put on a boyish pouting face, 'I don't know what I've done to be treated so shabbily. It's as if everything's changed and you don't love me anymore.'

Delia almost relented but somehow it was as if, all of a sudden, her passion was extinguished. 'Don't be silly,' she said sharply, 'Nothing's changed. I need to go.'

Flinging on her coat and grabbing her purse she raced off through the studio and outer room, banging the door behind her and letting out a deep sigh of relief. As swiftly as it had begun so it ended. Delia realised she never wanted to see Jan again. He was the past now. She was on a new journey to a future she must handle herself. If only she had a confidante. There was Bobby Jo, but she was much too young and already too pie-eyed about Xander to care about anyone else's love life.

It was a week or two later that Delia had the shock of her life. She had scribbled a quick note to Jan saying she was too

Life, Love, Death

busy at work to continue the painting lessons and instead had resumed her visits to the Museum of Modern Art on Tuesday afternoons.

It was there in the ladies' powder room that she overheard two women gossiping: 'Have you heard who he's taken up with? Some poor shop assistant from Queens? He must be desperate.'

Delia, sat in one of the cubicles, half listening and not paying much attention until she realised - shock, horror - that they were actually talking about her. She was aghast, but there was worse to come.

'You're kidding,' the other woman replied, 'what does he want with her? There's no money in it for him, surely.'

'Perhaps he's using her as a model.'

'You know these artists love to slum it with their models. Look at Toulouse-Lautrec and his prostitutes.'

'I can't think that's the case. Helena said she's mousy, middle aged and rather ingenuous.' By now Delia was practically biting her nails to the quick, berating herself for ever getting involved with Jan. How could she have been so stupid. But she had to hear the rest.

'That's it then – probably what he likes. Someone who adores him. Someone he can mould and use as his plaything.'

'I don't know about that. I believe he's quite smitten this time and tried to exhibit one of his nudes of her at the Betty

Life, Love, Death

Parsons Gallery in midtown, though I hear Betty wasn't too impressed.'

'Anyway darling, for the duration it looks as if we've been deprived of our leisurely afternoons of carnal delight. We'll have to wait for our beloved Jan to become bored with little Miss or Mrs Queens and want more adult company.'

They went off cackling together. Delia was left aghast, still standing in one of the stalls. Resting her head against the cool metal wall, she wept. She felt used, dirty, as if all her recently gained confidence and self-esteem had come crashing down. She supposed the two women were right. Due to her lack of experience, she'd put Jan on a pedestal and adored him – now he lay in smithereens at her feet. What had they meant about 'plaything'? Is that why he'd been attracted to her in the first place? Perhaps he'd seen her as untouched and unworldly, a vulnerable little creature to seduce and amuse himself with. An interlude between his various sexual forays with these rich, urbane women.

Standing in front of the mirror, Delia could hardly bear to look at herself. Feeling like a harlot, she hastily washed her red rimmed eyes and made efforts to repair her makeup, but her hand shook. She kept dropping her lipstick on the floor. When it rolled under the washbasin she left it, running out of the room and the building, afraid she would bump into someone who might know her. Later, back at home, she tried to tell herself that it was all over and forgotten. No one would ever know. She could go back to her former self, stay in the shadows, and keep herself to herself. But the thought of that nude painting niggled her. She would have to see it for herself, however painful that might be.

CHAPTER 28

It was a gloomy, rainy Tuesday in November when Bobby Jo, Joel and Delia sat down to lunch next. Both Joel and Bobby Jo were in a reasonable frame of mind, though preoccupied with their thoughts and in no mood to share. Regrettably Delia was not looking or feeling her best. Her clothes mirrored her mental state. The stark fitted black dress with a pristine white collar under the beige raincoat drained her face. The gloves had returned, but this time in black suede, and so had the hat, a plain cloche affair, pulled tightly over her plaited blonde hair. There were deep shadows under her eyes and more eyeliner than usual hiding swollen eyelids. Since her humiliation at the Museum, the crying had gone on for some time until Delia was all cried out and left feeling like an empty husk.

Bobby Jo sensed that Delia was not at her best. Not wanting to pry, she decided to try and cheer her up with lively stories from work. Her exuberance was infectious. Soon it seemed as if the whole place, including Addy, had woken up. Even Joel joined in saying, 'I's back at Smalls, Delia. I's were thinking of your advice and bumps into that old friend of mine, you remembers him, Benny? They's asked me back for extra gigs over Christmas. Wha'do'ya think?'

Delia did her best to look delighted for him, but it was a poor effort; still she managed to say, 'I'm pleased, Joel. This solves your Sergeant Mulroney problem for the time being.'

An animated Bobby Jo added, 'That's real swell, Joel. We'll come along again, won't we, Delia, before Christmas?'

Life, Love, Death

Delia barely moved her head to nod. She wanted this meal to be over, then she could go home and hide away in her apartment and stroke Monet for all he was worth. There were to be no more afternoons at the Museum of Modern Art, as who knew who she might bump into. As soon as she could she said a swift goodbye and scurried off as if the hounds of hell were chasing her.

'I wonder what's up with Delia?' a worried Bobby Jo said. 'She wasn't her usual self and what about those clothes? Maybe she was going to a funeral. What do you think?'

'I's 'don know. You's women have all sorts of moods and clothes. I's can't keep up. Anyways, young miss, it be her business. No needs for you to poke about in it.'

'I thought…,'Bobby Jo stuttered.

'Don' think. Keep your thinking for that there job of yours.'

'OK Joel, cool. I've got the message. I'm off now. See you later alligator or at least next Tuesday,' and she rushed off, red curls bobbing wildly round her head.

Joel groaned. All these young folk and their hip sayings made him feel his age. He could have a bit of peace now both women had gone. To celebrate his change of luck on the work front, he thought he would indulge himself and Betsy in something sweet. He called over to Addy, who shouted back, 'Be with you in a mo, old man.'

Rushing over, she said, 'I've got the very thing for you, Joel. What about a slice of coconut crème pie? I got some of that spray cream or chocolate sauce if you want a topping?'

Life, Love, Death

Joel grimaced, 'Plain does me, Addy.'

'Your lunch companions were in a rush today.'

'I knows. Don' know what the world is coming to. All this rushing around as if everything is speeding up. Makes me tired. That there young Bobby Jo, is like a whirlwind, prodding, noseying everywheres and getting to be a real New Yorker with them popular phrases.'

Addy grinned, 'You need to get with it, Joel. It's called being 'hip'. You're an old curmudgeon, but I love you.'

For a change, Joel laughed at himself, snapping back cheekily, 'Love you's too. How's that for an ole man?'

Addy went away smiling. It was good to see Joel chirpy. That's all she ever wanted was for people to be happy.

Back at the Trib, Bobby Jo was one very happy person too. As Xander was so busy, she thought he might have forgotten their lunch date, however she was wrong. 'I'm sorry, Bobby, I'm not going to be able to do lunch with you this week. There's too much to do. What about a drink after work tonight?'

Bobby Jo was thrilled, not only about the drink but the fact that he'd at last called her Bobby not Miss Roberta. Perhaps he was beginning to see her in a different light, more as a woman rather than a kid who'd been foisted upon him.

At home time, Xander came along with his coat on, evidently in a rush 'Come on, kiddo. Let's get this drink.

Life, Love, Death

Bring your briefcase with you. I want you to do a little job for me while I'm away.'

Bobby Jo, though not pleased to be demoted to 'kiddo' again, was overjoyed when Xander reached for her arm and tucked it into his. He hurried her along until they reached an out of the way back street bar, a real comedown from their night at '21'. Furtively, he pointed her in the direction of a seat far back in the depths of the room and went to order drinks without consulting Bobby Jo. It was all a bit hole and corner. Bobby Jo wondered what this was all about. Maybe she'd find out at last what sort of business Xander was involved in outside the Trib.

Back at the table he plonked down what turned out to be two whiskey sours though Bobby had no idea what she was drinking, only that it was too strong for her. After a few sips she pushed it away. Xander scoffed lightly, 'Sorry, kiddo, I should have got you a Virgin Mary. Anyway, perhaps next time, hey.'

Bobby Jo clung on to the 'next time' for dear life, oblivious to what Xander was saying. For some reason he'd moved closer and was talking in a half whisper: 'Miss Roberta, I'm going to tell you something in confidence. You must keep this to yourself, d'ya hear?'

Bobby Jo nodded, enthralled to have him so near but hardly listening.

Xander carried on, 'I've been helping illegals who come over from Mexico. You wouldn't believe the poor conditions they live under. Whilst I'm away I want you to deliver a package of forged papers for them to this address.' He shoved a

Life, Love, Death

sliver of notepaper towards her. 'Take this,' and Bobby Jo found herself being handed a large packet under the table. 'When no one is looking, put it in your briefcase. Tell no one. Be careful as Immigration Officers are everywhere. Do you understand?'

Bobby Jo must have looked stupefied so Xander repeated his last words, and gave her a little shake, 'Do you understand, Miss Roberta? You can see why I hold you in such regard. There aren't many people I trust as I trust you.' He squeezed her hand, 'You're a lovely girl. I'm lucky to have you in my life.'

This was unreal. Bobby Jo could hardly believe Xander was saying such wonderful things to her. Was he sincere or was this an act to get her to do his bidding? She didn't care, all she knew was that she yearned to be with him always.

'Let's go then,' Xander said. 'I've lots to do tonight.'

Bobby Jo felt a bubble of disappointment rise in her throat, but she swallowed it quickly. She'd been hoping they would spend the evening together, but it was not to be. However, as soon as they reached the Barbizon Hotel Xander pulled her into his arms, kissing her thoroughly and ardently, then hurried off shouting, 'See you when I get back, kiddo.'

A dazed Bobby Jo wondered if she would ever figure out this man. He was full of contradictions and capricious moods. She supposed if she wanted him, she would have to accept him as he was.

CHAPTER 29

Later that evening in another part of town, Hank O'Shaughnessy, G-man extraordinaire, leaned back against the wall balancing his chair on two legs, feet on the desk as he puffed away at a favoured brand of cheroot. Blowing wreaths of smoke far into the air, he beat out a slow tap on the arm of the metal chair with a half-chewed pencil. There was something suspicious here. It was so close he could smell it. All this talk of 'reds under the bed' had made him fractious and restless. Why couldn't he get a sniff of some Commie spies instead of this desk job checking out immigrants' credentials? He wanted to get his teeth into a big case. It was a waste when his senses were on the alert. He was sure he could be the one to uncover a spy ring. Something that would make his superiors sit up and listen, instead of treating him like a glorified office boy.

Hank took his mind back to last week and the unexpected incident he'd got involved in. At the time he'd wondered whether it had been a genuine gut reaction or plain animal attraction that had made him take notice.

It was last Tuesday. He'd dropped into a diner just off 6th Avenue. Sitting up at the counter he'd looked around and spotted an odd trio sitting together in a back booth. It was the redheaded girl who'd captured his attention. Why was such a vibrant young girl sitting with two rather fusty older people – perhaps her parents – though that couldn't be right as one of them was an elderly black man. They were engaged in an animated conversation, or at least the girl was. What on earth could they have in common? It was the girl who captivated him. She was so pretty, tossing her head with those red curls and bangs; he'd always been a sucker

Life, Love, Death

for girls with bangs. It was as if her enthusiasm spilled over, infecting the whole diner. Even the large ungainly waitress seemed to speed up. Yet his antenna told him there was something not right about the girl, something not kosher. Sure, he would like to get to know her better, but it wasn't that. It was as if she had something on her mind and all her chatter was a smokescreen. As a youngster he'd had a nose for secrets and for people telling lies. His Irish mother often told him he was psychic, but he thought that a load of twaddle. No FBI man worth his salt had time for anything unreal, but he desperately wanted to know more about the girl.

Trying to distract himself, he'd bitten into a cream cheese bagel and contemplated his afternoon. It was all dreary paperwork, none of which was urgent. His attention wandered back to the threesome in the corner. The girl was getting up, ready to leave. Perhaps he should follow her. What would be the harm? After all, he persuaded himself, it might even be for her own good. At any rate he could pick up some information about her. Trying not to look like a stalker and keeping a reasonable distance behind her, it wasn't difficult in the lunchtime crowds to track her bobbing red head. The girl moved off 6th, as if she was making for 7th Avenue. Finally, she disappeared into the Herald Tribune building. Hank was at a loss. Did the girl work there or was she visiting? He needed information. Years ago, he'd used an old contact in the building as a snitch. Now what was his name 'Frank something' – a boozed up old journo who'd seen better days? No doubt a few drinks would loosen the old chap's tongue. It wasn't easy to track him down. Eventually someone at the Trib mentioned he was usually to be found in the bar round the corner.

Life, Love, Death

Frank turned out to be a pushover. He was already three sheets to the wind when Hank found him and greeted Hank like a long lost relative. Thrilled to be contacted by a FBI man and knocking back a couple more bourbons, he managed to blurt out, 'Washa want, buddy?'

Hank described the red-haired girl whilst Frank slouched on his bar stool. The old man's rheumy blue eyes lit up, 'I seen that little gal. Sorta trainee reporter. She's got a relative friendly with the Reids or summat like that. These Protestant Republicans all stick together. Why d'ya wanna know?' He smacked his lips together lasciviously, 'Got some interest in her, heh? Bit young for you though. Green as grass.'

Hank shrugged, 'Just outstanding paperwork I wanted to clear up. Thanks, old friend.'

Later that afternoon, Hank was back at his post lurking outside the Trib building. His redheaded target finally emerged accompanied by a slightly older man who took her arm in a proprietary manner as they strolled down the street. Hank followed. The girl's companion looked familiar. He had dark hair and a sallow complexion as if he had Slavic blood. Picking up a newspaper, Hank closed in on them as they reached Times Square. They shot down a side turning to enter a small dingy bar. Giving them a minute or two to settle Hank entered and found a stool at the counter, observing them in the mirror. Ordering drinks they seemed in no hurry but sat close together like lovers. Hank was about to write this off as a lovers' tryst when he noticed the Slavic-looking man carefully reach into his coat and pass the girl a bulky package under the table. The girl looked around surreptitiously, then placed the packet in her briefcase. Intrigued, Hank could barely take his eyes off them. Could it

Life, Love, Death

be drugs, counterfeit money, or something else? His mind was buzzing. Within seconds, and before Hank had time to down his drink, the couple was on the move. He nearly lost them, then spied them heading towards Central Park. By the time he'd caught up with them they were already heading east on 63rd coming to a halt in front of the Barbizon Hotel for Women. Obviously this was where the girl was staying. Slowing down, he witnessed the man kissing the girl passionately before she darted into the hotel and the man loped off down the street.

That evening back at the office, Hank spent hours sifting through photos of wanted criminals, known reactionaries and Communists but came up with nothing.

So here he was, his intuition screaming at him that there was some sort of conspiracy or crime but what? Who could he tell when that's all he knew? He had no evidence and not an inkling as to what to look for. His colleagues would have a good laugh at his expense.

However, Hank made his mind up. He was not going to give up even if it meant using personal time. His best plan was to start with the girl. If she was as green as Frank said, all the better. She wouldn't suspect a thing. He would find someone to keep an eye on her, then insinuate himself into her life somehow.

CHAPTER 30

During the last week Delia had begun to put herself back together piece by piece. It had taken all her energy and fortitude especially when her day-to-day routine at Ohrbach's continually came under Mr Simmonds' close scrutiny. It was as if the man sensed her sudden defencelessness and was determined to reassert his position and dominance over her department. He would pull her up for the least little thing and she would go home each evening distraught and exhausted. Her only solace was Monet. She stroked the poor cat so much she was sure his fur would fall out and she'd end up with a bald cat. Even her Tuesday diner companions were of no real help. Joel was always grinning these day thinking about Blanche. Bobby Jo, well Bobby Jo was off with the fairies, sometimes gabbling about the latest film star or at other times reflective, thoughtful, and chewing her nails.

On this one particular Tuesday afternoon, Delia decided to take matters into her own hands. If she was going to get a grip on herself and her life again, she must see this so-called nude painting of Jan's. The Betty Parsons Gallery was on East 57th in Midtown and easy to get to. Delia loitered about outside trying to pluck up the courage to go in. Before she could open the door, a middle aged woman rushed out dressed in men's pants and shirt and waved the surprised Delia in. Was this Betty Parsons or a customer?

Inside there seemed to be no one on duty. Delia wandered round the gallery, gazing at the vivid modern art set off against plain white walls and a concrete floor. Delia had never been a lover of anything abstract or expressionistic, preferring the traditional. Yet she felt herself coming to life

Life, Love, Death

with all the shapes, the colours, the energy, and vitality of these strange configurations, as if they woke some primitive essence in her. It was the strangest emotion. Instantaneously, she felt a sense of familiarity and recognition linked to one of originality and freshness. At that split second, Delia knew where she belonged. Her illumination was interrupted by the reappearance of the woman who had swept past her at the door. Looking directly at Delia the woman said, 'Is there anything that interests you?'

Delia could hardly contain herself and blurted out, 'All of it. I'm speechless. I didn't realise art could be like this. The colours and shapes seem to swamp my whole body. I can hardly think or express myself.'

The woman laughed, 'That's exactly how I feel. I'm Betty Parsons. Back in '13, I visited the International Exhibition of Modern Art and was so inspired I felt it was a pivotal moment in my life. The excitement, the colour, the life. I felt as if I was a part of the paintings. I couldn't explain it either. I decided then and there that this was the world I wanted…art. My parents disapproved but here I am.'

Feeling she had met a kindred spirit Delia explained about the nude that Jan de Vries had painted of her. Betty frowned and thought for a minute, 'Yes, I do remember a bearded man coming in with a painting. A South African, I think. To be honest, I didn't think much of the painting. It was not the style of work I have here. But, he was extremely insistent and left it with me. I have a feeling I shoved it to the back of the storeroom, but I can find it if you really want to see it.'

Almost hysterical with relief, Delia began to laugh. So much for the great artist. Perhaps now she could put him in his

Life, Love, Death

proper perspective. He was the reject not her. She followed Betty to the storeroom. After some rummaging Betty produced Jan's painting. Delia had a shock to see her own body in the flesh, yet it wasn't really her, rather a version of her. To make matters worse there was a completely different head and shoulders, probably from another model.

'See what I mean,' Betty murmured. 'Bit of a mish mash, as if he had two different models in mind.'

Delia compressed her lips, 'Yes, I was one of those unfortunate models. Jan was a clever seducer making me think I was in love. Now I see it was plain lust. It's been a painful lesson.'

Betty patted her shoulder, 'We've all been there. If I told you how many romantic mistakes I've made, you'd think nothing of your own peccadillo. Anyway, time is going on. I think I'll close up for the day. Stay and have a sly late afternoon drink with me, and we can talk about our mutual misadventures.'

After a couple of whiskey sours, Delia felt herself opening up to this woman. They were of a similar age, but Betty had led a vastly different life. With her wealthy upbringing Betty had studied art, then moved into a marriage with a socialite followed by divorce and disinheritance from her family. After studying in France, she'd done jobs in galleries, then opened her own in '46.

Delia was in awe. Having sleepwalked through the first part of her life she knew she needed to make better choices or she would have nothing to show for her fifty odd years. She felt disappointed in herself and very much a failure.

Life, Love, Death

Fortunately for her, Betty was not of the same opinion and came up with a suggestion, 'Delia, seeing you're not happy at Ohrbach's, what about cutting your hours and coming to work for me part-time? I put on twelve shows September to May and close in the summer while I paint. But if you acted as my assistant, I could stay open all year. What do you think?'

Taken aback, Delia could hardly believe her luck. This could be her new life, a chance to enjoy her passion for art and escape the monotony of Ohrbach's. The two women agreed to discuss terms and meet the following week once Delia had a chance to talk to Personnel at Ohrbach's.

Delia was over the moon. Maybe Jan de Vries had done her a favour after all. She was growing up fast, learning from her mistakes and being offered a chance to give her life meaning. Would any of the men in her past life - her father, her husband, or her sons - be proud of the woman she was becoming? Probably not, they'd dismiss it all as feminine silliness and not be the slightest bit impressed about her burgeoning independence.

CHAPTER 31

The following Tuesday at the diner, Joel was in a good mood, Delia in an exceptional one and Bobby Jo, missing Xander, the odd one out. Each of them was absorbed in their own little world and their food when a tall dark haired man approached their booth, 'Any chance you kind folks might let me share your table?' he asked in a strange drawl. 'It's busy and I've little time for lunch.'

A deafening silence descended on the trio. An outsider was definitely not welcome. However Delia, always the lady, extended a hand, 'Please join us. I can see the counter seats are full.'

The man sat down, 'Kind of you, ma'am. I'm Hank O'Shaughnessy. Hope this isn't too much of an imposition,' he said, addressing himself to the other two at the table. Neither Joel nor Bobby Jo spoke. He raised a hand to catch Addy as she flitted by, prompting a raised eyebrow on her part when she saw where he was sitting. 'What do you need, young man?' she asked in a businesslike tone, thinking how dare he upset her favourite threesome, after all the trouble she'd gone to putting them together. They'd bonded like a club. This young man was an interloper and she had to force a smile.

'A burger and fries, Miss – oh and a cup of joe too – hot and black, if it's not too much trouble.' Hank tried some charm, sensing the underlying antipathy.

'All our coffee is hot, Mister, I'll thank you to know,' Addy spat out and shot off in a huff.

Life, Love, Death

'Did I say something wrong?' Hank asked affably. 'I always seem to put my foot in it without meaning to.'

'Not at all,' Delia said, 'it's Adelie's way. She's a heart of gold. We all love her, don't we?'

Joel grunted, 'Dunno about loving her. Going too far Delia, as usual.'

Bobby Jo remained taciturn, forking through her unappetising shrimp salad, her mind on Xander. Since his departure overseas she'd determined to get herself in shape for his return and cut out the 'dogs, hamburgers, and fries. Otherwise how would she ever compete with those slim soignée New York ladies.

'How about you, young lady?' Hank persevered. 'Do you approve of Addy?'

Shrugging, Bobby Jo said distantly, 'Okay I s'pose. Can take her or leave her. Don't care.' The table relapsed into an uncomfortable silence interspersed with the sounds of eating and Joel's constant struggle with his clacking false teeth.

Hank felt himself redden and grow hot under the collar. This wasn't going well. These three were clearly keen to get rid of him, making Hank wonder how he was ever going to foster a friendship with the young girl. Perhaps he had been too precipitate in thrusting himself into their company. Nevertheless, before long his opportunity came. Delia excused herself, rushing off saying she had business to sort. Joel too decided to absent himself. Hank was left with Bobby Jo and a chance to make progress. Looking directly at her, he said 'Sorry, I didn't get your name.'

Life, Love, Death

A recalcitrant Bobby Jo said sullenly, 'I didn't give it,' then thinking better of herself mumbled, 'Bobby Jo.'

Hank proffered his hand, 'Pleased to meet you, Bobby Jo. I'm Hank.'

Despite herself, Bobby Jo half smiled, 'I didn't think anyone in New York was that formal.'

Spotting the vestiges of a smile, Hank continued. Putting on a mock Irish accent he said, 'Well, we Irish are well brought up, my mauvoureen, so we are. Even my mammy would approve.' He watched carefully as Bobby Jo's mouth teetered on the edge of laughter. Carrying on, he said, 'I expect you were well brought up too. Where do you hail from?'

This time Bobby Jo couldn't help herself but reply, 'Oh, a small town. You won't have heard of it. Little Chute, Wisconsin. Seems a long time ago now,' she added wistfully.

'And how long would that be since you came to the big city?'

It was then Bobby Jo broke out in big smirk, laughing at herself, 'Why it's only six months. It seems a lifetime though.'

Hank nodded, 'I understand. Sometimes it can feel like that, especially if there are a whole lot of new experiences. New York is an exciting city after all.'

Bobby Jo's eyes lit up. Her earlier mood vanished. She took a long hard look at this young man. He was certainly good

Life, Love, Death

looking though in a different way to Xander. Tall, well-built with dark hair and bright blue eyes. He had a much fairer complexion than Xander and a more open countenance as if he was inordinately curious about the world and people.

Quite aware of her examination, Hank said playfully, 'Will I do?'

Bobby Jo blushed to the roots of her copper hair, 'I'm sorry. I didn't mean to stare.' Trying to recover her composure, she added, 'I've never met anyone Irish before.'

'That's alright, Bobby Jo,' Hank said with a twinkle in his eye. 'I've never met a copper head from Wisconsin before either.'

At that they both broke down, giggling in delight. Hank thought wow, I've made a made a breakthrough. Once they'd finished their food Hank said, 'I need to get back. Whereabouts do you work?'

Now more at ease with this handsome man, Bobby Jo was proud to say she worked at the Tribune.

Hank grinned, 'Why, that's on my way. Perhaps we could walk together.'

Bobby Jo was only too eager. Hank was easy to talk to and extremely willing to listen to her and her opinions. So very different from Xander. By the time they arrived at the Tribune building Bobby Jo felt loath to say goodbye to this attractive stranger.

Life, Love, Death

Hank, determined to exploit this perfect moment, said, 'Any chance we can see one another again? Maybe for a casual drink or a bite to eat.'

Bobby Jo was hesitant, then as if making up her mind, nodded, 'I don't see why not. You can ring me here at the Trib any day.' Despite her loyalties and feelings being entirely focussed on Xander, another man on the scene might wake him up and make him take more notice of her. It certainly couldn't hurt.

CHAPTER 32

Thanksgiving came and went, totally ignored by the trio at the diner. Bobby Jo had never had any intention of going home to the family in Wisconsin, Delia had other things on her mind and Joel never bothered to celebrate as the Pilgrims were not part of his history.

But Christmas was a different prospect. This particular Tuesday they did something they seldom did and that was to open up about their plans for the holiday. It was as if each of them now had a future to talk about.

Delia started it off, saying excitedly, 'I think my youngest son, the travel writer, may be coming home for Christmas. Mind you, it's a bit uncertain till the last minute. Otherwise, I've been invited to a Christmas Day party at the gallery. It's supposed to be a sumptuous affair full of artists and sculptors. What are you both doing?'

This was the first Joel and Bobby Jo had heard about the gallery. An affronted Bobby Jo asked, 'What gallery? Have you changed your job, Delia? You've kept that pretty secret from us.'

'I'm sorry, my dear. I would have told you sooner. It's all happened quickly. I'm still at Ohrbach's part-time but got offered a chance to work at this downtown gallery and jumped at it. It's always been a dream of mine.'

'Good luck to you, Missus. You's deserves a break,' Joel actually lifted his head from his plate and patted Delia on the arm. It was the most physical contact he'd made with either of them since they'd known him.

Life, Love, Death

'What about you, Joel, what are you doing for the holiday?'

Joel beamed the widest smile they'd ever seen. His wrinkles cracking into huge crevasses on either side of his face, his eyes glistening with emotion, 'Blanche, she's the singer at Smalls, you knows, asks me for the day with her family. They's a lot o'them 'cos she used to foster. Been a long time since I's was with a family likes that,' adding anxiously, 'I's jus' hopes I's can cope.'

Delia said reassuringly, 'Am sure it will be fine, Joel. You'll have such a good time.'

They looked at Bobby Jo who pulled a despondent face, 'I don't know yet what I'm doing, but definitely not going home.' Lately she'd felt confused. Since Xander's return from Indochina he'd been elusive, only asking if she'd delivered his package then ignoring her saying he was busy. This last package had worried Bobby Jo. It had the same 'To J from KM' on it but this time she'd had to deliver it to the Jefferson School of Science, some sort of Adult Education College on 6th Avenue. It was a strange place for Xander to be involved with. How did that fit with his work with the Mexican immigrants? What was worse it was as if someone was following and watching her. She'd been dying to tell Xander but always desperate for his approval, she didn't want to displease him.

The last few weeks she'd felt at her lowest and then, as if by magic, Hank had appeared. He'd taken her out to the theatre, bowling and all manner of things. The only catch was that he had secrets too. When Bobby Jo casually asked about his work, he'd shrugged and said, 'Oh, government work, a boring office job counting stats and filling in

Life, Love, Death

paperwork – dreary really.' Bobby Jo's sixth sense was aroused. She felt sure he wasn't telling the truth, but enjoyed his company too much to make a big issue of it. He was comfortable to be with, as if she'd always known him, a much less complicated man than Xander and a good friend to a lonely girl.

Trying to interpret the flitting expressions on Bobby Jo's face, Delia, always the romantic, said, 'Am sure there'll be an invite from some young man soon enough. There's Xander and, if I'm not much mistaken, that young man who joined our table a few weeks ago. He seemed taken with you. Now what was his name?'

'Hank,' Bobby Jo said reluctantly. 'In fact, I've seen quite a bit of him. Only as a friend. Nothing more.'

'But you never know,' Delia said with a gleam in her eye. 'Relationships often start with friendship.'

'All you's women thinks about is romance,' Joel grumbled.

Not to be thwarted a delighted Delia quipped, 'What about you and Blanche then? Is that a friendship?'

'S'none of your business, lady, I's telling you. I likes her and she likes me and that's all there is to it, not like this young 'un here and her's unrequited love for what's 'is name, Xander.'

At that Bobby Jo woke up, 'It's not unrequited. In fact, it's very requited,' she said with anger and passion, but her voice soon faded away saying, '… he's busy with important

Life, Love, Death

articles these days. I'm sure it'll be different soon.' On her way back to the Trib that day she wondered if it would.

A few days later, her spirits were lifted when, on impulse, Hank met her from work. Bobby Jo was so pleased to see him she threw her arms round him as if he'd come to rescue her, completely unaware there was a shadowy figure in an epauletted raincoat and fedora watching them from a doorway.

Xander scowled. This wouldn't do, this wouldn't do at all. What had happened to his devoted little admirer. She couldn't have found herself a boyfriend while he'd been away, could she? He really couldn't afford to lose this innocent as his courier. There was no time to cultivate anyone else. Competition was not usually his bag as he'd never had problems attracting and keeping women interested. In this case, he could see he would need all the stratagem at his disposal to win her back.

CHAPTER 33

As Christmas Day drew even nearer and winter temperatures began to set in, Xander raised his head from his Nixon articles and fixing a bleary eye on Bobby Jo said, 'Bout time we went out and took a professional look at the chaos out there. I hate Christmas, all that fake religion and materialism. All I want to do is hunker down and wait for the New Year. But Sam says, and we must do what Sam says, 'Get out an article about Christmas in the city.' I've no ideas what but I guess we'll think of something. Get your coat and boots on and that fluffy thing you call a hat.'

As much as Bobby Jo was only too eager to go out with Xander, she was disappointed to hear his views about Christmas. It had always been her favourite time of year with present giving after church on Christmas Eve, parties, and lots of delicious food. What would she do if she didn't go home? It would be a sad, lonely time in New York if Xander wasn't around. Choking back her upset, she said heartily, 'Shall I call Harry, we'll need shots.'

'Sure thing. You do that, Miss Roberta.'

Dejectedly Bobby Jo went off to call Harry. It was going to be like that again, was it? Back to their previous relationship. Would she ever know where she stood with Xander?

It started raining as they set off and all three were in a black mood, reflecting the weather. Xander seemed particularly edgy. As soon as they reached Times Square, he said peremptorily, 'You two go on to the Rockefeller Centre. Get Christmassy shots of skaters and the tree. I'll catch you up.'

Life, Love, Death

Without allowing for any arguments, he vanished into the crowds.

Bobby Jo and Harry were left looking at one another. 'Where do you think he's gone this time?' an irritable Bobby Jo groused. 'He's always doing this to us. What's it all about?'

'No idea, sweetie. He's a law unto himself. A man of secrets he never shares with me or the boys. I often wonder if he's got a second job or something. A while ago there was talk about him being a bit of a Red, but I can't imagine one working for a republican paper like the Trib. That's only gossip, young lady,' he put his finger to his lips, 'not to be spread around unless you want McCarthy breathing down our necks. No, he's probably got some honey stashed away and goes off to visit her.'

Bobby Jo recoiled as if she'd been shot. This wasn't what she wanted to hear. Maybe Harry was speculating. After all, a man who'd kissed her like Xander had must want her, not some other girl.

By now they were at Rockefeller Centre. Harry shot endless film of the skaters as Bobby Jo sat with her notebook, trying to pull herself together to write captions. Then they made their way back to Times Square.

Harry prompted Bobby Jo to talk to the shoppers, 'Find out what this year's toy fad is. Ask men what they're buying their wives.' Getting more enthusiastic and in the Christmas spirit, Harry said, 'We need a shot of some kid sitting on Santa's knee, so we'll head for Macy's. Then perhaps a pic of those Rockettes at Radio City. They always dress up as Santas for the holiday. I know someone who works

Life, Love, Death

backstage and can get us in. I don't know what Xander wants but he'll have to put up with what he gets. He's probably trying to keep us busy as a cover for what he's slunk off to do.'

It started to rain heavily, and the temperature was dropping rapidly when Bobby Jo heard the faint sounds of a Sax. 'Hang on a minute, Harry. I want to check something.' Surely it couldn't be Joel, not in this weather. But it was. Drenched to the skin, he and Betsy were doing their best to play to the crowds who were scurrying for shelter in doorways. He was a sad sight. Bobby Jo pulled Harry's arm, 'Look, that's a friend of mine. We can't leave him there. I've got money. Let's take him to that Choc Full o'Nuts and get him a hot drink and something to eat?'

Joel was none too pleased to be confronted by Bobby Jo of all people. 'Leave me alone, young 'un. Betsy and me is alright.'

'I thought you'd given up busking round here, Joel. What about Sergeant Mulroney? You don't want to be back in jail again.'

'None of your business, Missy. Jus' wants bit extra. A special Christmas present for some 'un.'

After a lot more persuasion and with Harry launching in as well, Joel gave in. Sitting down at the lunch counter, Joel knocked back a coffee and a nutted cheese sandwich. Afterwards, Bobby Jo touched his shoulder saying, 'Why don't we take you home? It's not the sort of day for you to be out.'

Life, Love, Death

The old man mumbled under his breath, but Bobby Jo wouldn't give up, 'What about Betsy? It can hardly be doing her any good.' She looked pleadingly across at Harry who nodded, 'Sure thing, if Xander can do the vanishing act so can we. Don't forget our deadline though, little lady.'

As they bundled themselves, Joel and Betsy into a yellow cab, Bobby Jo happened to glance across the road and see Xander talking to someone in a black Cadillac. Despite her energetic waving, he didn't seem to see them. After a minute or two, he got in the car and it drove off. As they made their way to the Village with Joel, Harry enquired, 'Who were you waving to?'

Thinking it wiser to keep her own counsel, Bobby Jo said, 'I thought it was someone I knew.'

They dropped a coughing, sneezing Joel at his basement. Refusing their offers of help or a doctor, the old man bade them farewell brusquely, 'No medics for me, Missy. You's go about your business. I's be alright here at home.'

Reluctant to leave him, Bobby Jo was obliged to return to the Trib with Harry. Back at the office, there was still no sign of Xander. Harry murmured under his breath, 'Looks like it's up to us again, sweetie.' By the time Sam came to check on them, everything was complete. He studied the sheets and hummed and hawed, 'Not bad, not bad at all and where's his lordship?'

Before Bobby Jo could utter a word, Harry stepped in, 'He took a cold. Felt unwell and went home.'

Life, Love, Death

Not impressed, Sam Murphy narrowed his eyes, 'I'll be having words. He spends too much time vanishing for my liking and don't,' he raised a warning hand, 'keep covering for him anymore or there'll be trouble for you two as well.'

A chastened Harry and Bobby Jo left for the bar round the corner. 'He'll get his comeuppance for sure,' Harry said gloomily. 'Now don't pull that face, little lady. You know it as well as me. I can tell you've a bit of a thing for him but he's not worth it. You'd be better off with that nice young man who was waiting for you last week.'

But Bobby Jo was not listening. Hank was okay of course but he wasn't Xander.

CHAPTER 34

Ten days before Christmas Delia and Bobby Jo arrived at the diner as usual, but there was no sign of Joel. Addy rushed over, 'Heard about Joel? He's in Bellevue. The silly old man tried to go out and busk in this cold and collapsed on the street. Can either of you go and find out about him? I'd go but I've got my hands full.'

Bobby Jo broke down, saying tearfully, 'It's my fault. I saw him last week. He wasn't well. Harry and I took him home, but he wouldn't let us call a doctor.'

'Don't worry, dear, you're not to blame. You know what a stubborn old goat he is.

'We'll go this evening and check on him,' Delia said reassuringly.

Addy nodded, 'Remember, he don' take kindly to being told what to do.'

That evening, Delia and Bobby Jo made their way down the dreary, disinfected corridors of Bellevue, Bobby Jo looking as if she was about to cry. Delia took her hand and squeezed it hard, 'I'm sure he'll be alright. He's a tough 'un is Joel.'

The ward was full to bursting with beds lined up in rows. As they tentatively made their way it was hard to recognise one sick man from another. Finally, they stopped a nurse. She pointed to a corner bed. A large black lady blocked their first view of Joel, who was sitting up in bed beaming from ear to ear as she whispered quietly to him. His expression changed when he saw who was approaching and he mumbled

Life, Love, Death

something under his breath to his companion. She turned, smiling broadly, showing large white teeth, and greeting them by name, 'Hi, I expect you're Delia and Bobby Jo. Joel's told me about your Tuesday lunches. I'm Blanche, the singer at Smalls, Joel's friend.' Ignoring Joel's grouchy expression, she spoke for him as if he was a child, 'He's delighted you've come. Please sit.' Whilst she busied herself finding chairs, they bent towards Joel and asked, 'How are you?'

'No need for you's to come, no need at all.'

Returning with the chairs, Blanche laughed heartily, 'Now don' you be so ungrateful, old man. You know you're pleased to see your friends.'

Joel took his telling off manfully, making efforts to smile at them. Delia chuckled inwardly. My goodness, Joel had met his match at last, though she couldn't help wondering what this relationship was all about.

However, the effort to cope with three women must have exhausted him, as Joel lay back on his pillows and closed his eyes. Blanche said softly, 'I think I've worn him out. They were worried he had tuberculosis, but it's just a nasty chest infection. He needs antibiotics, care, and sleep. Perhaps we'd better leave him to it.'

As the three of them walked down the corridor together, Blanche said, 'I think he'll be here till Christmas.'

Worried, Bobby Jo said, 'But he can't go back to that damp basement. I wish I could help but I live in a women's hostel.' She looked at Delia expectantly, who said instantly, 'He must come and stay with me. I only have a one bedroom

Life, Love, Death

apartment in Queens but he's welcome. I'm sure I can come up with a foldaway bed to sleep on.'

Towering above them, Blanche wrapped her arms round both their shoulders, 'Now don' worry your heads, you two. Joel will come to me in Harlem. I has a big enough place. 'Din I bring up a load of my foster kids there. He's already invited for Christmas anyways so what does it matter if it's a touch earlier. You both is welcome too if you don' be doing anything else.'

'Thanks Blanche, that's a real weight off my mind,' Delia said gratefully. 'I must say it would have been difficult as I'm hoping my son is coming for the holiday. You're sorted for Christmas aren't you, Bobby Jo? I expect you'll be going to Wisconsin.'

Bobby Jo faked a nod. She didn't want to mention the sore subject of not going home. After they said goodbye to Blanche at the subway, Delia remarked, 'Fancy that old rogue Joel. He certainly didn't let on about her and how gorgeous she is.'

A solemn Bobby Jo said, 'I think he did mention her and the Christmas arrangements, but I wasn't paying much attention. They seem to be exceptionally good friends though.'

As she made her own way home, Bobby Jo felt envious. Even Joel had a lady friend. All she could do was yearn after a man who didn't seem to want her. What was wrong with her? Still and all, there was Hank. He'd rung earlier that day saying he wanted to see her and would she have dinner with him.

Life, Love, Death

It was a joy and a relaxing experience to go out with him. He was always pleased to see her, taking her to such lovely restaurants, and not minding about being seen with her in public, unlike Xander with his hole and corner venues. It was plain there was something on Hank's mind. During the dessert, Bobby Jo asked, 'Is there a problem? You seem distracted.'

'I am. Probably work,' Hank said carefully and dismissively. 'But changing the subject, I've been wondering if you were seeing anyone else. I expect you have a lot of sweethearts.'

Bobby Jo didn't know how to react. Trying to be honest without hurting Hank's feelings, she said, 'Well there is …was someone at work. I did see him for a while but he seems to have lost interest.' She didn't add that she hadn't lost interest in him.

Hank heaved an enormous sigh of relief as if he'd rid himself of a heavy burden. Taken aback by the vehemence of it, Bobby Jo thought surely Hank wasn't that worried about her having another man in her life. After all they barely knew one another. Suddenly she felt uneasy, but the moment passed. Hank continued, 'That's good then. I wondered if you'd come visit my family during the holiday. I warn you they are a rowdy bunch, being Irish, but have warm hearts and will welcome you.'

Bobby Jo was not at all sure about meeting Hanks's family at this stage of their friendship, concerned about the implications. Prevaricating, she asked, 'Whereabouts do they live?'

Life, Love, Death

'Upstate New York. Not far from the city.' Assuming Bobby Jo's interest meant she was accepting his invitation, Hank said, 'Pack a bag. We'll stay a few days. What do you think?'

Bobby Jo wondered what she did think. She definitely didn't want to go home and it looked as if Xander had no intention of spending the holiday with her. That meant a few lonely days at the Barbizon Hotel holed up on her own. Why shouldn't she have fun instead. 'Okay, Hank. That would be great. I'd love to meet your family.'

Perhaps it would shake up Xander if she wasn't around and available.

CHAPTER 35
Christmas, 1953 – Part 1

Delia was disappointed and frustrated. Her son had sent a cable saying, 'Spending Christmas in Singapore with Veronica,' (his latest girlfriend). Expect OK with you Mom.'

Delia wondered where she'd gone wrong. Clutching the poor, almost balding Monet to her chest she whimpered, 'What did I do, Monet, to be slighted like this? Look at all those years I spent giving those boys everything, and my husband as well, and this is what I get. A brief message and I'm supposed to be 'OK' with that. I always felt like an outsider even in my own family. It was as if Gus and the boys were in it together, despite all that cooking, cleaning and entertaining I did with Gus's medical friends. Yet they all looked down on me with my Southern accent and my homemaker skills. Me, with a good degree from Vassar.'

Still stroking the protesting, mewing cat, Delia carried on, 'And what about my birthdays, do you remember, Monet?' Gus would say in that soft, doctor voice, 'Here's something you need, Delia, I'm sure you'll love it,'...and then present me with a beautifully wrapped gift, which would turn out to be a new vacuum cleaner, an automatic toaster or one of the latest gadgets, a microwave.'

Foisting the poor Monet into a more comfortable position on her knee, Delia continued, 'Didn't he ever appreciate the years I'd wasted working in fashion stores to fund him through medical school?' Monet started kneading with his paws, Delia squeezed him lovingly, 'Yes, I adored him, but I always felt isolated and alone. Fortunately, Dexedrine came along. It helped me cope with those unending days of

Life, Love, Death

boredom. I wasn't the only housewife who escaped into chemicals or alcohol. Violet, my next door neighbour, would lean over our white picket fence and slur out, 'Wha don' you come in for a little drinkiepoo, darl'. Do you the world of good.' I always refused. Dexedrine and gin was a lethal mix. A therapist is what I needed, someone to talk to, but Gus would never have sanctioned that.'

'Oh, very well Monet, get down. I suppose you want something to eat. Perhaps you've been my therapist all these years.' Cooking up the cat's favourite chicken livers, Delia carried on with her reflections, 'Now Gus is gone I can change. I'm free. Work at the gallery is opening my eyes to the world, and I've finally dispatched the Dexedrine into the garbage.' Laughing and patting the ravenous Monet, 'Maybe Gus did me a favour by dying or else I'd be a hopeless addict by now.'

Giving Monet a last pat, Delia picked up Simone de Beauvoir's 'The Second Sex' and carried on reading. Much of the author's thoughts mirrored her own, making her realise she must think differently now she was an independent working woman supporting herself. Liberation was hers and boy, was she going to enjoy it.

Accepting Betty Parsons' invite to her Christmas Day party, Delia decided to splash out on a new dress. Ignoring the staff discount at Ohrbach's, Delia made a sortie to 5th Avenue but was discouraged by the selection and the prices. Talking to one of the sales ladies, she was advised to, 'Check out a vintage shop in the Village. You'll see, it'll be worth it.'

Delia had always been nervous of the Village and its reputation; even that time she'd taken Joel home from jail

Life, Love, Death

she'd barely stopped. Plucking up her courage she took a cab to Bleecker Street. After foraging, she found a promising shop and there it was the dress of her fantasies. It was a long fitted dress in a black and gold sequinned art deco style. It was perfect, a good fit with a few sequins missing, and she could deal with them.

Excited and elated, Delia could hardly wait for Christmas Day, spending Christmas Eve shopping for long black velvet gloves and a headband. But, once dressed for the party due to start mid-afternoon, Delia began to feel tremors of apprehension. She had never found it easy to socialise at her and Gus' parties and prayed she wouldn't end up a wallflower. But as soon as she arrived at the gallery, Betty was there to meet her, gazing admiringly at the dress, 'What a stunner. You look like you've stepped out of the '20s. You'll be a big hit with my artists. They'll want you to model.'

The gallery was bursting at the seams. Men and women flocked around her, making Delia wonder why she'd been so nervous. The dress was the talk of the place. People wore a cornucopia of clothes and costumes. Everything from smart cocktail attire, tuxedos, ball gowns to velvet smoking jackets, paint smeared smocks, dungarees, and floppy hats. Delia began to feel at home, recognising some of the artists she'd got to know over the last month. Betty's 'Four Horsemen', Pollock, Rothko, Newman and Still, were there. They were her stalwarts and been with her since her early foray into Abstract Expressionism. Delia found it much easier to make conversation than she'd thought. At least she'd not had to prepare food for this party. Tables were laden with whole lobsters, meats, and salads of every kind and even an abstract ice sculpture. Betty flitted round

Life, Love, Death

talking to everyone but keeping an eye out for the shy ones. As the afternoon moved into evening, the party became riotous with drunken artists doing party pieces.

A jazz band was playing 'The way you look tonight' when an elegant man with silvered hair came up and asked Delia to dance. She laughed, 'I don't know if I can in this dress. It's very heavy and fitted.'

'Then I'm sure this piece,' he nodded to the band, 'will allow us to move at the right pace. I thought how charming you looked. The dress is exquisite.'

'Are you an artist?' Delia asked as they moved on to the floor.

'Good heavens no, I can barely draw a straight line. I'm James. I work for Christie's of London. Just on a quick visit to New York. Betty always asks me to her parties when I'm here. As you know, she's not keen on auction houses so I'm here under sufferance.'

'I know what Betty's like,' Delia smiled. 'I'm Delia. I work for her.'

'D'you know, I thought I'd seen you before. You look so different tonight – like a goddess.'

'Some goddess. I work for a living not live in a temple'. Delia found herself giggling, realising for the first time in her life she was flirting. They danced all night and into the early hours of the next morning.

Life, Love, Death

Finally, James said, 'I'm afraid I must leave. I'm flying back to London later today. Can I give you a lift home and can I see you again.'

Delia was attracted to this likeable, good-humored man but thought of the Jan de Vries affair. This time she would be careful and less gullible.

'I would like to see you again, James. You can reach me here at the gallery, but I don't need a ride. I'll stay and help Betty with the clearing up and go home later.'

Moving towards her, James took her gloved hands and pulled her towards him, kissing her on the forehead, 'I'll be in touch soon, goddess.'

Taking his leave of Betty, he whispered in her ear, 'I think I'm in love, my dear. Take care of your protégé until I return.'

Betty retorted, 'Keep your hands off Delia. She's an excellent assistant. I don't want to lose her. She's been through a lot. Don't mess with her or you'll have me to deal with. You know how you charm the women.'

James looked shamefaced momentarily, 'No, honestly, I'm quite genuine this time. Anyway, I think she's given me the brush off, so I don't know where I stand.'

A smirking Betty said, 'Good for her. 'Bout time you men were put in your place. Have a good flight home. I'll see you on your next trip but only if you don't come poaching my artists or my assistant.'

Life, Love, Death

After he'd gone, Betty refused Delia's offers of help saying, 'Not in that dress. Don't worry, Delia. I've cleaners coming later. They'll sort everything out. You go home. Put your feet up. A word of warning before you go – be wary of James. He's far too attractive for his own good. In that dress you can have the pick of the bunch. Enjoy some flirtations and dates for a change, it'll do you good. Goodbye, my dear, I'll see you bright and early in the New Year. I wonder what 1954 will bring?'

Delia made a face, 'It's got to be better than this year. In fact, I'm looking forward to it. I feel I'm being reinvented to become the elegant, worldly woman I've always wanted to be.' They both burst out laughing.

Betty remarked, 'Just don't make me your role model,' and kissing Delia on both cheeks added, 'here's hoping you get what you desire.'

CHAPTER 36
Christmas, 1953 – Part 2

Bobby Jo was doing her best to reconcile herself to spending Christmas with Hank's family though she would have much preferred Xander's company. Xander ignored her right up to Christmas Eve, not speaking to her or asking what she was doing over the holiday. He was in one of his surly, morose moods.

On Christmas Eve, Harry came over to wish them both the Season's Greetings, asking them out for a drink to celebrate and wondering what they were doing for the holiday. Xander shook his head, 'I don't celebrate. It's just another day, though I expect Miss Roberta has plans.'

Bobby Jo retorted, 'I do and I'm looking forward to them.'

Momentarily Xander was confounded, then jibed sarcastically, 'Going home to the parents, I expect? What's the name of that quaint town in Wisconsin you come from? Oh, yes Little Chute. I suppose it'll be a traditional Dutch Christmas there?'

'No, I've an invite from someone else.'

'Oh, and who would that be. Surely not your diner friends or some sweet miss from the Barbizon?'

'No,' Bobby Jo said unequivocally.

'H'm,' said Xander, 'Not telling Harry or me then. A big secret, heh?'

Life, Love, Death

'That's right,' Bobby Jo said merrily, taking Harry's extended arm and leaving with him.

'That's done for him,' Harry said cheerfully.' He won't like not knowing. 'Spect you've an invite from that nice young man you've been seeing.'

Bobby Jo tapped her nose, 'Maybe, then maybe not.'

'Well, whoever he is he's a lucky chap. Come and have a seasonal drink with me before I face a packed subway and my gang.'

Early the next morning, Hank picked Bobby Jo up from the Barbizon, 'It's not a long journey. About two hours if the roads are clear.'

In the car both Hank and Bobby Jo were engrossed in their own thoughts. Bobby Jo was wondering what she had let herself in for and Hank was having misgivings. Since asking Bobby Jo for Christmas on impulse, Hank had realised what a big step he was taking. During the time he'd been seeing Bobby Jo, he'd investigated hers and Xander's backgrounds. Hers of course was squeaky clean but Xander…Well, Xander not only had a Russian mother he'd never acknowledged but a secret life outside the Tribune. His journalist friends were Communists though they might of course just be paying lip service to its ideals. But what about Xander? Could he be a sleeper agent for Moscow and what was in that package Xander had given to Bobby Jo? Hank could feel tingles on the back of his neck, sure he was on the right track. However, he was in a quandary. His feelings for Bobby Jo had crept up on him in the last weeks. Now he was not

Life, Love, Death

certain whether he was using her to find out about Xander or because he was falling in love with her.

The journey went by so swiftly they were both in shock when they realised they had nearly reached their destination. Bobby Jo had never asked exactly where they were going as she was too fixated on Xander. Hank said, 'You won't believe this. I forgot to tell you. My mother lives in Hudson, named after the explorer, like your last name. My five siblings and me were brought up in Brooklyn. When my brother got killed, we were all grown and Mom moved out here.' He omitted to mention it was he who'd bought the house and still supported her.

Bobby Jo was jittery as they approached, feeling she was here under false pretences. She needn't have worried. As soon as they pulled into the driveway, the front door opened and a horde of people emerged. They rushed up to the car, hugging and kissing her before she had a chance to get out. Hank laughed, 'Oh, let the poor girl be. She'll think you're mad.'

'That we are,' said a tiny gray haired lady pushing her way through the throng, 'Welcome, Bobby Jo, to this house of Irish ruffians. They've had too much hooch already. Come in, my dear. We'll leave Hank to sort that lot out.'

'Thank you, Mrs O'Shaughnessy, that would be lovely,' Bobby Jo said taking the woman's arm.

'Call me Mollie, me darlin, everybody does. Now what is it to be? A drop of the hard stuff or a cuppa of the brown stuff?'

Life, Love, Death

'Definitely the brown stuff. I think it's a bit early for the hard stuff,' Bobby Jo countered, doing her best to join in the banter.

Mollie took a good look at Bobby Jo, 'I don' know. You look all in to me. Come awa' with me to the kitchen. It'll be a lot more peaceful. Let's leave that lot of hoodlums to their own devices.'

The two of them sat quietly in the rustic kitchen. Bobby Jo felt as if she was going to cry. Mollie put an arm round the girl and said, 'Go on if you need to. Do you the power of good. I expect you're missing your ma and pa. It's a sentimental time is Christmas.' Giving Bobby Jo a chance to compose herself, Mollie continued, 'This is the time of year I miss my Sean, my husband you know, and my boy, Connor.'

'If you don't mind my asking, what happened to them?'

'Course not, me darlin'. Sean was a New York cop and got shot by a druggie. After his death, with Hank away, Connor got in with a bad lot and was knifed. This is what made me move from the city. Of course, my four girls had married by then and many of them were living up this way. Now, I see me grandchildren all the time.'

It wasn't long before the whole crowd piled into the kitchen. The girls started preparing the dinner. Hank pulled Bobby Jo away, saying, 'Let's go for a walk. I'll show you the neighbourhood.'

'But shouldn't I do my bit?' Bobby Jo protested.

Life, Love, Death

'Nah, my sisters will fight it out between themselves and I do mean fight it out. They'll soon be shouting the odds at one another and quarrelling.' Seeing the shocked expression on Bobby Jo's face, he reassured her, 'It doesn't mean a thing. They adore one another. Mom will knock them into shape. Despite her size and her years, she's definitely in charge – a real major general.'

Bobby Jo burst out laughing, 'It's not like my home. Everything there is organised and calm, with never a raised voice and definitely no alcohol, well maybe a little jenever for special occasions.'

'That's why you'll have fun here. Dinner will be a blast.'

It certainly was. Bobby Jo had never experienced anything like it. Twenty adults and children packed themselves noisily round the enormous, scrubbed oak dining table. She found herself wedged between Hank and the local parish priest Father Paddy who'd arrived after Mass. He was a jovial white haired old gentleman who seemed to take the O'Shaughnessy family in his stride, ignoring their occasional blasphemies and rude jokes. He murmured softly, 'Well now, Bobby Jo. It's lovely to see Hank with such a pretty young lady. It's difficult for him being the eldest. He takes his responsibilities to heart. Then, of course, there's his job. His work doesn't exactly allow for relationships.'

Bobby Jo frowned, 'What do you mean, Father? What about his work? Surely a government office job wouldn't interfere with Hank having a relationship.

Recognising he'd said something he shouldn't, the old man shrugged his shoulders, 'I've spoken out of turn. Forgive me,

Life, Love, Death

my dear, it's senility setting in fast.' With that he turned to talk to Mollie who was sitting next to him. Having overheard some of their conversation the older woman looked worried until the priest patted her hand comfortingly. Bobby Jo, noticing all this interplay, wondered what was going on. She'd thought all along that Hank, like Xander, had secrets. Why couldn't people be more open and honest she wondered? But then was she herself being that honest and truthful about either Xander or her parents?

Doing her best to join in the fun and games after the meal Bobby Jo was wary. When one of the children took out a pretend gun and faked shooting his uncle, calling out, 'Like you, Uncle Hank,' to be immediately shushed by his mother, Bobby Jo had even more cause for concern.

The next few days Bobby Jo was kept busy with the O'Shaughnessy family, having no time to deliberate or talk to Hank who was always ankle deep in his nieces and nephews. On the ride home, Bobby Jo brought up the subject of Hank's job. 'Why are you so interested?' he asked. 'Honestly my job is dull, keeping track of immigration records and stats., nothing more.'

'But what about your nephew…? When he pointed his imaginary gun at you, didn't he say, 'Like you, Uncle Hank'?'

'Oh, that was make believe. You know what children are.'

That was the only response Bobby Jo could get from him. But she knew there was something else.

CHAPTER 37
Christmas, 1953 – Part 3

Joel was in a complete tizz. Now that he was on the road to recovery, Blanche was due to collect him and take him to her place. Looking in the mirror, he didn't like what he saw. His face, with its strange pallor, was thinner and more wrinkled than ever. His brown eyes had sunk deep into his head, and his grizzled gray hair was long and straggly. Pleading with one of the nurses, he managed to get her to give him a haircut and a shave. Then there was the matter of clothes. A few weeks ago Blanche had been to his basement and collected his clothes, but they were in such a state he was embarrassed for her to see them. Doing his best to talk to one of the friendlier nurses, he explained his predicament. Ransacking lost property, she found him a decent shirt that she washed and ironed for him and a pair of practically new Levi jeans.

When Blanche arrived he'd done the best he could to look presentable. The moment she saw him, her eyes twinkled in merriment, 'Well, I'm blessed. Is that really you, Mr Petersen, looking fine and dandy? Would never have recognised you. Now is you ready? My house ain't any palace you know but it's clean and comfortable. What's that you say? I's a bit hard of hearing from all that dang music.'

Joel muttered, 'Bound to be better than my place. Was ashamed for you's to see it.'

'Now don' you be worrying, old man. I's seen much worse in my day I can tell you and at least it's weather dry, ain't it.' She laughed out loud. 'Now let's get you back to mine. You can rest up. I's a nice little back bedroom set up for you

Life, Love, Death

special. These here dang hospitals are no good for the sick, you's never get a minute's peace.'

Taking the subway to 125th Street, Blanche insisted on carrying Joel's bag. He was too weak to argue or be embarrassed when she shamed a fit, young, white guy into giving up his seat. He felt his age once they arrived at Blanche's. The house had seen better days but maintained the elegance of a brownstone despite being surrounded by boarded up buildings.

'Don' you worry about the outside,' Blanche said nonchalantly, 'it's the inside that matters. I brung up a whole mess of foster kids right here. They did okay.'

She was right as ever and Joel was astounded to step into light airy rooms, attractively decorated and furnished with comfortable chairs and couches. A warm, inviting kitchen spanned the width of the house. He sighed deeply. It had been a long time since he'd seen beauty and comfort, if ever. 'Far out,' he managed to stutter, taking a leaf out of Bobby Jo's vocabulary, 'a wonder.'

'I don' know about that,' Blanche said in an offhand way, but she smiled, secretly pleased at the compliment. 'Let me take you to your bedroom. Can you manage the stairs?'

'Course I's can,' Joel growled. 'Not in my dotage yet,' however he was badly out of breath by the time they made the first floor.

Blanche pushed open a door. 'Here you are. Why don' you take a rest. I'll bring up tea. The main bathroom's right next door.'

Life, Love, Death

The room was decorated in pale lemon with a large bed in the centre covered with a blue and yellow comforter. A pair of new pyjamas lay on the pillow. All the woodwork and cupboards had been painted white. Joel felt warmed by the lightness of it all and the comforting yellow glow.

Without a word, Blanche turned and left. Joel, too exhausted to take his clothes off, removed his shoes, lay down and was asleep in no time. Some hours later he was awakened by a knock on the door. Blanche arrived with tea and biscuits. 'I looked in earlier but you was sound asleep, so I left you. If you hear a lot of crashing and banging downstairs, some of my kids have arrived early for Christmas. Though of course they're not kids anymore. When you feel up to it come down and meet them.'

Joel was not at all enthusiastic about meeting her brood, as she called them, preferring to stay in the yellow bedroom, but thought he ought to make an effort as she'd been so kind.

On his arrival in the kitchen, he was dismayed to find it full to bursting with noisy young people. Before he knew it, they'd shepherded him towards the most comfortable chair and sat themselves down round the kitchen table. 'I bet you wonder who we all are,' they said in unison, laughing noisily. 'We're Mama Blanche's 'Misfits'. That's what she calls us when she's cross.' They each got up, came over and shook Joel's hand. An attractive redhead said, 'I'm Nancy. I work at Macy's.' By the time they got to Steve who was a New York cop, Joel was bemused. Blanche's 'Misfits' were of varying races and colour. It was as if Blanche had gone out on the streets of Harlem and collected up a smattering of the most diverse children she could find.

Life, Love, Death

Seeing Joel's astonishment, Blanche shrugged, 'I worked for the Children's Bureau in my thirties and wanted to help all them lost babies, so enrolled as a foster mother. It was hard at the start. Now I have the large family I always wanted. They're a rowdy bunch,' she playfully swatted Levi's black curly head, 'especially this one, who never stops talking. You wouldn't believe he's studying to be a Rabbi. Don' know how his congregation will ever get a word in.' Everyone chuckled as Levi stuck out his tongue. 'Now who's gonna help me fix supper?' There was a show of hands and everyone rushed round doing their own thing.

Joel sat back and closed his eyes. If this was family life he didn't know whether he would have coped or not. On the other hand, it was unexpected bliss to be looked after like this at his time of life.

CHAPTER 38

On the run-up to New Year, Xander was feeling the pressure both in and outside work. Sam Murphy was showing his disapproval verbally, 'Look my lad, you're walking a fine line. If I hear you've disappeared again and left that poor child, Roberta, and Harry to cope and cover for you, it'll be curtains. I may have threatened before but next time it'll be passed up to Mrs Reid and that won't go well for you. Roberta is her protégé, so watch out. This is your last chance, d'ya hear?'

Outside work, Xander's journalist friends were just as dismissive. Even Jasha, tracking him down in his black Cadillac, had been curt and peremptory, 'Get in, Karl, I'm not pleased with you. Sometimes it's hard to believe you're one of us. You don't mind taking our handouts but with what result? I'm starting to wonder if you're double crossing us.'

Xander exploded violently, 'You know I'm loyal. Look what I've done for you already. I'm completely dedicated to the Party. How can you talk to me like that when I'm putting my work and my personal life on the line? You're the one who dumped me in a capitalist Republican newspaper and gave me that stupid code name. Sometimes I don't know who I am. I'm not even being truthful to my fellow comrades and leading this double life is getting harder and harder.'

'Calm down, comrade, I believe in you even if those at Moscow Central are sceptical because of your American father. But we need information and recruits desperately. Our numbers are falling due to Senator McCarthy. Everyone

Life, Love, Death

here is paranoid about being labelled a Communist. We've had to find extra funds to prop up our base at the Jefferson School. Since Comrade Khrushchev took over and the hydrogen bomb was tested in Kazakhstan, it's become urgent to find scientists to help with plans for a super bomb. You must develop contacts in the scientific community. This is no time to slack.'

Affronted, Xander snarled, 'Look here Jasha, I've been working hard but it takes time to build assets. The ones you want are in Mexico and Princeton. It's difficult for me to travel outside New York and keep my job. Don't you have other agents in those areas?'

'Of course we do,' Jasha snapped back, 'but I'm based in New York and I don't have access to them. Anyway, I hear you've been cavorting round town with some girl, wasting our money at the '21' Club. How is that developing assets?'

'Roberta is my courier; I'll have you know. She's been useful to me when I don't have time to deliver messages to you. If your other agents and I all met up on a regular basis it would help the exchange of information.'

'That's never going to happen, my friend. Everything, and I mean everything, goes through me. I can't afford to put any of my people in danger. Keep on doing your job. We'll say no more,' Jasha shrugged. 'That's it, now get out,' and Xander was dismissed.

Xander was disgruntled and resentful about being reprimanded by both sides. However, he'd long ago committed himself to the Party and had to grin and bear it. Once into the New Year perhaps he would be able to pull all

Life, Love, Death

the strands he'd been working on together. But he was going to need Bobby Jo. Since the holiday she'd been keeping her distance, apparently a lot happier and more cheerful. What was noticeable was she'd stopped watching Xander and waiting for his every move. Xander wondered if he'd lost her. He would have to do something about that. In-between Christmas and the New Year, Xander took to shadowing Bobby Jo home to the Barbizon. It was clear there was another man in the mix, although this young man himself appeared furtive and slippery. He often looked in windows to see if he was being followed, cutting down back lanes, jumping on buses or vanishing down the subway. This was not the normal behaviour of the average young man. Who was he? Could he be an agent of some kind, and who was he working for? Was Jasha playing fast and loose and having him followed or was a G-man on to him or Bobby Jo?

Xander's instincts were primed but he didn't want to catch the attention of either Bobby Jo or the young man. Deciding on different tactics, he said casually, 'Miss Roberta, are you booked for New Year's Eve? If you're not I'd very much like to take you to a dinner and dance at the Stork Club. Then perhaps we could take in the 'Ball Drop' at Times Square. What do you think?'

Bobby Jo bit her lip. Part of her wanted to go, but another part of her was upset about the way Xander had ignored her so much recently. It was as if he'd dumped her. Regrettably she was still crazy about him. Despite Hank's attentions it was Xander who made her heart flutter. 'I don't know,' she said scathingly, 'I had the feeling you were tired of me and that's why you've been cutting me.'
A flabbergasted Xander didn't know what to say. This little girl was really growing up and showing her fangs. 'Nothing

Life, Love, Death

of the sort,' he protested. 'I've been under a lot of pressure. It's made me rather distracted and distant. I'm sorry. I didn't mean to hurt you.'

'Far from it,' Bobby Jo said coolly. 'I certainly wasn't hurt. I've been pretty busy myself with other things. But thanks for the apology, much appreciated.' It was a revelation to hear Xander apologise. This was not something he ever did.

'So, what about it?' Xander continued. 'Are we on for New Year's Eve?'

'Why not,' Bobby Jo said with a shrug, 'I've no other invites as yet.'

Playing hard to get, Xander thought, we'll see about that. He was going to have to work hard to get back the old, adoring Roberta. It would be a challenge but he always loved a challenge.

That evening Hank was waiting outside the Tribune as usual, 'Before we go for a meal, Bobby Jo, how about doing something special on New Year's Eve? Maybe go somewhere posh for dinner and then on to Times Square. It's always lively before they drop the ball.'

A disconcerted Bobby Jo couldn't believe her luck, two identical invites. It was too much. Trying to let Hank down gently, she said, 'Yes, that sounds great. Unfortunately, I've accepted another invite.'

Shaken and slightly hurt, Hank said, 'I suppose it's that guy you work with, the one who'd supposedly forgotten all

Life, Love, Death

about you. I thought since Christmas and meeting my family you were my girl now.'

Blushing and indignant, Bobby Jo retorted, 'I don't know what gave you that idea. I'm my own person and choose whom I go out with.'

'If that's the case, I'd better take you home smartish and we'll go our separate ways,' Hank said in a huff.

Bobby Jo didn't know what to say. Hank had been good to her, but Xander…She'd never wanted to admit it before, even to herself, but she knew she was truly in love with that strange sinister man who often disregarded her. The drive back to the Barbizon was brief and tense. When they arrived Hank sprang out, like the gentleman he was, and opened her door. Pecking her on the cheek, he drove off without a word. Bobby Jo felt guilty and remorseful about the way things had ended. However, as she made her way to her room, all she could think about was what to wear to the Stork Club? It had to be something different to the emerald taffeta dress. This time she might need Delia's help.

Hank felt devastated on his way home. He'd never been in love before. This little redhead had really got to him even though he knew he'd been playing with fire. If his supervisor found out he was seeing someone linked to a likely Communist agent, he'd be for the chop. What was he to do? Bobby Jo was obviously far more involved with this Xander than he'd thought. He'd deluded himself that his attentions might have distracted her. But it was not to be. Now there was little chance he could save her from herself. He had no choice but to come clean and admit everything to his supervisor.

CHAPTER 39

Hank, never a man to procrastinate, made an appointment with his superior for New Year's Eve. This was to have been the very evening when he'd planned to take Bobby Jo out and propose. That was history now of course. Making his way to the Field Office on that freezing December morning, Hank tried to formulate what he was going to say without implicating himself. Saying he'd been bored, decided to follow a girl from a diner and was now in love with that same girl who was maybe a Russian agent's courier, would hardly do his career any good.

Hank's supervisor had been in the service almost as long as J. Edgar Hoover and was not a man to be trifled with. He greeted Hank curtly, leaving him standing in front of his desk whilst he dealt with paperwork. Eventually he said, 'Sit, young man. Tell me what this is about.' The more Hank explained the more Senior Special Agent Brewster scowled, 'This isn't good, Hank, and doesn't reflect well on you.' Hank, though relieved to be addressed by his first name, was not reassured by Brewster's words.

Lightening his tone, the older man said, 'We all make mistakes. I suppose considering your age it's easy to make a fool of yourself over a girl. Now we have to deal with the fallout. One positive thing you've done is possibly uncover a Communist agent, though albeit inadvertently. That's in your favour. I'm going to put one of my best men on Xander Smith. We'll discover what he's up to and see if he has a contact with Moscow Central in New York. In the meantime, use your relationship with Bobby Jo. Find out how involved your girl is and what she's doing for this man. There's to be no warning her off or you'll be out of a job, or at the very

Life, Love, Death

worst, doing time at Rikers. Be on your guard. Keep your head. Report back on my private number. We'll see if there are any other agents involved. This could be a coup for us.'

Throughout this homily Hank never uttered a word. Feeling humiliated, he was grateful to have got off so easily. It was going to be difficult to re-establish his relationship with Bobby Jo but his job and his father's memory were on the line, and he must do whatever it took. He would have to be tough and hard-headed, and not let his emotions blind him to whatever Bobby Jo was doing.

That evening, a jubilant Bobby Jo was being handed into a stretch Porsche limousine by Xander. It was luxury itself as they drank champagne and made their way to the Stork Club on East 53rd. Goodness knows where Xander had got such a vehicle. Bobby Jo didn't care. She lounged back decked out in a red velvet cocktail dress studded with rhinestones and sequins, its wide skirt cinched at the waist, and a fur stole she'd borrowed from Delia thrown over her shoulders.

Doing his utmost to be attentive, Xander kept refilling Bobby Jo's glass. By the time they got to the club she was tipsy. This was exactly what he wanted, and this time he was going to be sure she was his for the taking. His dutiful little courier would be back where she belonged, making every effort to please him.

At the Club, the owner Sherman Billingsley, a former bootlegger, greeted Xander warmly as if he were an old friend. He showed them the Cub Room and Table 50 where Walter Winchell wrote his columns and broadcast his radio programmes, before escorting them to the dining room.

Life, Love, Death

Bobby Jo was in a haze from the champagne and Xander had to order for them both. Barely aware of the food, she found herself mesmerised by Xander's constant gaze, his thumb repetitively stroking the palm of her hand. Once the meal was over, Xander gestured for the bill.

'Are we going to Times Square now?' Bobby Jo whispered.

Ignoring her question, Xander bundled her into the fur wrap, calling for their car. As soon as they settled into the inviting warmth of the back seat, he pulled her close, murmuring in her ear, 'I thought we might go to my place first. But of course, if you'd rather freeze in Times Square…'

Bobby Jo shivered, 'No, your place would be better.' One part of her champagne befuddled mind thought he's never asked me there before, and felt a tiny quiver of excitement. Perhaps this meant their relationship was moving forward. She had no time to think as Xander pulled her to him and began to kiss her thoroughly. Bobby Jo's head was spinning when they pulled up in front of a walk-up in the East Village. As they alighted Xander had to half carry and half drag an intoxicated and breathless Bobby Jo up the three flights to his studio apartment. Once there, he deposited her on the one and only couch. She lay back, closing her eyes, too confused to think.

Xander disappeared into a tiny kitchenette, bringing out a glass of some strange, coloured liquid, 'Here, drink this. It might help.'

Unable to raise her head, Xander had to prop her against his shoulder whilst Bobby Jo drank the foul tasting potion. 'This helps me get over a hangover,' he said, blithely. 'It's a prairie

Life, Love, Death

oyster. I won't tell you what it's made of, it might put you off.'

Bobby Jo could barely get it down. As soon as she did, she fell fast asleep. Xander shook his head in disbelief. What a child she was. Pulling down the wall bed, he picked Bobby Jo up and laid her gently on it, covering her with a comforter. Stretching out on the couch he watched her sleep, continuing to knock back half a bottle of brandy.

Xander wondered if he was as callous as he made himself out to be or whether it was the result of his childhood. It had never been easy. First of all, growing up with his sick mother in Russia, then moving to the US as a teenager to live with his American father's unwelcoming family. Once the Cold War had started, he'd never been sure where his loyalties lay, feeling like a split personality. He never knew whether he was Karl, the Communist partisan and agent, or Xander, the journalist, hedonist and lover of women. There was a lot he loved about living in America, yet at the same time hated the profligacy and the materialism. At heart he was a Marxist. However, recently he'd started questioning whether the current Soviet government still held fast to those same principles.

Bobby Jo stirred and moaned in her sleep. Xander forced himself into action. Carefully and skilfully, he undressed the sleeping girl. Taking off his own clothes he slid into bed beside her. Somehow, quite naturally without waking she turned and moved into his arms. He had a few moments of compunction at what he was doing to this naïve young virgin, but they were soon over. Sex was one thing, but love meant little or nothing to him. His mother had never shown him any affection even though he'd adored her. He'd

Life, Love, Death

certainly never been in love himself. Bobby Jo had to fit into his plans, otherwise he had no need of her. She had a part to play. He was damned sure he was going to make her play it. It was his destiny. He had to fulfil it to the bitter end whatever the outcome would be for either of them.

NEW YORK NEWS, 1954
WORLD NEWS
Indo-China War ends; France gives N. Vietnam to Communists
Roger Bannister runs 4 min. mile in UK!
U.S.A NEWS
Ellis Island closes
U.S. Hydrogen Bomb tested on Bikini Atoll
Supreme Court rules: Segregation in public schools unconstitutional
Senator McCarthy censured by Senate – end of Communist witch hunt
President Eisenhower signs the Communist Control Act
EVERYDAY NEWS
TV dinners introduced.
The first transistor radio produced for sale
Fashion: Bubble/ pencil skirts, nylon fabrics, slacks
Music: Frank Sinatra, 'Rock around the Clock' (Bill Haley)
Toys: Betsy McCall Doll, Dick Tracy Siren Squad Car
TV: 'The Lone Ranger', 'I Love Lucy'
Films/Books: 'Lord of the Flies', 'White Christmas', 'The Caine Mutiny'

CHAPTER 40

The first Tuesday of 1954 at the diner was like an old pals' reunion. Neither Delia nor Bobby Jo had seen Joel so happy. In fact, they were quite sure he'd never smiled at them so much in all the time they'd been together. He was irrepressible, shouting to Addy, 'Happy New Year. Are we's gonna to get any service over here or should we's take our custom elsewhere?'

'Not so much lip, you old goat. I'll be with you in a mo.' Addy's tone was curt but they could see she was trying not to grin.

Delia and Bobby Jo chuckled out loud, 'What's got into you, Joel? You look so smart and cheerful. Are you fully recovered now? What sort of Christmas did you have at Blanche's?'

Bobby Jo added, 'Are you two an item?'

Life, Love, Death

'What's all these here questions. Not you's business, ladies. Keeps you's noses outta my life.' Not really rattled, the old man actually grinned at them for the very first time, showing a pair of immaculate white dentures. The two women were flabbergasted. What with the teeth and the old man's obviously new houndstooth wool sports coat and immaculate corduroy trousers, it was hard to believe it was the same man. His hair had been styled and cut, and short shrift had been made of his stubbly old chin.

Addy came bustling over, 'Now what can I get my favourite customers at the start of a new year?'

Joel piped up before the other two could speak, 'Pancakes and maple syrup all round and cups of joe. I's treating. It be a special occasion,' he flashed a gleaming smile.

Delia was not at all sure she wanted to indulge in pancakes so soon after Christmas but didn't want to be a killjoy. Bobby Jo was delighted, 'What's the occasion, Joel?'

'There ain't an actual special occasion but I's bin receiving such kindness from Blanche's family I's want to share it with you's two. I supposes you's my family, well sorta,' he mumbled into his chest.

Thrown off balance, a disconcerted Delia didn't know how to react to such a backhanded compliment. Realising how much it took for Joel to express his emotions, she patted his hand reassuringly, saying, 'Tell us what's been going on.'

A misty eyed Joel said, 'Well as you's knowed I's stayed at Blanche's all over Christmas. They's was so kind to me with presents, a lovely room. Such a lotta food. Now they's bin

Life, Love, Death

down, cleaned me basement and given me so much furniture I's dunno myself. The old place be a palace.' The old man was so overcome he could barely speak, continuing brokenly, 'I's dunno why they's did it. I's no one…such good stuff 'an all. I's an old man…not worth bothering 'bout.'

'Of course you are worth bothering about,' Bobby Jo said vehemently. 'Everyone is worth bothering about. We all want someone to care for us.' She suddenly had a flashback of herself in Xander's arms, and couldn't help grinning and saying to herself, 'he really does love me after all'.

Delia nodded in agreement, 'Of course, Bobby Jo, we should all care for one another as best we can.' At that point the pancakes arrived. Both Joel and Bobby Jo concentrated on pouring streams of maple syrup over them. A wincing Delia rationed her syrup, thinking of the calories she'd consumed over the holiday and on Christmas Day. After the gallery party there'd been no contact from James until yesterday when a large bouquet of flowers arrived at her apartment. With it came an apologetic letter saying he'd had to go abroad for work but was looking forward to renewing their acquaintance when he came to New York later in the month. Accompanying the bouquet was a small velvet box with a gold and diamond brooch moulded in the shape of a goddess. Delia didn't know what to think. On the one hand she was annoyed he'd found out where she lived, probably down to Betty, and on the other hand flattered he'd taken so much trouble with the brooch.

Dragging her attention back to the present, Delia realised Joel and Bobby Jo were deep in conversation about President

Life, Love, Death

Eisenhower and Senator McCarthy. Trying to join in, she asked, 'What are you two talking about?

An unusually talkative Joel piped up, 'This little gal says there's talk the President hates that there Senator's guts but he be keeping quiet till he brung him down. What does you's think?'

'Hardly,' Delia protested. 'I think the President is too honourable to play such dirty tricks. It's plain conjecture. The President has never said a word about the Senator to the press. In fact, they're both Republicans and, if my memory serves me right, they campaigned together in '52.' She turned to Bobby Jo, 'You need to be careful about chit chat, Bobby Jo. This is how the 'Red Scare' started. Decent people's reputations were ruined overnight.'

'Delia, you're not in favour of that horrible man, are you? Wasn't he the one who started the 'reds under the bed' nonsense? I think everyone should be free to believe in whatever they like.' By now Bobby Jo had worked herself up so much her face had turned the colour of her hair.

'Calm down,' Delia said. 'I think the President knows what he's doing. We should leave politics to the government. They know best.'

'But do they?' Bobby Jo was determined not to give up. 'I think we, as voters, have every right to question our politicians and the government.' Fleetingly she thought of Xander. If he was a Communist as Harry said, then didn't he have a right to his own beliefs? But then again had she been colluding with him by delivering those mysterious packages? They weren't anything to do with Communism,

Life, Love, Death

were they? No, of course not, they were just publicity leaflets to help poor illegal immigrants. Although Xander could be tough and cynical, Bobby Jo was convinced that was all a façade. In her heart of hearts she was positive he was kinder and far more selfless than he appeared. After all, wasn't he doing his best for the Mexicans.

Joel, amused to see the two women going head to head, started guffawing, 'I's didn't know you's two had it in you. All that passion – wasted on this old man.'

At that, the three of them sat back laughing. Always the pacifier, Delia said, 'Let's forget our differences and start the New Year with a toast even if it's only coffee. What shall we drink to?'

'What about love and excitement?' Bobby Jo said waving her cup in the air.

'Dunno about any of that,' Joel griped. 'I's only wants a comfortable bed and summat to eat.'

'Well,' said Delia. 'I don't know what the year will bring but I want to go on working at the gallery and becoming my true self.' Privately she added, perhaps there might just be a handsome Englishman around to help me do that.

The three of them clinked coffee cups. Each smiled complacently thinking to themselves that 1954 was going to be a good year for each of them. It was, wasn't it?

CHAPTER 41

In the last few weeks of January Delia was on cloud nine. James had arrived from London, intent on feting and feasting her all over town. There were Broadway shows, private boxes at the opera, concerts at Carnegie Hall, private viewings at the Guggenheim and the Museum of Modern Art, as well as visits to little-known artist studios. There were dinners at exclusive clubs and weekends at Long Island, Westchester, and Maine.

Delia was determined not to get carried away but enjoy it for what it was, her experiences with Jan de Vries always uppermost in her mind. They had been hard lessons to learn. This time she must be more in charge of her feelings. Nevertheless, it was difficult not to get excited with the novelty of it all, the flattery, the constant attention, and the chance to do all the things she loved. Gus would never have indulged her in this way. It was a whirlwind of pure pleasure and self-indulgence.

Seeing Delia's ecstatic face every day at the gallery, Betty would shake her head and say, 'Don't forget, I warned you. James is a charmer, a seasoned veteran in knowing how to please a woman. Bear in mind all that charisma comes from years of practice.'

However it was too late for warnings as by now Delia had practically thrown caution to the wind for the second time in her life, not even crossing her fingers to hope things wouldn't go wrong. James, sensing the last vestiges of her insecurity, would reassure her, 'Look my dear, we are both mature adults. Don't take any notice of what other people think or say. Enjoy our time together.'

Life, Love, Death

The weeks moved on and Delia suddenly found herself with her second lover. James was totally different to Jan de Vries. He was thoughtful and loving, wishing to give her every satisfaction. There was no humiliation or superior treatment, it was all pleasing and calm. Delia couldn't help but wish and hope for a future with this man.

One morning, as they lay in bed in Queens, James said, 'I'm considering buying a flat in Manhattan. What do you think? I'm tired of hotel living, even at the Waldorf Astoria. I want to be able to relax at home when I come over.'

Delia said quietly, 'It's not up to me. You have to decide something like that for yourself.'

'But it is up to you, my darling girl. I want us to live there together. Then when I'm in London I can think of you there waiting for me.'

Perplexed, Delia was unsure what James was suggesting, 'Do you mean as your mistress?'

'No, not in the terms you mean. As you know I never want to marry but I would like us to live together, though we have the Atlantic between us most of the time.'

'I can't do that, James. I have my flat. It's my only security and there's Monet.'

James burst out laughing, 'I think Monet will settle in anywhere as long as he's fed. As for security, I don't think you understand, I'll be putting the apartment or co-op in your name. I wouldn't dream of making you give up your

Life, Love, Death

security but I do want to make our relationship more permanent.'

Delia frowned, 'It's generous of you, but what if we break up or you find someone else? What happens to me then?'

'My dear Delia, despite my reputation which I'm sure Betty has kept you well informed about, I feel at peace and settled with you and think about you all the time even when I'm in London. If that means love, then I think I love you.'

'I'm sure you're sincere, James, but you've probably been in love many times before. For me there was only Gus. I loved him dearly despite his failings.' Too ashamed to mention her sexual escapade with Jan, Delia consigned that episode to the past. Something she'd rather forget.

Over the next days, James was adamant about finding an apartment despite Delia's misgivings. He was a decisive man who expected to get what he wanted with a minimum of fuss. Before she knew it, Delia found herself being escorted around a range of top end apartments in the city.

After seeing half a dozen beautifully appointed and furnished apartments, James said, 'The agent is going to show us this one last property. If it isn't the pièce de resistance, I'll eat my hat.'

Delia giggled nervously, 'You never wear a hat,' and gaining confidence quipped cheekily, 'you're much too vain about that magnificent head of hair to cover it up.'

James' eyebrows shot up, delighted to see Delia beginning to unwind. She'd been so uptight throughout the viewings;

Life, Love, Death

he'd begun to wonder if he was pressuring her too much. He scoffed, 'I don't know, Delia. I think all these apartments have gone to your head and not with a hat on.' He bent and kissed her on the cheek, 'This is the most relaxed I've seen you since we started out. I love it when you knock me off my pedestal. The conceit comes with the job, I'm afraid. We auctioneers are an arrogant crowd, so used to being the centre of attention.'

The last co-op they were viewing turned out to be a complete surprise. It was in Sutton Place on 57th Street, only a stone's throw from Delia's work at Parsons. James was bursting with pride as they entered the building. He nodded to the porter, waving away the agent as they made their way up in the private elevator up to the penthouse. This was the one he was sure Delia wouldn't be able to resist. The views over the East River and the city were to die for.

Delia felt as if she was in a trance. Surely this spectacular place wasn't meant for her. She was speechless with the wonder of it all. The apartment was partially furnished with artwork. She stammered, 'Where did all the art come from? Was it the previous owner's?'

'No, I took a gamble,' James said sheepishly, 'and had some of my collection shipped here. I was pretty certain you'd like this last option. But don't worry, I can have it removed if this isn't for you.'

'No, please don't,' Delia gasped. She could barely breathe, still taking in the views and all the space. What a contrast to her tiny one bedroomed apartment in Queens. There were two bedrooms, two bathrooms, a library, a modern kitchen, as well as a light, airy living room extending through glass

Life, Love, Death

doors to a deck. Shocked, Delia said, 'But this is too much even for two of us and the cost...'

'Don't worry – it's the perfect location for us both and as for the cost... Over the years I've collected a great deal of art and much of it has proved to be a good investment. Should we check the bedrooms now, do you think?' he smirked behind the newly arrived agent's back.

Delia, feeling playful, tapped him on the behind as they scurried toward the other end of the apartment. They started behaving like newlyweds, chuckling and chasing one another round the rooms as if they were on their honeymoon.

The previous week, Delia had taken Betty Parsons into her confidence, asking her advice. Wrinkling her brow, Betty had declared, 'Wow, that's a turn-up for the book. I've never known James go this far. You really must be something special, my dear. An apartment, you say, and in your name. You've got nothing to lose. Go for it. This chance may never come again.'

Delia blushed, 'I don't know. It's like being a kept woman, sitting around waiting for James to arrive.'

'But you won't be, Delia. You've your own life here You could give up that awful Ohrbach's' job and help me out full-time. Then I can get back to painting.'

'But I won't have the status of a married woman. Gus would turn over in his grave at the thought of my living in sin.'

Life, Love, Death

Betty looked at Delia searchingly, 'But did you truly want to get married again? Be honest with yourself. You want to be a modern woman. This way you have your freedom and independence, together with the attentions of a man who sees you infrequently and therefore spoils you. Don't you deserve that now?'

'I suppose so,' Delia mumbled weakly. 'I can feel myself giving in, but I'm apprehensive about the future.'

'Pooh,' Betty snorted. 'None of us knows what the future will bring. Stop fretting is my advice. Take it or leave it, it's up to you,' and with that Betty whisked off to lunch with one of her recalcitrant artists.

Back at the penthouse, Delia was suddenly aware she hadn't been listening to either James or the agent, being too preoccupied with Betty's advice. It was apparent James was in the process of finalising everything. Turning to Delia, he said, 'I've a lawyer lined up for tomorrow so we can complete and get you moved out of Queens as soon as.'

It was all happening in a flash. Delia felt elated yet perturbed. Had she done it again and given up her hard won grip on her life to yet another man, and how would that work out?

CHAPTER 42

The following Tuesday Delia had absolutely no intention of telling either Joel or Bobby Jo about her change of circumstances. However, there was a glow about her even Joel recognised as he mumbled, 'You's look different, Delia. Can't put me finger right on it but it's summat, I knows. What's up?'

'Nothing, nothing at all,' Delia said shortly. 'Everything's the same.'

Bobby Jo raised her head from her plate of hot dogs and chilli fries, giving the blushing Delia a penetrating look, 'Goodness, Delia. You look radiant, as if you've just run off and got married. There's something almost bridal about you.'

'Rubbish,' Delia snorted, 'I don't know what's got into you two. I'm the same dull, old, cautious Delia,' though she knew she wasn't anymore. Attempting to distract them, she asked Bobby Jo, 'How are things with you and Xander?'

'Wonderful,' Bobby Jo exclaimed. 'I feel I'm getting to know him at last. We've become closer,' she added smugly.

Joel gave a dirty laugh, 'Bet it's real close, little Missy.'

How right he is, Bobby Jo thought. Since New Year's Eve everything was sweetness and light. Xander was far more tactile, insisting on taking her out for meals and drinks, with them ending up at his apartment for nights of non-stop passion. Bobby Jo was in a haze of desire, barely able to concentrate on her work. Her parents, who had almost given

Life, Love, Death

up hearing from their one and only daughter, would send plaintive pleading letters which Bobby Jo invariably dispatched to the garbage. No-one and nothing was going to distract her during this special time with Xander. Hank had made several attempts at reconciliation, but she'd rebuffed him each time.

On that Tuesday afternoon, when Bobby Jo returned to work, Xander took her to one side, 'I need a favour, angel. Cover for me. I need to go out on urgent family business.' He stroked her cheek and squeezed her waist.

'But what about Sam? Didn't he say you were on your last warning?'

Xander wrinkled his nose, 'Oh that. I'd quite forgotten. Say I've gone out to see a contact about an assignment that may be significant,' and laughing added, 'tell him it's something to do with the hydrogen bomb, that'll rev him up.'

Bobby Jo nodded, 'Okay, I'll do my best. Can I help? You know I'd do anything for you.'

'I know, sweetie. But this is private and confidential though I might need you later. Be back end of the afternoon.'

Since his last run-in with Jasha, Xander had become increasingly angry and upset. Moscow Central was expecting too much of him. How was he, on his own, going to find the scientific assets they wanted. Disillusionment had set in. What was this all about anyway – Russia competing with America in the arms race to be the first to produce a superbomb? The Soviet government and Khrushchev were no better than the American government and Eisenhower. A

Life, Love, Death

bomb would hardly help the Russian people. This was not what he'd signed up for when he'd been ordered to work at the Trib as a cover. Then again what about all the sacrifices he'd made in his personal life, or what there was of it. He was sure Jasha wasn't playing fair with him. There were bound to be other agents in New York who could undertake this work. Clearly Jasha didn't wholly trust him. Well, if Jasha was running a cell he was damned if he wasn't going to find out who was in it and what they were up to.

Jasha hadn't been pleased when Xander rang his direct line, and even less pleased to hear Xander's request for the latest bugging equipment. 'Didn't I tell you, Karl, not to ring me. This number is for emergencies only. I always get in touch with you. Use the drop if you want to contact me. Anyone could be listening in. Why do you want this equipment?'

Xander gave him a long explanation about finding a possible asset at the National Science Foundation in Washington, someone with contacts at the Atomic Energy Commission. It sounded plausible, even to Xander's ears. Jasha said he would do what he could and arranged a meeting for that afternoon in Central Park at the usual bench.

Later that day, a distracted Xander hurried to the rendezvous point. In his haste he failed to notice a thick set man who had been trailing him since the Trib. Once Xander sat down the man strode past him making for a hot dog stand where he leaned against the counter, eating and chatting to the owner, keeping Xander in view. Jasha took his time to arrive. When he did he sat at the further end of the seat from Xander clutching a metal suitcase. After a desultory greeting, Jasha said angrily in a low voice, 'This is clumsy, comrade. We're exposed here. I don't like it. I've

Life, Love, Death

brought what you asked for. You better come up with the goods after all the trouble I've been to.'

Xander simply smiled, refusing to be goaded by Jasha's bullying tone. After a moment or two, a jumpy Jasha got up and rushed off, leaving Xander to pick up the suitcase.

The burly man at the stand nonchalantly finished his 'dog threw away his soiled napkin in the nearest bin, and strolled after Xander as if he had all the time in the world.

A sweating Xander raced back to the office, concerned about Sam noticing his absence. Bobby Jo grinned, saying, 'You're off the hook. Sam's gone up to see Mrs Reid.' She looked questioningly at the suitcase, 'What's that?'

'Nothing for you to worry about, cherub. Only some equipment I need. We might as well wrap up for the day.' He kissed her hurriedly on the cheek. 'Sorry, can't see you tonight. I've work to do. Catch up tomorrow.'

CHAPTER 43

Every Tuesday it seemed as if Joel grew in confidence. Gone was the grumpy, grizzled old man that Delia, Bobby Jo, and Addy were used to. In his stead was a cheerful, shaved, smart, elderly man quick to make jokes and exchange quips with Addy, who was totally flabbergasted by the change. She would have liked to think it was she who'd brought it about but Delia and Bobby Jo set her straight – confiding in her about Blanche.

Joel was now spending every weekend with Blanche and 'The Misfits'. He'd even started to get to know each one of them by name. Curiously, he'd become particularly friendly with Steve, the white New York cop. They would play checkers together, and occasionally Steve would play his clarinet with the old-timers at Smalls. Though only in his thirties, he had plenty of time for the old man, loving to hear stories of the old days.

Joel talked openly to him about Prohibition, 'They's was good and bad old days: speakeasies on every corner, bootleggers selling high price booze, illegal stills, bathtub gin but also the Mafia, gangsters, and corruption. I's could tell you's many a tale but maybe's best forgotten.'

One day Joel had confided in his new friend about his arch enemy Sergeant Mulroney. Steve chuckled, 'He's not a man to be crossed, Joel. Busking's been illegal since the Mayor banned it in '36. If I were you I'd stick to the Village. You'll be off his beat there.'

Joel protested, 'But all the tourists are in Times Square. That's where there be money.'

Life, Love, Death

Steve patted Joel's shoulder, 'Look Joel, you've got Smalls and Mama Blanche looking out for you, there's no need to put yourself and Betsy through this foul February weather. You've been hospitalised once; you don't want that again, old friend, do you?'

Joel nodded. Usually never a man to be told, he was always prepared to listen to Steve. They were buddies. It was as if Steve was the son he'd never had though more likely the grandson he'd never had. It was a joy to play at Smalls with him. At last everything in Joel's world was good.

It was later that week the unforeseen happened. Joel and the gang were playing their usual Thursday night gig. Everyone was on top form. The music was buzzing. Suddenly, without warning, Benny Carter, who'd been perched on a high stool with his trumpet, keeled over and fell to the floor. There was a shocked silence, then pandemonium, as people rushed to help with cries of, 'Is there a doctor in the house?' and 'Someone call 911.' But it was too late. Benny was pronounced dead at the scene.

Joel was stricken and had to be helped from the stage by Steve. He sat the old man down, giving him a glass of brandy. Joel kept repeating in a low groan, 'He were one of my oldest friends. It can't be true. What will I's do without him?' All the old gang surrounded them, just as stunned and upset.

The manager made an announcement, 'Regrettably, ladies and gentlemen, I'm sure you understand but due to this tragedy we are closing Smalls tonight in memory of our good friend Benny Carter. We'll let everyone know about the arrangements for his funeral. In due course, I'm sure the

Life, Love, Death

management will want to dedicate a memorial evening to all his years with us. Benny was an exceptional trumpet player.' There was a low murmur of sympathy from the audience as they left quietly, heads bowed.

Steve whispered in Joel's ear, 'Why don't you come back with me to Mama Blanche's for the night. It's too much for you to go home to the Village and be on your own.'

But Joel refused, 'I's need to be with my old friends now, Steve, thanks all the same.'

'Then I'll stay with you. Why don't I get everyone a round of drinks?'

The old men gathered together drinking till the early hours as if they never wanted to leave. When the shock wore off, they began to reminisce about their old band mate. 'D'ya remember when old Benny ate himself sick over them pork chitlins when we was on the road down south, threw up in his trumpet case and carried on playing. He'd eat anything that lived and breathed would Benny.'

Joel was far away in his own memories of Benny when he heard his name mentioned linked to Desirée's. 'Weren't you a bit sweet on that gal, Joel?'

Joel said shortly, 'That were long times ago. She's went off with some trumpet player, I's think.' Still loyal to her, he didn't want to tell them how she'd ended up. That was none of their business.

Steve was agog with all the old musos' stories. He was certain there was more Joel could tell. These musicians were

Life, Love, Death

from a different era, bringing prohibition and the jazz age to life. He was envious of their camaraderie. Sure, cops had some of that but it wasn't the same - mostly it was just with your fellow beat cop. These guys had been on the road living and playing together. The session began to wind up as many of the old men needed their beds. Despite Joel's initial protestations, Steve whisked him away to Mama Blanche's and tucked him into his old bedroom.

Before he left the room, Joel clutched Steve's arm, 'I's like to go like that. Promise me, Steve – no hospital. I's want to play till the end. Bury me in de ground with my Betsy by my side.'

'You've got a good few years yet, Joel. Don't be worrying about it. Get some sleep. Mama Blanche will cook you up a feast in the morning.'

'Dunno, Steve. I's this bad feeling. Summat is comin'. I's know it. I's feel it.'

'It's tonight, Joel. It was a shock losing your old friend like that. Don't worry, you've got us. We'll look out for you.'

Steve closed the door, but he could still hear the old man mumbling, 'It's comin'. I's know it. I's feel it.'

CHAPTER 44

The next week at the diner, Joel was still dogged by visions of death pursuing him. Never keen to divulge anything too personal, he blurted out, 'My old friend Benny Carter dropped dead last Thursday at Smalls when we was playing.'

Delia and Bobby Jo were shocked. Ever compassionate, Delia said, 'You must be upset. What a terrible way to go. Was he ill?'

'Dunno, seemed fit to me. Not terrible way to go – the best. Still working. That's what I's want.'

Having no experience of death, Bobby Jo didn't know what to say. She laid a comforting arm on Joel's, but he brushed it away, 'Thanks, young 'un. I's don' need sympathy. I's alright.'

'I'm sorry,' Bobby Jo said, biting her lip. 'I never know what to say when someone dies. I don't like to think about anyone close to me dying either, in fact I never want to think about death at all.'

'Me neither,' Delia said. 'All I do know is I want to die in my own bed with dignity. I don't want to be cut up and used for those transplants I keep hearing about in the news.'

'We's all have to die. It be jus' a fact of life, but I's know summat is comin'. It's comin'. I's know it,' Joel said forcefully.

Life, Love, Death

Bobby Jo shivered, 'Can we please change the subject? I'm looking forward to the rest of my life.' She nearly added 'with Xander' but thought better of it.

Delia was thinking the same. She didn't want to think about death either. Life was too exciting for her at present. It had never been so good. She, James and Monet had settled into a routine in the new apartment. Monet's fur was flourishing now he was not subjected to Delia's interminable daily stroking, and he'd taken to James with more enthusiasm than Delia had thought possible.

Last month when James arrived, he'd said glumly, 'I really should go to the Rockefeller cocktail party and make contacts but I'd far rather stay home with you both.' Grinning boyishly, he added, 'and that's exactly what I'm going to do.'

Delia often regretted she and Gus hadn't had this same comfortable intimacy through all those years, but he was either on call, socialising, or exchanging shop talk with his hospital colleagues.

Of course, there were still a few sticking points in hers and James' relationship, one in particular. She had yet to tell her sons about this unconventional liaison. Her sons took after their father and would probably be stuffy and priggish about her situation. Goodness, how much she'd changed. In the past, she wouldn't have dreamt of criticising her sons like this. She'd always adored and doted on them - maybe too much. They'd never recognise their once submissive, housewifely mother in this glamorous creature floating round in a diamanté tea gown, drinking cocktails, and flirting with her handsome lover. To add to this, she'd

Life, Love, Death

become more radical in her thinking thanks to Betty Parsons. These days Delia was a passionate devotee of Mrs Eleanor Roosevelt's daily column 'My Day' in The New York Times. It's down to earth charm concealed subtleties about humanitarian issues, civil rights, and women's equality that Delia had never ever thought about before.

Surprisingly, an open-minded James was only too willing to encourage her interests. One day he said, 'Look Delia, if you want to do something more practical and political rather than just reading about ideas, why don't you join the 'Women Creating Change Club' in the city. I think your hero, Mrs Roosevelt, is its vice president. Go, find out about it.'

'You wouldn't mind?'

'Of course not. You're your own person. You can do and think what you like.'

This was so different from what Gus would have said, Delia was pleasantly surprised. She got a very different response from Betty Parsons who scoffed, 'They're probably a bunch of do-gooders. Posh ladies with nothing to do but lunch. Before you know it, Delia, you'll be sitting on committees and hosting charity events. I thought you had more about you than those WASPs.'

But Delia was not put off. She had to start somewhere. When she went along to the headquarters, she was amazed to find out how much they'd already achieved. Some of it was hardly revolutionary but at least they were beginning to influence legislation. Before she knew it, it was exactly as Betty had said, and, she was coopted on to a special

Life, Love, Death

committee looking at tenants' living conditions in Manhattan. These were strong women with something to say. It was a revelation to Delia. All her life no one had ever asked her opinion. Her father had dictated, her husband expected her to fall into line and her sons dismissed everything she said as female nonsense. James was different. When she came home with strong opinions or lapsed into a feisty argument he laughed, saying, 'I knew there was a passionate thinking woman in there somewhere. Try not to become too independent or too liberated or you might not need me anymore.'

Delia had smiled ruefully, 'As if that would ever happen. It's just that I've been let out of my cage and want to try my new wings.'

Pulling her close, James teased, 'Don't fly away, my darling girl. I don't want to lose you as soon as I've found you.'

Shocking herself out of her daydreams and back to the diner, Delia realised she'd completely forgotten all about her lunch companions, so absorbed was she in her own life. They weren't still talking about death, were they? Apparently they were. Joel was now talking about where he wanted to be buried, 'Have to be the Village. I's wants my Betsy with me. We's grew up together and we's going to spend eternity together.'

Trying not to giggle behind her hand, Bobby Jo said, 'I don't think they'll let you do that, Joel. I know people are dressed in their Sunday best in their coffins, but I can't see an undertaker letting you lie there with your Sax.'

Life, Love, Death

An immovable Joel, with a mulish expression on his face, said, 'That's gonna happen. I's 'spect you's two, as my friends, to makes sure it does, or I's will come back and haunt you's.'

Paying close attention now, Delia said soothingly, 'I assure you Joel, I will. I promise. We both will, won't we Bobby Jo? Betsy should be with you in the afterlife, and we'll think about you every time we hear a Sax playing.'

CHAPTER 45

Bobby Jo was frustrated. Things had been going so well with Xander since the New Year. Now he was back to his former self, moody, secretive, and remote. He made no efforts to ask her out or even to take her to bed back at his apartment. It was all business. Sometimes she wished she still had Hank. He'd been easy to talk to, but it looked as if he'd finished with her as these days he never rang. Determined to confront Xander, she marched up to his desk and said, 'I don't know what I've done wrong, but I won't be treated this way.'

A bewildered Xander looked up, 'Whatever do you mean, honey? I thought we were good.'

'You've ignored me for weeks as if I'm of no account. I suppose all you wanted was sex,' Bobby Jo spat out.

Xander blinked, 'What had happened to his innocent, little country girl? She'd grown up without him noticing. 'Don't be silly, sweetie. I'm busy at the moment,' adding hastily, 'I thought you were my sweetheart, or was I mistaken?' It would never do to antagonise his little courier.

A placated Bobby Jo calmed down, 'Well that's alright then. But Xander, why do you have to be so secretive? You can trust me. I can help and really want to. Is this about the illegals?'

'That's it,' Xander was quick to agree. 'Look, my cherub, I will need you soon. Be patient. In the meantime, why don't I take you out tonight and bring you up to date. I've heard there's a new Ukrainian restaurant opening in the East

Life, Love, Death

Village. Shall we try it?' He'd have to get creative, Xander thought, if he was going to carry on stringing Bobby Jo along. Anyway, his whole life was a fiction; a little more wouldn't be hard to come by.

Bobby Jo seemed satisfied letting Xander return to his machinations. He'd finally got to grips with the bugging equipment he'd borrowed. His next goal was to track Jasha's movements. This proved more difficult than he thought. Xander had left messages at the drop but there'd been no response so far. It was mid-afternoon before he had a cryptic message telling him to meet Jasha and his driver in Times Square again. Jasha was not in a good mood. He was having doubts about Xander and was none too pleased to have his afternoon interrupted. 'What is it now, Karl? This better be important. I've another meeting to get to this afternoon.'

Xander gritted his teeth but said evenly, 'It's about the Atomic Energy Commission...'

'I know, I know. You told me last time,' Jasha interrupted curtly.

'Well, if you'll only listen. I think I've found someone there who has a contact at the University of California in the Radiation Laboratory at Livermore.'

'What on earth is that?'

'It's a new lab set up by two guys called Lawrence and Teller in competition with Los Alamos to develop magnetic fusion.'

Life, Love, Death

Jasha sat up straight, 'Well done Karl, that's more like it. Can you find us an asset? I can supply you with anything you need – money, equipment. Name it!'

'I'm okay at the moment. I'll let you know if I need anything, though money is always welcome.' Xander smirked inwardly. He might as well make the most of the Soviet's open coffers. They said goodbye and arranged the next meeting.

No sooner had they gone than Xander set off after them in his own car. He was worried his Buick wouldn't catch up with the black Cadillac but was in luck, spotting it travelling south towards the Battery. In a split second they took a sharp turn through back streets, making their way towards some derelict, boarded-up warehouses, and stopping in front of one of them. Jasha hastily ran into one of the buildings, leaving his driver leaning against the car smoking a cigarette.

Xander making sure his car was well hidden and carrying the metal suitcase, sneaked behind the Cadillac and into the building after Jasha. Once inside, Xander could see an elevator ascending to the fifth floor. Finding a staircase, he ran up the five flights. Sneaking along, he turned a corner, nearly running into a group of men and one woman standing drinking coffee at the entrance to one of the rooms. Jasha stepped out of the elevator in front of them, calling the group to order in the room without closing the door. They pulled out chairs and sat round a dirty metal table. Xander positioned his antennae, leaning against the corner out of sight. The conversation was in Russian and Xander though not fluent, could pick up the gist of it. After formalities,

Life, Love, Death

Jasha said, 'English please, comrades, we are in America. We must practise.'

The conversation ambled on with a lot of broken English. Xander, fiddling with his headphones, wasn't paying attention until he heard the name 'Karl' mentioned and realised he was the subject of their conversation. They seemed to be arguing as to whether he was a double agent or not. Feeling bile rising in his throat, Xander could hardly contain his rage thinking of all his years of loyalty to the party.

One of the men said, 'What do you expect, Jasha? Karl's half American. Spent most of his life here. This contact he's found could be a trap, something to draw us in and make sure we all get caught.' The others agreed.

Xander, recognising the man's voice, was desperate to see his face. Risking a look, he was astounded. It couldn't be could it...but it was... Of all people, his journalist friend Stefan from the Daily Worker. Not only that but he recognised the woman too. It was Edith in her usual thick tweed jacket and trousers. He couldn't believe it. Had they been spying on him all along when he'd thought of them as friends and comrades? In all the years he'd known them they'd never let on they were actual agents for Moscow Central. He'd just thought of them as Marxist idealogues not activists like himself.

Jasha was the only one to protest, 'But Karl's worked for us for years and been useful. I might have a few misgivings myself but I've no real cause to mistrust him.'

Life, Love, Death

An older man said, 'Comrade Khrushchev says these are difficult times. We must develop the super bomb ahead of the Americans. This is our chance. Most Americans don't want to hear about another bomb. Attitudes have changed since Hiroshima and Nagasaki. Even Oppenheimer is against it. We need to find some sympathetic scientists to work for us. Why not let one of us work with Karl and watch him?'

Jasha scowled, 'No, comrades. I need to keep the cell separate. That's how we do things. I'll deal with Karl in my own way. Carry on exploiting the anti-bomb propaganda with the Americans. That's essential at the moment.'

None of this was of any interest to Xander. The arms race was of little consequence. All he thought about was his people, the Russians, and what they meant to him. He'd never felt a strong patriotic allegiance towards America despite living and growing up there. Nonetheless, if his so-called comrades were intent on thinking of him as a double agent, so be it. That's what he might as well be.

Slipping quietly out of the building as the group began to knock back vodka, and making his way back to the Tribune, Xander thought he caught a glimpse of a car following him. It was unlikely to have been one of Jasha's people but it could be the Feds. Maybe they were on to him at last. He would have to be more careful in covering his tracks, and make better use of Bobby Jo. If he were to make a deal with the Feds, he wanted it to be in his own time and on his own terms.

CHAPTER 46

Spring was finally showing itself. The threesome at the diner were aware of an air of optimism lifting their spirits. At last Joel had left all thoughts of imminent death behind, Delia was relishing her new life, and Bobby Jo was feeling hopeful about her relationship with Xander.

The night at the Ukrainian restaurant had been memorable with pierogi and beef stroganoff washed down with lots of beer. Later, Bobby Jo remembered Xander hadn't mentioned anything about his work with the illegals or what he wanted her to do. He was in a good mood, teasing and joking with her. As usual they ended up back at his apartment making frantic love.

Unexpectedly that very day, Hank had rung wanting to meet up. Bobby Jo was flustered, surprised to hear from him after so long, and agreed to meet the following week. She made up her mind to tell him she was with Xander now but was still curious to know what he wanted, considering they'd parted on such bad terms.

Back at the diner, all three sat contemplating their thoughts as Addy breezed up bringing glasses of water. She was on good form, 'Now come on folks, what will you have today? That Frankie may have his faults but he sure can cook. He's thrown together his special Manhattan clam chowder. How about a bowl of that, a Salisbury steak or Irish stew for a change?'

Joel shook his head, 'My usual Addy, please.' It was such a change to hear Joel say 'please' that Addy did a little curtsy

Life, Love, Death

in acknowledgement, 'Your wish is my command, sir,' she wisecracked. 'Now what about you two?'

Always keen for a new experience, Bobby Jo said, 'Chowder, please Addy, and rolls.'

Delia smiled, 'You're in a good mood, Adelie, must be the time of year. I think I might have a change from my usual 'rabbit food', as Bobby Jo calls it, and try some of the Irish stew as it's nearly Saint Patrick's Day.'

'Good for you,' Addy replied. 'A change is good as a rest or so my mama used to say. We all need something to shake us up occasionally. Be back in a jiffy, folks.'

Joel wasn't entirely sure he wanted change, although, his life had been drastically transformed since meeting Blanche. He'd been completely accepted and adopted as part of her family now. All the children cosseted him when he was there, and he had finally begun to understand what it was like to be loved. There was no question though that Steve was his favourite. They would play all the old tunes together to entertain the others and many of the 'Misfits' would sing or dance.

A few weeks later, Joel was staying at Blanche's as usual for yet another weekend. On the Monday, he said, 'Thanks Blanche, I's must get back. I's getting too comfortable here and might not wanna leave.'

Blanche laughed, 'Don' you be silly, old man. You can stay forever if you wants. There's plenty o'room. One more makes no difference to me.'

Life, Love, Death

Joel was adamant, 'I's never outstays my welcome thanking you's, Blanche.'

'Well then, let my Steve escort you to the subway. There's bin a bit o' trouble here lately. At least if you're with a uniformed cop you'll be alright.'

Joel agreed, always willing to spend time with Steve. As they were about to cross the road outside Blanche's house, a burly black man, swaying on his feet, called over the road jeering, 'What you doing with that whitey, old man, and a cop at that?'

Steve said, 'Take no notice, Joel. He's either half-cut or out of his mind on coke.' They kept on walking and talking.

So absorbed were they in their conversation, they never heard the man creep up behind them. Before they knew it, he had hold of Steve. Initially Joel was frozen with shock, then rage took over. He threw his frail body between Steve and the assailant. Feeling something sharp press into his body, he managed to thrust the man off Steve who by now had collapsed on the floor. It was then Joel realised the man had a knife. Steve lay gasping on the ground. is eyes rolled back into his head and then he was still. Their attacker, seeing what he'd done to a cop, took fright and ran off. Joel lay down beside Steve and cradled him in his arms. He could feel his own strength ebbing away, unaware of the blood trickling down his side. Stroking Steve's face it was as if Joel's long buried emotions came to the surface and he was holding the son he'd never had.

The hullabaloo brought a small crowd. Someone ran to tell Blanche and call an ambulance. Blanche rushed up the street,

Life, Love, Death

puffing and panting. Kneeling down she pulled Steve towards her, wailing as if her heart would break, 'My son, my son, my darling son.' Noticing Joel for the first time, she put out her hand. Joel, too weak to take it, whispered, 'I's tried to save him. I's tried…' then he too was gone.' Blanche leaned over Steve's body, kissing Joel on the cheek, 'I know, I know. You did your best. You're together now.' She fell against them sobbing and weeping as if she'd never stop. It took two ambulance crew to help lift her.

Refusing to go back to her house she sat on a chair on the sidewalk until the two bodies were loaded into the ambulance. Finally she let one of her children take her home, insisting on carrying Joel's bag and Betsy, both of which had been thrown into the road during the fracas.

Back at Blanche's the Misfits sat around holding one another's hands in shock and disbelief. Steve had been one of Blanche's first foster children, the one to look up to and take advice from, and Joel, though they'd only known him a short time, had become a beloved grandfather.

Blanche was in such a state of distress she had to be sedated. But her last words to everyone before she fell asleep were, 'You must tell Delia and Bobby Jo. They're his friends. He'll want them to know, and Smalls of course…'

The Misfits looked blank. They'd never heard of Joel's friends before. Whenever he'd stayed with them he never mentioned anyone. How would they ever find them and who were they?

CHAPTER 47

The following Tuesday, Delia and Bobby Jo sat in Leo's in complete ignorance. They commented, 'Strange Joel isn't here. He's always first.' They waved to Addy who was making her rounds with glasses of water and coffee. 'Adelie, my dear,' Delia said. 'Do you know what's happened to Joel? He's not ill again, is he?'

Addy shrugged, 'Don' know where that old man is. I must say it's unlike him. Don' worry. I'll ask around.'

They were both well into their meals when she came back. There was a distraught look on her face and she was waving the Harlem News. 'Look, look here, you two. I can't believe it. It's Joel. He's dead!'

Delia rapidly ran her finger down the columns and read aloud the headline, 'Black hero defends white cop'. All the details were there. Bobby Jo gave a piteous cry, slipping off her chair in a dead faint. One of the customers lifted her back on to the chair and pushed her head between her knees. Then with Addy and Delia fanning her and another customer holding smelling salts under her nose, Bobby Jo revived and was given a glass of water.

Delia was shaken too, suddenly looking pale and drawn. Addy helped her sit, calling to Frankie to bring the brandy. Frankie grumbled under his breath, brooding about why there was so much fuss over one old man's death. He'd never liked having Joel in the diner despite him being a friend of his late father's. Perhaps this was good riddance.

Life, Love, Death

Once they'd recovered, Bobby Jo and Delia sat and looked at one another. 'I don't know what to do or feel,' Bobby Jo said plaintively. 'It's as if a close member of my family has died.'

'I know what you mean,' Delia said. 'He could be an 'onery old man and certainly was when I met him, but he changed when he met Blanche. Oh goodness Blanche…she must be devastated. I must go and see her. We could both go, couldn't we?'

'I suppose so,' Bobby Jo said reluctantly. 'I wouldn't know what to say though. I always feel awkward if someone's ill or has died.

'I know it's difficult but try and put yourself in their place. It's no good ignoring the hard things in life,' Delia said, firmly. 'Just be with the person, hold their hand. Tell them how sorry you are. Shall we go this evening?'

'But Harlem…Isn't it dangerous particularly after what's happened to Joel?'

'We'll take a cab. We'll be fine,' Delia said in a steady voice. 'We can't not go. Joel was our friend.'

Arriving at Blanche's that evening Delia wondered if they were doing the right thing, but the door was flung open by a beautiful redhead who welcomed them warmly, 'Am I glad to see you two. Blanche was fretting, wanting us to get in touch with you, but we had no idea how to. Mama Blanche hasn't been well since the deaths. She's depressed and listless, not speaking or eating and staying in bed all day. We're worried about her. She refuses to see a doctor. Perhaps you two might talk to her and ease her mind.'

Life, Love, Death

Bobby Jo looked alarmed, 'I don't know what we could do,' but was shushed by Delia who said, 'Take us to her. We'll do our best.'

Minutes later they were shown into a large brightly coloured room dimmed by drawn shades. The only sign of Blanche was a large recumbent shape in the middle of the bed. Delia opened the shades. The figure on the bed groaned, 'No light. Leave me alone.'

Sympathetically, Delia said in a soft voice, 'We can't do that, Blanche. We've come to help.'

'Who is that? I can't see clearly.'

'It's Delia and Bobby Jo. Joel's friends from the diner. We were shocked about him and your son and wanted to see you. What can we do for you?'

'I don' need anything. I've lost Steve and Joel. I's alone now.'

'But you're not. You have the most wonderful family – what do you call them? Oh yes, 'Mama Blanche's Misfits'. They're here to lend a hand and so are we, aren't we Bobby Jo?'

'Yeah,' Bobby Jo said feebly, not sure in what way she could do anything.

There was a knock on the door. One of the Misfits brought in tea and cake. 'Y'all need to eat,' she announced.

Blanche moaned and sighed but sat up in bed. Delia persuaded her to have a drink and some cake. Soon there were signs of life in the handsome woman's face. With only

Life, Love, Death

the hint of a smile she said, 'I never thought I'd see you two white ladies drinking tea with me in my house.'

'But we're friends,' Delia insisted. 'We were all Joel's friends. None of us had known him long. He meant a lot to each one of us, and particularly to your son Steve.

'I know,' Blanche said tenderly. 'They was great buddies. Peculiar how that came about and now they've died together.' Large, sorrowful tears ran down her face.

Delia stroked the big woman's hand, 'What can I do for you?' she asked tenderly.

'There's funerals to arrange,' Blanche broke down completely. 'I can't manage.'

'Don't worry,' Delia reassured her, 'We'll talk to your family and work it out together. Lie back and rest.'

On the landing Bobby Jo whispered, 'I don't know anything about arranging funerals...'

'Don't worry. I expect Steve's will be a police funeral and we can arrange Joel's. Let's talk to everyone. Sort out who does what. It'll be easier that way.'

'If you're sure,' Bobby Jo said uncertainly.

'I am,' Delia said with assurance. 'Don't you remember we promised Joel when he kept predicting his own death that we would carry out his wishes. That was uncanny, as if he knew what was coming.'

CHAPTER 48

In the end, it was James who was to resolve many of the problems relating to Joel's funeral. The New York Police Department organised Steve's. It was a formal, sombre affair with uniformed police lining the way and Steve's hearse led by a solitary cop car with a flashing light. Blanche, adorned in a long black veil, was in a terrible state but her grief-stricken children accompanied her to the poignant service at Trinity Church and the interment. A solitary musician from Smalls played 'The Last Post' on Steve's clarinet, as he was laid to rest in full dress uniform.

Joel's funeral a week later was a very different affair, in fact a riotous one. James, through his many contacts, had been able to secure a plot for Joel at Greenwich Cemetery in the Village. Smalls brought their musicians to parade up Bleecker Street, in the style of a good ole New Orleans send-off, followed by crowds of Village people tapping their feet and dancing. Delia shed a tear thinking how much Joel would have loved it. He'd have grumbled about the fuss, but inwardly been pleased. Blanche and her family had petitioned the police to recognise the old man's courage and so he lay in his casket, Betsy by his side, the Medal of Honor pinned to his chest. At the graveside the pastor couldn't get a word in, as old musicians kept interrupting wanting to say a final goodbye to their friend. When everything had been said and dirt had been thrown on the closed casket, the band played Joel out to Scott Joplin's 'The Entertainer'.

Delia had never been to such a lively affair. Bobby Jo, with little experience of death or funerals, couldn't believe the contrast between the two occasions.

Life, Love, Death

The next weeks sitting in Leo's was hard for them both. It was as if Joel's ghost sat between them. At times they thought they could hear the clack, clack, clacking of those false teeth grinding their way through 'those danged spikes of crispy bacon'. Both were off their food, pushing it round the plate in a dejected manner.

'Anything I can get you, ladies?' Addy said quietly, feeling sad and woebegone herself. On the day of Joel's funeral she'd changed her usual stained apron for a clean one, standing on the stoop for ages wishing she could be at the funeral, and totally ignoring Frankie's screams of 'Service, service. Get a move on, Addy. What's got into you? I can't do all this on my own.' In the end he was forced to abandon the kitchen and serve the meals himself.

The three of them felt as if some precious part of the diner had been lost. It was remarkable to think how much space Joel and Betsy had taken up in their lives. Now they were gone for ever.

Addy said sorrowfully, 'That old man bin comin' here for years and years – every Tuesday, like clockwork. He were like a fixture. Years ago, he and Leo grew up together in the same Brooklyn tenement, both musicians, Leo with the piano, then drums. They was in the same band for a time 'til Leo buys the diner. Long before I come here, Leo says to Joel, 'You're always welcome. You have a seat for the rest of your life.' Surreptitiously, she put her hand to her mouth and whispered, 'Frankie's granddaddy was black like Joel, Leo being half and half, but that Frankie don' know. I might have to tell him one day.' She laughed raucously and maliciously.

Life, Love, Death

Delia and Bobby Jo were taken aback, 'Did you never want to tell him, Adelie?' Delia asked. 'Particularly when he was so unpleasant and unkind to Joel.'

'Nah, I were always waiting for a moment when he tried to kick Joel out for ever, then I were going to spring it on 'im. But I lost my chance,' she said sadly. 'I'll bide my time now.'

As the two women left, Delia squeezed Addy's shoulder, 'We'll both be here next Tuesday. See you then.' Bobby Jo was silent as they walked up the street. Delia took her arm consolingly, 'It's tough when someone dies. At least Joel had a great departure. He was loved by more people than he ever knew. I thought I would go and visit Blanche this week as she's still not well. I'm worried about her. What do you think? Do you want to come?'

'I don't know, Delia. I feel low and don't think I would be any good. I'm very down, and don't know what's happening with Xander.' All of a sudden, the thought of Hank popped into her head. With everything that had been going on, Bobby Jo remembered she'd never turned up for their meeting. What must he have thought of her? Anyway, it was too late to bother now. She couldn't think about him. Xander was of more importance to her.

Troubled about the girl, Delia hugged her feeling uneasy about the turmoil she could see in Bobby Jo's eyes, 'I'm always here for you, Bobby Jo. Ring me if you change your mind about going to Blanche's or want to talk.'

They parted, promising to be back at the diner the following Tuesday.

CHAPTER 49

Over the last weeks, Xander had had to time to reflect. He knew he was a loner when it came down to it yet belonging to the Party had given him a sense of camaraderie, all fighting for the same cause. Now he had to go it alone again. He was sure he was being followed but didn't know by whom. This particular day on his way home from work, he stopped his car at a newsstand, grabbed a copy of the Trib and walked up the street. Turning into an alley, he waited, knuckleduster at the ready. A minute or two went by. A thickset man came round the corner. Xander stepped into the man's path, 'What's going on? Why are you following me?'

The burly man blustered, 'I'm not…just going this way.'

'Stop right there,' Xander advanced menacingly. 'There's nothing up here but a dead end. What are you, Feds?' he brandished his knuckles at the man's face. 'If so I wanna see your boss.'

Paling, the thickset man nodded reluctantly, 'Why not. Come with me,' and trying to recover the situation said sneeringly, 'He'd like to meet you too, I guess. I'll drive.'

'No, I don't think so. I'll follow in my car. I like to know where I'm going.'

At the field office, Xander was shown into a large empty room with a table and two chairs. 'Wait there,' the man gestured to one of the chairs.

Life, Love, Death

After a considerable time, he returned ashen-faced. Any earlier bravado he'd shown had vanished, and he mumbled, 'Follow me.'

Sitting alone in yet another gray soulless room, Xander started to have second thoughts. Was he doing the right thing? Throwing his lot in with the Feds was a big step. What about Mother Russia? He'd been a patriot from the time he stood at his mother's knee. Now he would be a traitor and rootless. What sort of future could he have? He was still absorbed in his own thoughts when Senior Special Agent Brewster slipped into the room. Without Xander noticing, the Agent observed him for a time before he spoke, 'It's good of you to pay us a visit, Mr Smith. You've certainly piqued our interest.'

Brewster sat down on the chair opposite, remaining silent. He was a man one could miss in a crowd, yet there was something steely about him. Never a man to be crossed or ignored, he sat patiently waiting, his unreadable face showing no expression. Xander shuffled nervously in his chair, confronted by this maddening indifference. Feeling the pressure, he blustered, 'Why was that man following me?'

'I'm sure you know why,' Brewster replied calmly. 'Stop prevaricating, Mr Smith. Tell me why you're here.'

'If you know so much about me, why don't you tell me,' Xander mocked with bravado.

'No doubt, Mr Smith, you've come to do a deal with us.'

'So, what if I have. How can I trust you Feds?'

Life, Love, Death

'We can reciprocate, Mr Smith. How can we trust you, a Soviet agent or spy if you prefer that term?'

Xander was shaken to hear himself described like that. He'd always thought of himself as a patriotic comrade, a believer in a cause, a free, independent spirit not someone who worked for a government and certainly not a spy. Now he was about to offer to actually work for another government.

Registering Xander's discomfiture, Brewster said gently, 'I'm sure in the past your motives have been pure, Mr Smith. Here I'm afraid we deal in facts, evidence, and information. What do you want from us and what are you willing to give in return?'

A shaken Xander tried to pull himself together, mumbling, 'I want immunity. In return I can give you vital information.'

Brewster smiled in an alarming way, 'I think, Mr Smith, you are in no position to call the shots. This is how it will be. You will maintain your present position with Moscow and work for us at the same time. What the movies call, I believe, 'a double agent', but we shall be planning the strategy and you will be carrying it out and reporting directly to me.'

Not at all sure this was what he wanted, Xander nodded. He had little in the way of bargaining chips. At this juncture it dawned on him he desperately wanted to get out of the game altogether and have a fresh start. It would take some doing but he knew he could pull it off. Money was all he needed. 'Very well,' he said wearily. 'There's a cell operating in New York. I can point you towards them, but I'll need money and lots of it.'

Life, Love, Death

Brewster sucked in his cheeks ruefully. It always came down to cash in the end. No doubt the Russians were also paying him liberally. There really was no such thing as idealism or patriotism when moolah was involved. 'Very well, Mr Smith. We'll provide you with what you need. You must give us details of the people involved and when and where they meet. I'll keep my best man on your tail, entirely for your protection and our insurance purposes you understand.'

Xander grinned, 'Surely not that big gorilla you dumped on me today.'

'No,' Brewster said resolutely, 'I've someone far better in mind. You won't even know he's there. After all, we are thinking of your safety and welfare. I wouldn't want anything happening to you.'

'Worried about your investment?' Xander gibed, full of swagger now he'd achieved his aim.

'Always, we look after our own people as long as they behave and even then, of course, we have the means to take care of them altogether,' Mr Brewster said ominously.

Xander was cheerful and optimistic as he departed, confident that he was clever enough to outwit both the Feds and the Soviets. He would find himself a location far away from them both, indulge himself, and enjoy 'a lotus-eating' life with plenty of wine and women. Didn't he deserve it after all these years of dedication to the Party?

CHAPTER 50

Bobby Jo wasn't herself these days. At the diner, Delia and Addy noticed how miserable and subdued the girl was. Addy remarked, 'That poor girl. She's taken Joel's death bad. We'll have to watch her. Death comes hard to young 'uns, don' it? At her age no one thinks they gonna die, life stretches before them.'

Delia nodded, 'It's been a blow to us all, particularly the way Joel died, though he was so brave. I find it hard myself,' she wiped away a stray tear.

'Now don' you start, Mrs Gray, or we'll all be at it.' She went away mumbling, 'I was fond of that old man in my way too. He bin comin' here so long.'

Delia made up her mind to take Bobby Jo in hand, 'Why don't you come to the gallery one afternoon? I live nearby. You can come home with me for lunch. What do you think?'

Bobby Jo looked up and gave a half-hearted smile, 'That sounds lovely, Delia. I didn't know you'd moved. I thought you lived in Queens.'

Delia frowned, thinking there was much Bobby Jo didn't know about her life, but wasn't inclined to tell her just at that moment. James was not due back for another week or two, so there was no reason to mention him. 'I moved into an apartment near the gallery. It's convenient. Please come – perhaps Saturday? You won't be working at the paper, and I only work half day.'

Life, Love, Death

They agreed on a time and the thought of it appeared to cheer Bobby Jo up. It was a relief for Addy and Delia to see the young girl leave with a spring in her step again.

On the Saturday, Bobby Jo turned up at the gallery. Delia showed her round the pictures, but they weren't to the young girl's taste, and they soon set out for the apartment at Sutton Place. Bobby Jo's eyes nearly fell out of her head when she saw the penthouse. 'Goodness, Delia. Have you come into money or something?' Realising what she'd said she quickly apologised, 'I'm sorry, Delia, that was rude. It's none of my business.'

Delia reddened, 'It's not quite like that, my dear. As it happens, I own the apartment, but it was a gift. I never told you or Joel but I met a lovely man. We live here together when he's in the country. I'm sure you'll be shocked. Your poor parents would be scandalised to know we're not married and not intending to marry. I've been married once. That was enough.'

Bobby Jo collapsed in a fit of coughing. An alarmed Delia ran round getting water and patting her on the back. When she recovered, Bobby Jo said, 'I'm not shocked, Delia. It caught me unawares and made me laugh. That's why I was choking. It's so unlike you and so out of character. I can't believe you kept all this from us for so long but I'm happy for you. You deserve it after working for that terrible man in that awful store.'

'I still do work,' Delia said indignantly, 'but now it's doing something I love. Anyway, no more about my disreputable liaison. Sit down, have something to eat and tell me what's going on with you.'

Life, Love, Death

Bobby Jo grimaced, continuing to cuddle and stroke Monet, 'Nothing as exciting as your life. I don't know where I am with Xander. Then there's Hank, do you remember him? I was supposed to meet him but forgot due to what happened to Joel.'

'I remember him well. He was that gorgeous young man who came to our table in the diner once. Didn't you spend Christmas with him?'

'I did, and absolutely adored his family. He was alright too. We dated but there was something he didn't want to tell me. Like Xander he had his secrets and I was tired of men like that.'

'What now?'

'I don't know. I have a secret too and not one I ever wanted,' Bobby Jo said, hanging her head.

'What do you mean?'

'I'm sure, Delia, you'll be the one to be taken aback if I tell you but I need to tell someone.'

'Go ahead, Bobby Jo. I'm very different to the old Delia you first met a year ago. Nothing but nothing surprises me now.'

Bobby Jo blurted out, 'I think I'm pregnant. What shall I do?'

Delia was actually dumbfounded, completely caught off guard. Before she could stop herself, she asked, 'Who's the father?'

Life, Love, Death

'Xander of course,' was the reply. 'Hank and I didn't have that sort of relationship.'

'I'm sorry, my dear. You're right. I was surprised, but it happens. What can I do? Have you seen a doctor to have it confirmed? What about Xander? Have you told him?'

'No to the doctor I'm too embarrassed and no, I haven't told Xander. I'm afraid he'll leave me.'

Delia bit her lip, 'Didn't you use any form of contraception? I thought you modern young women were up on all of that.'

Mortified, Bobby Jo said, 'Perhaps I'm not that modern after all. It was the night at the Stork Club. I was very drunk and didn't understand what was happening, but I'm crazy about Xander. I never thought about consequences.'

Putting her arm round the young girl, Delia was furious to think Xander had taken advantage of such an innocent. But it was too late to think of that now. It was time for action. 'I'll make an appointment first thing on Monday with my doctor. He's very understanding. At least we'll know for certain, and how far along you are. What about your parents? Will they support you?'

'I doubt it. I've cut off all contact with them since I've been here. They would never approve of me bringing a baby home if I'm unmarried. I'd have to have it adopted and I don't know what I want...' Bobby Jo broke down crying hysterically.

Life, Love, Death

Taking charge, Delia said, 'Stay the weekend. I'll ring the Tribune on Monday and say you're sick. We'll go to the doctor's together and decide what to do after that.'

Tucking the sleeping girl into bed in the guest room, Delia poured herself a large whiskey and soda and sat back wondering what to do. Should she ring Bobby Jo's parents? Should she confront Xander who should have known better? If only James was here, but he was currently scouring Europe for a Cedric Morris painting to buy for Christie's. Lamentably, this was something she'd have to sort out on her own.

CHAPTER 51

As it happened, the very parents Delia was thinking about were on their way to New York. They'd tried every way possible to contact their errant daughter but had come up with a wall of silence. In desperation, they rang Mrs Reid at the Tribune who was out of the country and been referred to Sam Murphy. He was sympathetic and said he would talk to Bobby Jo. After he spoke to them, he began to wonder if Xander was to blame. He should never have given that rogue Xander such a greenhorn. Goodness knows how he might have corrupted her.

For the Hudsons, the train journey to New York was a long and anxious one. On the way they discussed what to say to their daughter. Mrs Hudson was weeping once they reached Grand Central, and the decision was made to check in to the Lexington. They would dine early, sleep and confront their offspring in the morning when they were both rested and in a calmer state of mind.

The next morning with no time to waste they set out for the Barbizon Hotel. There was no sign of Bobby Jo even at that early hour. The Hudsons, becoming increasingly agitated, took a cab to the Tribune offices. They were shown into Sam's office demanding to see their daughter. As it was not yet nine o'clock and with no sign of Bobby Jo, Sam was at a loss. He pacified the couple with coffee, regaling them with stories about their daughter's work and what a natural writer she was. But there was no consoling Mrs Hudson who began to sob copiously, pleading, 'Mr Murphy, Mr Murphy, where is our daughter. She's our only child. What's happened to her?'

Life, Love, Death

Sam left messages at the front desk telling them to look out for Bobby Jo. At last they rang with a message. A lady had telephoned early that morning saying Bobby Jo wouldn't be in today as she was sick. But it was a mystery as to where Bobby Jo was, although Sam had his suspicions. The Hudsons were persuaded to return to their hotel and wait. No sooner had they left than Xander arrived and was told to report to the editor urgently. A dishevelled and grumpy Xander made his way to Sam's office to be confronted with the raging, mouth frothing and haranguing figure of his editor. Wondering what he'd done this time he stood motionless, waiting for the storm to die down, impatiently cracking his knuckles behind his back.

'What have you done with that girl?' Sam screamed. 'I've had her parents here for over an hour accusing me of selling her off to the white slave trade.' Finally noticing Xander's state of dress and lethargy, he said more evenly, 'Wake up, man. Pull yourself together and enlighten me.'

Xander shook himself awake, 'What girl and what parents? Sam, I've no idea what you're talking about.'

'That trainee of course, your trainee. What's her name – Roberta or is it Bobby Jo? I'm confused with all her names.'

'Oh, her,' Xander said nonchalantly. 'I don't know where she is. Isn't she here?' He looked at his watch, 'She's usually punctual.'

'No, no she's not here. Are you stupid or something? That's the problem. Why do you think I'm this upset? Some woman rang up and left a message saying Bobby Jo wouldn't be coming in today as she was sick, and I have no idea where

Life, Love, Death

the girl is. You must know something, after all you're working with the child and my spies tell me you've been escorting her round town.'

Xander blinked hard. How much did this wily editor know? Plastering a smile on his face, he said guilelessly, 'Okay, I've been showing her round, but I don't know where she is at this particular moment. She must be with friends, I suppose.'

'Well stop supposing and get out there and find her. Her parents, the Hudsons, are staying at the Lexington. They expect to hear from you by the end of the day. Use your contacts, d'ya hear me, otherwise there'll be hell to pay when Mrs Reid finds out. They're friends of hers.'

A surly Xander slunk out the door, banging it hard behind him. What the devil! Was he to spend his valuable time looking for some danged girl when he had urgent business of his own. Ignoring Sam's orders, Xander returned to formulating his next move to becoming a free man.

Back at their hotel, Mrs Hudson was so distraught her husband suggested they return to the Barbizon and wait for Bobby Jo's return. It was six in the evening when Delia delivered a pale Bobby Jo back to the hotel. The doctor had confirmed she was six weeks' pregnant. On their way back in the cab, Delia squeezed Bobby Jo's hand, 'It'll be alright, my dear. You have time yet. We'll talk things through when you're rested. Shall I come in with you and see you to your room?'

'No thanks, Delia. I appreciate all you've done. I need to be alone and think.'

Life, Love, Death

'Very well, dear. I'll see you at the diner tomorrow. Ring me if you need anything,' Delia hugged the distressed girl, 'I'll come straight over.'

Head bowed, Bobby Jo waved the cab and Delia goodbye and entered the foyer. Her parents were sitting right opposite the revolving door. Alarmed, Bobby Jo cried out. Mrs Huson rushed over and took her in her arms as Bobby Jo burst into tears, whimpering, 'Why are you here? I'm sorry. I'm sorry I've not been in touch. What are you doing here?'

'We were worried, Bobby Jo,' her father said sternly. There's been hardly a word from you since you came to New York. It's as if you've disowned us or are ashamed of us. We love you and only want the best for you, you know that.' Observing gaggles of girls standing round gawping, he added, 'Shall we move to your room, young lady. We seem to be making a spectacle of ourselves.'

Once in her room Bobby Jo did her best to recover, drying her eyes and wondering what to say. Studying her parents it was as if she saw them for the first time, recognising how much older they seemed. She could never tell them about her situation. It would be too cruel and break their hearts. Being their only child and a late one at that, they'd had so many expectations of her. Maybe if she was engaged or about to get married it would be a different matter, but Xander was hardly marriage material, even she could see that.

Attempting to reassure them, Bobby Jo embarked on a long explanation of how she'd been staying with a woman friend for the weekend, had felt unwell and her friend had rung the

Life, Love, Death

Tribune for her. 'It was probably something I ate. I do love trying lots of different food,' she said airily. She then went on to tell them how well she was doing at the Trib, how much she loved being a journalist and what a great mentor she had.

'We've been there and know all this,' her father said dryly, 'and met your boss, Sam Murphy. He seems an OK sort of guy and quite fatherly towards you. What about this other guy, a mentor or something? Mr Murphy didn't rate him at all.'

Trying to gather her thoughts, Bobby Jo said, 'Oh, that's Sam's way. He's a bit of a taskmaster and doesn't like it when Xander disappears.' This was the first time she'd said Xander's name out loud. A convulsive tremor, she couldn't control, went straight through her.

Mrs Hudson, quick to spot her reaction, said forcefully, 'I think it's time you came home with us, Bobby Jo. We don't like you being alone in the city and the type of people you're meeting. Journalists are exposed to all sorts of distressing and bad experiences. We don't want this for you.' Changing to a more imploring tone, she said, 'Please come home with us, Bobby Jo. Forget all these ideas about being a journalist. Settle down in Little Chute. I'm sure there's plenty of nice boys that will make you a good husband.'

Bobby Jo flinched, 'I'm sorry, Mom. I don't want to come back to Little Chute and certainly not marry 'some nice boy'. Inwardly she thought perhaps that's my problem, I'm only attracted to the bad ones. Of course, Hank was a good man despite his secrets, yet all she craved for was Xander.

Life, Love, Death

Standing resolute against all their entreaties, Bobby Jo tried to reassure them, 'Honestly, I'll keep in touch this time. I really will. I do love you both.' Referring back to her father's earlier words she added, 'I'm not at all ashamed of you or want to disown you. I'll have time off this summer and…' (crossing her fingers behind her back) 'will come home to Little Chute and catch up with everyone.' She smiled widely trying to be convincing.

The Hudsons, seeing their efforts had ended in failure, had no choice but to take their leave. Mr Hudson pressed a fifty dollar bill into Bobby Jo's hand, and kissing her on the cheek said, 'You'll always be my little girl. Remember that.' He practically had to drag his crying wife, who was still holding on to Bobby Jo, out the door. With a heavy heart, Bobby Jo watched them make their way down the corridor to the elevator wondering if she would ever see them again. What was her future to be?

All of a sudden, she felt a deep sense of loss and grief as if she'd not only said goodbye to her parents but also to her childhood. The realisation came as a shock and hit her hard. She was now an adult whether she liked it or not and was about to become a mother, a parent even. How would she cope? More importantly, how was she to break the news to Xander?

CHAPTER 52

On the Tuesday morning after her parents had left, Bobby Jo turned up at the Trib at her usual time. Xander glowered at her, 'Have you any idea what you put me through yesterday? Sam was on my back telling me to track you down. He really put me through the wringer. Where were you?'

'With a friend,' Bobby Jo said sullenly. 'What's it to do with you? These days you never bother where I am or who I'm with.'

'Don't be silly,' Xander replied, attempting a pacifying manner. 'Of course I care about you. Aren't you my girl? Calm down. Tell me everything. I'll make us coffee. We'll have a good chat. It's not busy today so Sam won't bother us.' He smiled in his usual devilishly charming way, managing to elicit a slight response. 'That's my girl,' he said patting her on the head. Bobby Jo, though not thrilled to be patted like a child or a dog, was placated and even more so when he returned and put his arm round her kissing her neck. 'Now sweetie, what's been happening?'

As Bobby Jo regaled him with the story of her parents' swift departure, Xander sighed heavily masking his relief with a yawn. The last thing he wanted was two angry parents in the wings. Once her saga was over Bobby Jo hesitated. She was on the verge of telling Xander about the baby then thought better of it. If as he said she really was 'his girl' maybe she had nothing to worry about and he would stand by her.

Life, Love, Death

Later at lunch in the diner, Bobby Jo smiled when Delia asked solicitously, 'How are things?'

'No need to worry, Delia. Xander and I are on better terms.'

'You told him?'

'No, it wasn't the right time.'

'Be careful,' Delia warned. 'Time can run away with you. You need to decide whether you're keeping the baby or not. Why didn't you tell your parents? I'm sure they would have supported you.'

Alarmed, Bobby Jo exclaimed, 'I couldn't. They would never have felt the same way about me. They'd be too shocked. They're such upright people and devout churchgoers, I can't tell them ever. You won't tell them will you, Delia?' she begged.

'Certainly not. It's none of my business, but I'm worried about you. There aren't many options for unmarried girls these days.' Wondering if she should be more direct, Delia continued, 'You know it's illegal to have an abortion or try to get rid of the baby yourself, don't you?'

Bobby Jo recoiled, 'I would never do anything of the kind, especially to Xander's baby. No, I've every intention of keeping it.'

Delia's eyebrows shot up, 'But what about work? What happens when they start noticing or if you develop morning sickness?'

Life, Love, Death

'Oh, I'll be fine. I'm fit as a flea,' Bobby Jo said casually as if it was of no account. 'I feel well. There'll be nothing like that.'

'You'd be surprised,' Delia said ironically. 'Sometimes sickness can go on for months. When I had the boys…'

Bobby Jo interrupted, 'Let's talk about something else. When is James coming to New York? Can I meet him?'

It was obvious Bobby Jo was trying to pretend nothing was out of the ordinary, making Delia even more concerned. Bracing herself, she answered Bobby Jo's question, 'He'll be back next week,' and couldn't help grinning broadly. 'We might take a trip together. He has some time off – so maybe we'll go to the Rockies or Mexico. I can't wait.'

'What about the gallery?'

'Betty isn't painting at the moment. She'll step in for me. It's not too busy yet. Summer is more hectic.'

Bobby Jo could see Delia was glowing with anticipation and felt a pang of envy. If only it was like that for her and Xander. After lunch, feeling dispirited about her predicament and more anxious than she would admit, she dragged herself wearily back to work.

In another part of the city, Hank was also feeling miserable. It was as if he'd been completely abandoned by both Bobby Jo and his boss. His orders were to keep in contact with Bobby Jo but every time he rang her she was evasive. She'd never even turned up for their meeting after Christmas. Senior Special Agent Brewster was just as elusive. He either

Life, Love, Death

cancelled appointments with Hank, or, when a dogged Hank insisted on meeting, was extremely guarded, 'Look, Agent O'Shaughnessy, (goodness, Hank thought, it's back to formality. That's not a good sign.), 'there's a big operation about to take place. Due to your liaison with Miss Hudson you can't expect to be briefed. The fewer people who know the better. All I want from you is an insight into Miss Hudson's involvement. Is she a naïve pawn or a Communist sleeper?'

Hank, mortified at being sidelined, became red-faced with fury, protesting loudly, 'Bobby Jo's a complete innocent. She fancies herself in love with that Xander Smith, that's all. It's a schoolgirl crush. She'll soon get over it.'

'And that's why you're not involved in this case, young man. It's written all over your face. You're in love with the girl. I'm sorry for you. I know how frustrating unrequited love can be. This is why I have to keep you out of the game. It's for your own good. Find out where that girl stands then I'll be willing to listen.'

Showing the angry Hank out of his office, Brewster stood at the window rubbing his chin and reflecting. He was never going to let Hank know Xander was now working for them. The girl, well, she was of no account, probably a mere bystander used as a courier. If she got caught up in the action it would be her own fault. Brewster just wanted to make sure Hank didn't upset his plans and warn the girl. After all, you can't depend on a man in love. Lovers could be unpredictable. In the long-term, Brewster decided, he'd rather hold on to a trained agent like Hank than waste time and effort on some stupid slip of a girl who was infatuated with his double agent.

CHAPTER 53

On that same day back at the Tribune, Bobby Jo was called in to Sam Murphy's office. She barely had time to enter before he got up, came over and put a friendly arm round her shoulders, 'Whatever's been going on with you, young Roberta? I've had angry parents, an even angrier publisher, all demanding to find out what I've done with you, as if I've murdered you and buried your body.'

Bobby Jo sat down heavily on one of the editor's leather backed chairs, 'I'm sorry. It was nothing. Nothing at all,' she emphasised. 'I was staying with a friend for the weekend. On Monday I felt sick – something I'd eaten probably, and she rang in for me.'

'Good, that's alright then. These things happen. We'll forget about it. In future, be a good girl and keep your parents informed. They were furious, almost hysterical well at least your mother was.' He laughed, 'I thought they were going to have my head cut off and served on a plate.'

Bobby Jo got up to leave.

'Not so fast, young lady. We still have Xander Smith to talk about. I hear you and he are dating or are 'an item', as they say these days, and certainly seeing the town together. I'm not happy about that. He's not to be trusted, particularly with a young girl like you.'

Bobby Jo, knowing she could hardly admit the truth, feigned indignance, 'Xander has helped me a lot. Yes, we have gone to a few clubs together but he's been an absolute gentleman, and it's really my private business.'

Life, Love, Death

'Very well, Roberta, be advised. Things and people aren't always as they seem. You're still very inexperienced. I wouldn't like to see you get into trouble. Remember my door is always open.' He shrugged and chuckled, 'I mean metaphorically of course, but if I can help at any time I will.'

Down in the office, Xander's ears might have been burning if he hadn't been too involved in scheming and plotting. His mind was focussed on money. The Feds and Moscow Central, though they didn't know it yet, were going to be his sponsors – his financiers and bankers. But he needed a couple of good tales to reel in both Jasha and Brewster. Of course, both men were motivated by ambition, each in his own way. Jasha wanted to appear indispensable and invaluable, not causing any trouble for his Moscow masters whilst he continued to enjoy New York's fleshpots. Brewster on the other hand was looking for promotion, wanting a big coup that would propel him up the career ladder. Catching a Communist cell in New York could do it.

Tackling the Jasha situation first, Xander decided to contact his two drinking buddies from the Daily Worker. Considering how they'd betrayed him, he'd no compunction in using them as gofers. Initially they seemed surprised to hear from him, probably feeling guilty, but they agreed to meet him for a drink at lunchtime. They arrived late, but Xander had already set up drinks for them – double vodkas in both cases.

Edith smiled, saying in an ingratiating way, 'We haven't seen much of you, Karl. What have you been up to?'

Life, Love, Death

'This and that,' Xander said carelessly. 'But I have a few difficulties. Things are hotting up for me. I may have to make a swift departure from these shores.'

At that, Stefan who had been slouched down gloomily staring into his glass, sat up with a start, 'What sort of difficulties?'

Xander bent towards them and whispered, 'You know being a proclaimed Communist is dangerous these days.'

'But it's not as if you're actually working for Russia,' Edith said quietly. 'You merely believe as we do in the principles of Communism. Stefan and I as reporters for the Daily Worker are probably more at risk than you.'

Xander, aware he had to shock them out of their apathy and make them go running back to Jasha and the cell, said, 'What if I told you I was a spy and work for Moscow Central?'

The two sat back aghast. This wasn't how it was supposed to be. They were incredulous, too traumatised to speak, thinking about the consequences for themselves and Jasha. What if this crazy guy ran amok in New York telling everyone he was a Russian spy. Doing their best to laugh it off, they said, 'But you aren't, are you?'

'No, of course not. After all I wouldn't tell anyone if I was, would I?' Xander, nearly broke down in fits of glee seeing the expression on their faces.

Suddenly, knocking back their drinks in one gulp, they both got up to leave, 'Sorry Karl, we've got to get back. We've got

Life, Love, Death

a deadline to meet. Give us a ring, and we'll meet up when we've more time.'

Edith added, warningly, 'I'm sure your problems will sort themselves out. Don't do anything crazy. Let us know straightaway if you decide to leave the country.' Xander nodded. Once they were gone he ordered another double vodka. That had certainly woken those two up. No doubt they would be in immediate contact with Jasha. None of them would want the publicity of a spy scandal. As for Brewster, he was easily dealt with; after all, one of his Feds was already following Xander and would keep his boss up to date.

Jasha was a trickier proposition. He would expect information on Xander's mysterious asset before parting with any more money. Maybe this was where Miss Roberta could assist. He needed to turn on the charm once more, captivate her, and make her his again.

CHAPTER 54

The next Tuesday at the diner, as Delia and Bobby Jo settled down for lunch and Addy stopped bobbing about chatting and serving them, Delia said, 'I don't know how to tell you this, Bobby Jo. James is back. We're going on the road trip I mentioned. As the weather's so good we're setting off the end of this week for a month. I feel I'm letting you down just when you need me, but James is so excited about seeing more of this country I don't want to let him down either.'

A distraught Bobby Jo stared down at her plate trying to hide her tears, 'I'll miss you, Delia. You've been like a mother to me these last weeks. I don't know what I'd have done without you.'

Delia winced inwardly. She'd hoped her mothering days were over. Nowadays she wanted to enjoy being single without responsibilities or dependants, with only a lover to please. Placing her hand over Bobby Jo's, she said consolingly, 'It's only a month. I'll keep in touch. We can come back at any time. As things are better with Xander, perhaps you could tell him about the baby?'

'I don't know,' Bobby Jo said, 'though he did call me 'his girl' the other day and was thoughtful and kind. A month is a long time. How big will I be? What if people start to notice? What about morning sickness?'

Nonplussed, Delia was baffled. She'd done her best to talk candidly to Bobby Jo over the last weeks, but it was as if Bobby Jo had only just woken up to the realities of it all. 'Won't you reconsider telling your parents?'

Life, Love, Death

'Absolutely not,' Bobby Jo shouted, 'I can't, I can't.'

'I think then,' Delia said firmly and baldly. 'you have no choice but to tell Xander. You'll have no one else to turn to if I'm not around.'

Bobby Jo folded her lips tightly, 'I'll see,' she said stubbornly.

Delia could do no more, and with nothing else to say they ate the rest of their lunch in silence. Before they parted, Delia pulled a reluctant Bobby Jo to her in a warm embrace. Placing an envelope in her hand, she whispered in Bobby Jo's ear, 'Here's our itinerary if you want to contact me, the key to my apartment, and money to keep you going. My doctor will be expecting you this week. Make sure you ring for an appointment. All your medical care is paid for in advance.'

Bobby Jo burst into tears, 'You've been so good to me, Delia. I know I can be obstinate, but I appreciate everything you've done. After all we're comparative strangers.'

'Hardly, my dear. I think we're strangers who've become friends now. Even Joel would say that if he was here.'

'I do miss him. I know he was a bad-tempered old man some of the time, but he gave good advice when he was in the mood. At least at the end of his life he found happiness with Blanche and her family.'

'Hold on to those memories,' Delia said. 'There was something about him that pulled at all our heartstrings. I miss him and Betsy too. Anyway, it's no use being sad. You

Life, Love, Death

have a new life to look forward to, Bobby Jo. Concentrate on that.'

'Thanks, Delia. I'll try. Have a wonderful trip. Send me postcards.'

Delia felt terribly guilty as she walked back to the gallery, wishing she didn't have to leave Bobby Jo at this time. There was a nagging feeling of foreboding looming at the back of her mind, but she couldn't quite work out what it was. Then she remembered. It was something Joel had said After the sudden death of his friend Benny Carter, he'd turned to them both at the diner and announced he knew, 'Summat is comin'. It's comin'. I's know it. I's feel it.' Delia shivered, aware of that same apprehension. But what it was she had no idea. She wasn't worried about herself or James. They were old enough and mature enough to cope, but Bobby Jo was a different matter.

At the Tribune, Xander was putting the finishing touches to his campaign. The first stage was to provoke Jasha. Using their usual letter drop, he left a cryptic message saying, *'Feds on to me. Got key to Hydrogen Project. In hiding. Need money. Courier will collect. Await contact for further info.'* Pleased with himself he sat back and greeted Bobby Jo warmly when she returned from lunch, 'Did you meet your friend? Delia, isn't it?'

Thrilled he was taking an interest in her life, Bobby Jo said, 'Yes, she and her, I'm not sure what to call him, 'boyfriend', are going off on a month's road trip.'

Xander could only just about hide his satisfaction. Good, that was another hurdle out of the way. Bobby Jo had

Life, Love, Death

become far too dependent on that Delia for his liking. Now he had Bobby Jo all to himself again. 'Shall we go out for dinner tonight?' he proposed and was reassured to see Bobby Jo's rather glum face light up. At the same time as Bobby Jo was thinking this might be an opportunity to break her news to Xander, he was plotting on a means to lure Bobby Jo back to her courier duties.

Later that night, once they were comfortably ensconced on one of the rooftop restaurants and enjoying the early evening warmth, Bobby Jo rehearsed in her mind what she was going to say. It would be better to wait till after their meal when Xander might be more receptive. But the occasion presented itself sooner than she expected when Xander said, 'I'll order champagne shall I or would you rather have a cocktail?'

'Water, please,' Bobby Jo replied, feeling nausea rising in her stomach, aware it was nerves rather than pregnancy symptoms.

'That's not like you,' Xander teased. 'You never turn down a drink. Is there something wrong?'

Bobby Jo decided to go for it there and then. Gulping down a glass of water, she stammered, '…I'm…I'm having a baby.'

Xander's face was a picture. His expressions changed from sheer bewilderment to complete disbelief. Finding his voice at last, he said, 'What do you mean?'

'A baby…I'm having a baby,' Bobby Jo said patiently. Now it was out in the open, she felt so much better and more in

Life, Love, Death

control. It was almost laughable, watching the fleeting emotions darting across Xander's face.

'I take it it's mine,' he said hoarsely.

'Of course, who's else would it be.'

'I thought maybe that fella Hank you told me about?'

'No, that was just a friendship.'

Xander, caught off balance for probably the first time in his life, had to think quickly. Always keen to exploit everything to his own advantage, he decided this state of affairs could be exactly what he needed.

'I'm sorry my darling girl, it was the shock threw me for a minute. I'm genuinely pleased if you are. Is this something you want?'

'Most definitely. I didn't know how you'd react. I thought you weren't interested in a permanent relationship let alone a family.'

'Seriously Roberta, you've got me wrong. There's nothing that would make me happier than to settle down with you.'

Before she could say another word, he was down on one knee, 'Will you marry me, my darling girl?'

Bobby Jo was stunned, spluttering, 'Yes, I will. I will.' At that, Xander drew her into his arms and kissed her thoroughly while the bar staff and customers cheered.

Life, Love, Death

An ecstatic Bobby Jo was stupefied. It was everything she'd dreamed of – the man she loved and a baby. She sat holding his hand and dreaming of their future together in the classic small house with the white picket fence. Too excited to eat, she scarcely listened to what Xander was saying to her.

'My own dear girl, I've a few issues to sort. You'll have to resume your courier duties. There's money to be collected that will set our family up for life. Will you do this for me?'

Not registering any words other than 'our family', Bobby Jo nodded, 'I'll do anything for you, Xander my darling. Name it.' She glowed with so much love that even Xander was entranced.

'We'll buy an engagement ring later next week,' he said tenderly, knowing full well his machinations would be complete by then.

Bobby Jo floated home on a cloud, too absorbed in her fairy tale romance to notice anything, and wishing Delia was there.

CHAPTER 55

At the letter drop, Jasha was hot with rage. His Russian temperament didn't take well to being crossed. Edith and Stefan had wasted no time in telling him what Karl had said. He was exasperated with Karl and his tricks. They'd have to find some way of controlling him or Jasha's future in New York could come to a bitter end. Being recalled to Moscow would be no life at all. Now there was this enigmatic message from Karl. What was it all about? What was the money for – to bribe someone or to enable that wretched Karl to flee the country? Jasha was in a bind. He desperately needed the information but distrusted the man. Weighing up the odds, he decided to believe in Karl and hope for the best. There was no difficulty with money. Moscow was quite prepared to provide endless dollars provided they could strengthen their communist cells and beat America in the arms race. Calming down, Jasha began to think rationally. Perhaps there was some advantage in all this for him and extra money too.

A few days later he received the call from Xander. Snorting down the telephone, he growled, 'What's this about?'

Xander interrupted, 'It's clear enough. I need money?'

'What for?'

'Be quiet and I'll tell you. I can't say much on the telephone, and I'm being followed. It's of absolute importance I get this money or I won't be able to go any further with the contact. He wants twenty thousand.'

Life, Love, Death

There was a gasp from the other end. 'You mean dollars? I'm not sure I can get that amount of money,' Jasha's voice cracked.

'Then you can say goodbye to your soft option here in New York. I expect your Russian masters will be delighted to welcome you back to Moscow.'

'No, please no. I'll get it. Give me time.'

'You've got a week. I won't be available to collect the money. I'm sending a trusted courier.'

'Not that Roberta girl? Does she know what this is about?'

'She knows what she needs to know. You can rely on her. We're engaged.'

There was a long silence as Jasha took in this nugget of news. An engagement – h'm - that might be a good thing. It would make it more difficult for Karl to up and leave. 'Very well. I suppose, congratulations are in order. Tell me where and when to meet her.'

'Be at the Blue Ribbon Café on West 44th Street at eleven in the morning a week from today with the money packed up in a gift box. Sit down at her table as if you know her. Give her the gift and say, 'Roberta? Congratulations on your engagement. Don't open the gift now. Wait and do that with your fiancé,' then leave.'

'But how will I know her?'

Life, Love, Death

'She has bright red hair, well more copper these days, and bangs and will be wearing a pink suit.'

'But what about my information?'

'I'll leave a note at our usual place once I receive the money and give you an address where we can meet face to face.'

'It seems an awful lot of trouble to me. I can't see why we can't meet now.'

'You're not the one in danger, I am. We'll do it my way or not at all.'

Jasha backed down, 'I'm sorry. I'll do what you say. Take care, my friend.'

Xander grunted in disgust as he put down the telephone. 'Friend' indeed! Certainly not! Now all he had to do was contact Brewster and set up the final act.

The meeting with Brewster was easy enough to handle though the agent blanched at the mention of twenty thousand dollars. 'Why so much?' he asked warily.

'Its expenses and a great many bribes,' Xander said carelessly. 'But if you don't want me to go ahead, feel free to cancel everything.'

'No, no, please carry on,' Brewster said hurriedly, his eyes gleaming with the anticipation of the recognition he might receive from even the great J. Edgar himself.

Life, Love, Death

'Very well,' Xander said confidently. 'I'll need the money by this time next week. Then I'll give you a date, time, and venue. I need to lie low, so gift wrap the money in a box and have it delivered by messenger to Miss Roberta Hudson at the Tribune building. Make sure it's put directly into her hands.'

Looking confused, but knowing full well who the girl was, Brewster said, 'Who's that? How is she involved in all this?'

'Roberta is my fiancée. She's helping me out and will be expecting the box.'

A thoughtful Brewster said nothing. The girl was certainly up to her neck in it and no way as innocent as Hank thought. Poor devil.

At that very moment Hank was in his office worrying about Bobby Jo. He'd tried to contact her so many times and been stonewalled. Should he try once more? To his amazement he was put straight through to her and she seemed delighted to hear from him. He could hear the excitement in her voice and was encouraged. However, his expectations were dashed when she merrily said, 'You won't believe it, Hank, I'm engaged.'

'Who to?' he asked miserably.

'Xander my work colleague, of course silly, who else. I'm over the moon, so very, very happy.'

'Congratulations,' Hank struggled to articulate the word as it stuck in his throat.' Not that scoundrel Xander Smith, he groaned to himself. She'll regret it.

Life, Love, Death

'You'll come to the wedding, won't you?' Bobby Jo continued. 'You're one of my best friends in New York and have always been good to me. I'm sorry I didn't treat you well but be pleased for me.'

'Of course. All I ever wanted was for you to be happy.' There was no more to be said. Hank couldn't wait to tell Brewster, hoping he might find a way to stop the engagement.

But he was out of luck. Brewster was unbending, 'I'm sorry, Hank. I know how much this must stick in your craw, but the girl's 'made her bed' as they say. There's nothing I can do about it.'

'But you could if Xander was working for you,' Hank persisted, suspecting Brewster wasn't telling him everything.

'That's not your business, Agent O'Shaughnessy. I have warned you before. Keep out of this. Have no further dealings with that girl or you might be looking at a prison sentence.'

Hank ground his teeth. He was convinced Bobby Jo was the love of his life. How could he abandon her? What was really going on? Was she in trouble? Was she in danger? He knew he would stand by her whatever the cost.

CHAPTER 56

The week after Delia and James departed for their road trip, Bobby Jo didn't feel like going to Leo's to eat alone. Instead, she ate a sandwich at her desk, fantasising about her prospective engagement ring. Xander hadn't mentioned it since, seeming too busy with comings and goings. He'd talked about her resuming her courier duties, but she hadn't paid much attention.

Eventually, he sat down opposite and said, 'I need you to do me a favour, my darling. An old friend has heard about our engagement and wants to give us a present. He's only in town briefly, and I've far too much to do. Could you be very kind and go to the Blue Ribbon Café at eleven tomorrow. Do you remember that little place we used to go to for coffee? My friend will arrive, call you by name and give you the gift. Bring it back. We'll open it together. Wear that pink suit I like so much.'

A starry eyed Bobby Jo was only too willing to agree. What struck her as odd as when she brought back the gift, wrapped in gold paper and red ribbons, Xander consigned it to a locked drawer and didn't refer to it again. The next day, Bobby Jo was called to Reception to collect another gift wrapped parcel. Again, when she brought it back, eager to unwrap it, Xander did the same thing as before – placing it in the same locked drawer. Exasperated, Bobby Jo said, 'Aren't we going to open these presents, Xander?'

'Not at work, sweetie. We'll take them home and open them together.'

Life, Love, Death

At the end of that day there was no sign of Xander, so Bobby Jo dragged her weary body back to the Barbizon and lay down for a nap, wondering where he was. Her pregnancy was at last showing symptoms - mainly tiredness, as Delia had said. There were still no signs of sickness and though she studied her stomach every day in the mirror there was little showing. Bobby Jo just wished she knew what Xander was thinking, and more importantly what he was up to.

In fact, Xander was doing his best to be cunning. The note he'd left at the letter drop was bound to antagonise Jasha and make him react. Hopefully in the anticipated way. It was a bit of a gamble, but Xander had spent his whole life taking risks so what did another one matter. He had the money from both sources now but he was uneasy about provoking Brewster, who would be a dangerous enemy. It was better to give him what he wanted, then Xander would be in the clear. Provoking Jasha was a whole different ball game.

The note to Jasha had been curt and to the point, '*Meet me Friday midday at Ellis Island. All will be revealed.*' Xander, knew full well that Ellis Island was on the point of closure. Jasha would know this too and be furious. Xander was gambling on the chance that Jasha would propose an alternative meeting place where he had back-up.

Xander's speculation paid off. Jasha was beside himself with rage. What was Karl playing at? Why arrange a meeting in such an out of the way, obscure place no longer open to the public? Jasha started thinking. Perhaps Karl had an ulterior motive – to get him on his own and kill him. After all, Karl knew nothing about the cell and probably thought Jasha was

Life, Love, Death

isolated in New York with no Russian embassy to back him up. Well, two could play at that game.

Jasha left a response, saying, '*Cannot make that meeting place. Meet you same time but at...*' then gave the warehouse address where the cell usually met.

Xander was triumphant. Everything was working out well. Jasha would call the cell, who would probably want to confront and kill him. All Xander needed to do was give Brewster and the Feds the nod. Then it would all be set up. The only fly in the ointment was Bobby Jo. She would need to be handled carefully. Hers was a key role. He must make certain she was ready to carry it out.

Bobby Jo was clueless. She wandered about in a dream, imagining her future life with Xander. Sam Murphy, who was unaware of their engagement, despaired of her. Day by day, her assignments fell apart and her pieces had to be rewritten. Summoning her for the umpteenth time, he said, 'What's wrong with you, Roberta? I had such great hopes of you. You're letting me down.'

Bobby Jo hung her head, making no response. Xander had warned her not to tell Sam about their engagement. 'It won't look good for either of our careers,' he'd said sternly.

All Bobby Jo could say was, 'I'm sorry, Mr Murphy. I'll do better. I really will.'

'I hope so,' he said seriously, 'otherwise I'll have to talk to Mrs Reid and that will be the end of your traineeship.'

Life, Love, Death

Back at her desk, Bobby Jo wished Xander was around. Where on earth could he be? She was feeling emotional these days. It must be the pregnancy but all she felt like doing was crying. Journalism had been everything to her. Now, obsessed with Xander and the forthcoming baby, she couldn't even do that well. To cheer herself up she looked at all the postcards Delia had sent her from their trip. On the last one, Delia had written, '*Having a wonderful time, but always worrying about you, my dear Bobby Jo. Take good care of yourself and the b… Thinking of you always, lots of love Delia and James xxx*'. Rereading it again Bobby Jo broke down and, putting her head on the desk, wept as if her heart would break. She needed Delia and her practical common sense now more than ever.

CHAPTER 57

Friday morning dawned, and Xander was up early. This is the day, he thought, freedom is on the horizon. All his chess pieces were in position. When he arrived at the office, he was faced with a tear stained Bobby Jo who whimpered, 'Where've you been? I needed you yesterday. I thought as we're engaged, you'd be here to support me.'

Xander sighed heavily and, fixing a reassuring smile on his face, took Bobby Jo's hand, 'I'm here now, my darling girl. Tell me all about it.'

'I've had such a telling off from Sam. He's threatening to terminate my traineeship if I don't improve. You're never here these days. I don't know what I'm doing.'

'Look, sweetie. He does this all the time. It's usually me that's on the carpet or the floorboards or whatever,' he joked lightly, trying to draw out a smile. But it was no good, Bobby Jo sat on his desk and wailed, 'I'm not happy. I feel so tired with this (she patted her flat stomach) and I miss Delia.'

Taking her in his arms, Xander patted her back soothingly. 'Everything will be fine, believe me. You're exhausted and perhaps a bit stale at work, but I've got a story that's going to cheer you up. It's a real humdinger. I can't tell you anything at this stage. Be ready to go out with me at eleven this morning. Then you'll see. In the meantime, I'll find you a spare office where you can put your feet up and have a rest. How does that suit?'

Life, Love, Death

Cheered up by Xander's attentions, Bobby Jo said, 'I knew you'd understand. You can be so thoughtful, that's why I love you. I'm dying to know about this story.'

'All in good time, all in good time,' Xander mumbled as he escorted her down the corridor and settled her in an empty office.

Prompt at eleven, he came and woke her, 'We must be going. We can't be late.' Bundling her into his car, he said, 'We're going to meet some important people. I want you to do exactly what I say.'

'Oh, I will, I will,' Bobby Jo said enthusiastically.

'I'll have to park the car out of sight, and let you go in first. Are you alright with that?'

'Absolutely. Where are we going?'

'To some warehouses at the docks.'

'Will it be dangerous?' Bobby Jo asked, not liking the sound of the place and unconsciously stroking her stomach.

'Not at all,' Xander said assertively.

On arrival, Xander took a swift look round. A few cars were parked already, and he recognised Jasha's. Checking his watch, he murmured, 'Perfect timing.' Kissing Bobby Jo on the cheek, he said, 'Go into that building. Take the elevator to the fifth floor. I'll be right behind you.'

'Couldn't I wait for you outside?'

Life, Love, Death

'No, I want to keep us undercover. You'll be fine. Trust me.'

Bobby Jo did as she was told. Once out of the elevator, she had no idea where to go. Should she wait for Xander or not? Hearing voices, she moved in their direction. Without warning a door swung open, and the man she'd met at the at the Blue Ribbon Café was standing there. Relieved to see Xander's friend, she smiled at him and stepped into the room. A lot of men in black overcoats and one mannish looking woman were sitting round a metal table. They stared at her in stupefaction.

All of a sudden, there was a clattering of footsteps on the stairs. Thinking it was Xander, Bobby Jo turned instinctively but a gun was pressed to her back and she was pushed to the floor. Chaos ensued. People started shouting, yelling, and screaming. Bullets began flying. Bobby Jo found herself dragged onto the landing, a pair of handcuffs clipped round her wrists. Pulled to her feet, a trembling, shaking Bobby Jo stuttered, 'What's happening? Where's Xander?'

A tall nondescript man wearing an FBI vest stepped in front of her, 'Wouldn't we both like to know. I'm Senior Special Agent Brewster. I'm afraid Miss Hudson, your friend Xander has deserted you…well, and me too if it comes to that.'

'But who are these people? What is this about?' a distraught Bobby Jo asked, as the black coated men, the woman and Jasha were led away in cuffs.

'This my dear, as if you didn't know is a Communist cell. We've been after them for a while. Luckily for us your friend Xander decided to turn double agent and betray them.'

Life, Love, Death

'But what do you mean...Xander...a double agent? I don't understand.' By now Bobby Jo was hysterical. 'I know nothing about Communist cells. Where's Xander? He's my fiancé. We're engaged.'

'Not anymore, my dear. He was a Russian spy, as you must have realised if you were engaged to him, and you were his courier. I'm sorry to say that though he's got away you'll likely be serving time at one of America's more exclusive penitentiaries.'

Before he finished talking, Bobby Jo fainted dead away. It was hours before she woke. It was then she was forced to face the brutal knowledge that not only was she lying in a strange hospital bed, her wrist cuffed to the rail, but she'd lost Xander's baby. She was a prisoner, a criminal, a traitor. Yet she was innocent, had done nothing illegal except fall in love with the wrong man.

Thousands of miles away in a small South American country, with no extradition treaty, sunning himself at a beach bar Xander was enjoying his liberty and the fruits of his labour. Counting out bundles of dollar bills, he said, 'Another Manhattan, barman, if you please. Keep 'em coming.' Turning towards the slowly setting sun, he raised his glass, 'Let's see now. Who should I toast? First of all, to my two generous benefactors, the American and Soviet governments. Then, my dear comrades in the Party. Jasha of course, never to be forgotten. Finally Special Agent Brewster, definitely can't leave him out. Oh, but there is someone I've missed. Here's to you, dear little Miss Roberta, my ex-fiancée. I could never have done it without you. All the very best for your future wherever that may be, from your beloved Xander (alias Karl Marx).'

CHAPTER 58
Sixteen Years later…26 August, 1970

Surprisingly, the day was as hot a day as that June day in '53 when she'd first met Joel and Bobby Jo at Leo's. Delia, wishing she'd worn more sunscreen, could feel that self-same sun burning into her face making her feel nostalgic. Who would ever believe the difference that year had made to their lives. Had that random meeting turned them into catalysts for one another? It was like an intertwined relationship that never resulted in anything permanent yet had all the impact of a marriage and a divorce.

In the years that followed, there'd been so many catalysts in the bigger picture of America's history. Rosa Parks not giving up her seat in the bus to a white man sparked not only the civil rights movement but started women thinking about their rights. The Montgomery Bus Boycott led to the founding of the Southern Christian Leadership Conference. Martin Luther King Jr., its leader, initiated The March on Washington. His famous address 'I have a dream' paved the way towards the Civil Rights Act of '64 and the Voting Rights Act of '65. The birth control pill allowed women choices and control over their lives. Betty Friedan's '63 book, 'The Feminine Mystique' got women questioning their accepted societal role of marriage and children, inspiring a second wave of feminism.

Now at nearly sixty-seven, Delia felt unconstrained and free as if she'd swallowed the elixir of youth. How else would she, Bedelia Gray, that prim Southern matron, be walking in a demonstration with fifty thousand women down the Avenue of the Americas on the 50th anniversary of women's suffrage. Yet here she was carrying a placard

Life, Love, Death

proclaiming, 'Women's Strike for Peace and Equality'. She, who'd never had a rebellious bone in her body or stepped out of line neither in her childhood, nor at Vassar, nor even in her marriage. What had those two people in the diner done to her? Yet their lives too had been upended. It was hard to imagine Joel, as infirm as he was, defending a white cop against a man of his own colour and race and getting knifed for his pains. It'd been a tragedy but a heroic one. Poor Blanche never recovered from losing her son Steve, dying shortly after from pneumonia.

More devastating was the thought of Bobby Jo, that exuberant, lively, young girl prosecuted under the 1917 Espionage Act, and sentenced to ten years at Rikers. Could she have knowingly betrayed her country or just been a gullible victim? Delia never believed Bobby Jo knew who or what Xander was. She and James had done their best to persuade the authorities of Bobby Jo's innocence, but times were against them. Still in the grip of the Second Red Scare and the passing of the Communist Control Act that summer, Bobby Jo's fate was sealed.

Poor Bobby Jo, her twenties had been swallowed up in prison but Hank, leaving the FBI immediately after her conviction, waited for her. Finally released after six years, Bobby Jo married him and they settled with their young family on a farm back in Wisconsin. How her life had come full circle. Whether Bobby Jo still hankered after Xander, Delia never knew. Maybe by now he was a distant memory never to be reclaimed.

…And Xander, he'd vanished into the mists of time possibly to a South American country or some other obscure location. Though as time went by, he had fewer countries to hide in.

Life, Love, Death

Of course, he might not be alive if the Feds or the KGB had caught up with him.

Out of the three strangers who had become friends at the diner, Delia was the only one left standing. A woman who at last had found her voice. She now owned Betty's gallery, still lived in Sutton Place, and had found a purpose in life. Of course, there was no James anymore to fill her lonely evenings. His early heart attack had taken him from her, but he was always with her in spirit and she wanted for nothing now she was a wealthy woman.

On Sundays, she would visit Trinity Churchyard, sit by James' grave, and tell him about her week and how much she missed him. Afterwards she would take the subway to the Village and visit Joel's grave at Greenwich Cemetery. She and Blanche had arranged a simple memorial stone which said, 'Here lies Joel Petersen, musician, devoted to his Betsy.' All those years back, it'd been a struggle with the undertaker to get him to agree to place the old Sax in the coffin with Joel, but he'd been no match for her and Blanche.

Delia was still a smart, glamorous woman. These days her life was less about painters and sculptors and more about causes and ideals. Her friends, of all colours and denominations, included feminine activists like Betty Frieden, Gloria Steinem, and Dorothy Pitman Hughes. She was someone who was listened to, someone confident enough to speak for herself.

As they passed the old diner tucked down a side street off 6th Avenue, Delia smiled ruefully. Who was sitting in their booth now? What would the future hold for them? What about Adelie? Was she still shouting orders in that grimy,

Life, Love, Death

stained overall. Delia wondered if she would ever know what unknown forces had brought the three of them together that Tuesday in June so long ago and kept them linked every Tuesday for a year. It was a mystery. Three complete strangers whose lives had overlapped for a moment in time, and then were torn asunder by events, never to be the same again.

BOOKS BY ROSEMARY HAMER

THE CHRISTMAS HOUSE (2015) - a dramatized version of the author's mother's early life. Set in an Aberystwyth boarding house from the Great War through to 1957. Dora grows up in a complicated family with a secret. Will the secret finally come out and how will it affect Dora's life?

THE SHADOW SHAPER (2018) - twenty year old Eleanor is drawn into the murky world of spying during the Cold War, falling for her enigmatic colleague, Paul. Travelling from remote Scotland to war torn Central America, Eleanor realises her survival is at risk from a hidden force.

PORTRAIT OF A DEATH (2019) - the journey of a painting of a mysterious lady as it passes through the decades and hands of four sets of characters from Paris via London ending up in New York. The story unmasks lives fraught with passion, jealousy, suspicion, terror and ultimately murder.

KENSHŌ, House of Secrets (2021) - Kenshō House, home of the Blenkinsop family, with its own ghostly history is the guardian of times gone by, acting as a bridge between Japan and England, maintaining its silence and unwilling to give up its mysteries.

ABOUT THE AUTHOR

Rosemary Hamer comes from Aberystwyth, Wales, has travelled extensively and followed three different career paths including running her own business. Now retired, she lives on the Wirral and concentrates on writing.

Printed in Great Britain
by Amazon